OYSTERS &
CHOCOLATE

OYSTERS & CHOCOLATE

Erotic Stories of Every Flavor

EDITED BY

Jordan LaRousse and

Samantha Sade

HEAT

HEAT
Published by New American Library, a division of
Penguin Group (USA) Inc., 375 Hudson Street,
New York, New York 10014, USA
Penguin Group (Canada), 90 Eglinton Avenue East, Suite 700, Toronto,
Ontario M4P 2Y3, Canada (a division of Pearson Penguin Canada Inc.)
Penguin Books Ltd., 80 Strand, London WC2R 0RL, England
Penguin Ireland, 25 St. Stephen's Green, Dublin 2,
Ireland (a division of Penguin Books Ltd.)
Penguin Group (Australia), 250 Camberwell Road, Camberwell, Victoria 3124,
Australia (a division of Pearson Australia Group Pty. Ltd.)
Penguin Books India Pvt. Ltd., 11 Community Centre, Panchsheel Park,
New Delhi - 110 017, India
Penguin Group (NZ), 67 Apollo Drive, Rosedale, North Shore 0632,
New Zealand (a division of Pearson New Zealand Ltd.)
Penguin Books (South Africa) (Pty.) Ltd., 24 Sturdee Avenue,
Rosebank, Johannesburg 2196, South Africa

Penguin Books Ltd., Registered Offices:
80 Strand, London WC2R 0RL, England

First published by Heat, an imprint of New American Library,
a division of Penguin Group (USA) Inc.

First Printing, May 2009
10 9 8 7 6 5 4 3 2 1

HEAT is a trademark of Penguin Group (USA) Inc.

LIBRARY OF CONGRESS CATALOGING-IN-PUBLICATION DATA:

Oysters & chocolate: erotic stories of every flavor/edited by Jordan LaRousse and Samantha Sade.
    p. cm.
    ISBN 978-0-451-22682-2
    1. Erotic stories, American. I. LaRousse, Jordan. II. Sade, Samantha.
III. Title: Oysters and chocolate.
    PS648.E7097 2009
    813'.01083538—dc22   2008054601

Set in Adobe Garamond
Designed by Ginger Legato

Printed in the United States of America

To Joe, our beloved SD. Thank you for your love, support, encouragement, financial backing, impeccable business sense, and ever-flowing tequila. Without you, this book never would have been possible.

ACKNOWLEDGMENTS

Our company began as three friends and an idea, and it would never have blossomed the way it has if it weren't for everyone who joined in on the adventure. Before the book came the Web site. Utmost gratitude goes to Brent Weaver and Steve Thiel, owners of HotPress Web (www.hotpressweb.com), the rockin' designers of OystersandChocolate.com, and the ultimate masters of our little piece of the Web. Thank you for taking our many spankings and for always loving your poor, but oh-so-grateful girls. And, of course, with this goes a big hug to both Erick Stubbs and Steven Waller. Thank you, Emmanuelle Alspaugh, our extraordinary agent—you are the perfect ambassador of erotica, and not a day has gone by that we haven't thanked the heavens to have you on our side. Thank you to Lindsay and to Penguin Group—it is literally a dream come true to work with you. Our writers—we will always be indebted to you—for giving us the beautiful, sexy, steamy prose that blends so well to create this erotic cocktail we call an anthology. Joe and Tre', thank you for being such amazing partners, for your patience and support, and for all of the inspiration you've given us over the many nights, mornings, afternoons . . . and beyond. Heather, our mistress of publicity—we are indebted to you for your passion and professionalism, and for holding our hands and ordering us wine when the interviews get too scary. Thank you to our beautiful Christi, for being our loving friend and companion on this amazing journey. Thank you to our beloved Jill; your support and enthusiasm have kept us going. Thank you to sexy and sassy Alanna, the ultimate "junior oyster." Thank you to Shoshanna and Noah, the best siblings an erotica purveyor could ever ask for. Much love to Eden, who has always been Jordan's greatest motivation to succeed. Thank you, Jocelyn, for being our feminist ally and for always supporting the notion that a woman's right to choose begins with her right to enjoy sex the ways she wants to. Our love and thanks to all of our amazing friends who continue to loyally read our newsletters, listen to our interviews, and come to our parties (Duffs—this means you). You all are the best! Thank you, Mom(s)—both of you! You both engendered in us a healthy respect and love for our bodies and our sex lives. A big thanks to Dad, whose pride in our endeavor makes us smile. Mike and Mary, your support and TLC have meant the world. Grandma Debbie, thank you for your blessings from beyond; we know you understand now. G'pa—thank you for loving us "even though" we edit and write erotica; we'll always cherish the copy of *The Marquis de Sade* that you gave us.

ACKNOWLEDGMENTS

Before the book and before the Web site came the women who needed erotica. Thank you, women, for being your sexy selves and for being such an intelligent, dynamic, fun, and eager audience!

Why the different flavors? Just as a chef employs a plethora of tastes and textures to excite the tongue, this book explores the many different ingredients necessary to excite the mind and body. Each flavor of erotica in this anthology is a note on the broad spectrum that is human sexuality. From the tender and loving to the sultry and dark, the human erotic palate is varied and complex. It is our desire that you read, explore, learn, and enjoy. We like to ask our readers, What turns you on? In other words, What's your favorite flavor?

MENU
Four-Course Amuse Bouche $69

VANILLA

a classic, sweet, and romantically decadent dish

DIRTY MARTINI

a distinctive, exciting cocktail with a naughty twist

LICORICE WHIPS

*a wild and strong-flavored course that spanks the tongue
with heat and bite*

OYSTERS

*firm and sensual—with deep, round cups, sweet scents,
and exclusively feminine flavors*

CONTENTS

Contents

OYSTERS &
CHOCOLATE

HIS DESK

by Terri Pray

Claire smiled and traced her fingers over the smooth surface of the large, warm wooden desk. Polished and loved, the oak desk had been in the office for as long as she had worked here. She'd rarely entered the office without finding him sitting behind it, his dark gaze intently fixed on his latest project, deal, or idea. Walking into his office and knowing he wasn't there felt odd.

A soft shiver claimed her limbs and she glanced back toward the door.

How many fantasies had she indulged in that had included this desk? The feel of his hands gripping her hips, the relentless pounding of his sex as he'd pinned her to the wood. Images of her with her panties down around her thighs, the touch of his hand against her bare buttocks as he delivered a series of sharp, stinging slaps, causing her to cry out in sensual pleasure.

The memories of those dreams sent a subtle torrent of clenching desire through her pussy.

Now . . . now he wasn't here, and she could bring those fantasies to life, or at least one of them, if only in a small way, but that was all she could ever hope for. What she wanted, what she craved to share with him, could never happen.

A forbidden love.

Or lust.

Either way, she knew it was wrong.

Was it so wrong to dream about the man whom she worked for?

A man like him didn't deserve to be alone. In all the years she'd worked for him he'd been kind, considerate, and thoughtful. But she'd also seen the other side of him: the demanding, forceful, work-and-deadlines man-in-charge who sent shocks of delight through her being.

He was untouchable; she knew that. In-house relationships weren't permitted, according to the terms of her contract. Something about preventing accusations of sexual harassment, but it meant that when it came to Simon Harris, all she could ever enjoy were her own private little dreams.

It just wasn't fair.

He was single, available, attractive, with dark eyes and salt-and-pepper hair. Hair that her fingers always itched to brush back from his face. How many times had she mentioned that he needed a haircut to tidy up those loose ends? She could see his smile even now. The small nod and wave of his hand that meant she was to find a place in his busy day to fit one in.

She could have spent a lifetime listening to his voice, looking into his handsome eyes. But they could share nothing more than coffee and the occasional chat between them, a joke, a laugh; apart from these things, it was all business. As single as he remained, he was her boss, which wiped out his available status, at least as far as she was concerned.

Six long years—if it hadn't been for the occasional heated look she'd caught out of the corner of her eye, she'd never have known of his interest in her. An interest he kept under firm control.

Would he have said something if they hadn't been working together? Suggested a brief encounter, or a permanent one? She'd never know—not unless she left her job and then dared to ask him. No, she wasn't about to do that; she needed the paycheck, and she'd worked damned hard to get this far in the company.

They both had.

So they were both trapped by the rules of the company. This left her only two choices: Shut down her desires for him (and thus deny a huge part of herself), or make him the focus of her deepest, most intimate fantasies.

She knew what her choice had to be.

Claire turned and walked through the office, locking the door and drawing the blinds before she returned to stand in front of his desk. A subtle quiver ran through her body. She could almost imagine him sitting there, his hands steepled, elbows on the desk, his dark gaze taking in every inch of her body.

"Like what you see, sir?" A soft tremble touched her words as she focused on the chair, his chair. She lifted her hands

3

slowly up from her waist and cupped her breasts. "I know you do. I can see it in your eyes. The question is: Would you like to see more?"

His smile played through her mind. The way his gaze narrowed and his lips parted softly, just enough to urge her to continue. Her nipples peaked against her blouse, and heat rippled through her core as she focused on the chair. She tweaked her hardened nubs and groaned, her inner walls clenching with her need to explore, to please him, to please them both.

His aftershave . . . she could still smell it in the office, that seductive, musky scent that permeated the desk, his chair, even the blotter he used on a daily basis. She breathed it in, drinking in his presence.

Footsteps echoed through the corridor beyond the office, and she froze in place.

God, no, she couldn't be caught in here. There'd be too many questions—ones she wasn't ready to answer. Even if she wasn't fired, she wouldn't be able to cope with the rumors. Her heart pounded against her rib cage, and fear stilled her hands as she waited, even if it didn't cool the heat in her sex.

The steps hesitated close to the door and then moved away, slowly at first, then at a steady pace, and finally disappeared.

Though her heart pounded in her ears and her breath came short, she didn't want to stop now. She tugged at the buttons on her blouse, opening them one by one until the fabric parted, fully exposing her lace-covered breasts. Her nipples were rock hard. Fear hadn't killed her passion; indeed, she felt more aroused now. She ran her hands slowly over her full breasts and gasped. Even this light touch set her desire aflame. Her clit and nipples throbbed as one, linked by an unseen chain.

She looked up, her gaze fixed on the desk. He was still there, in his chair. He watched; in her mind's eye, he watched every move she made. Good, she wanted him to watch, needed him to enjoy it, and had no desire to rush the moment. Especially not now.

Who knew when there would be another chance? He was out on a business trip, and the rest of the office had taken the opportunity to leave early.

"Shall I dance for you? Would you like that? Your own private striptease? No smoke, no men howling at me, just you, me, and the dance?" Heat flushed through her cheeks, her fingers tight on the edges of her blouse. "Yes, I think you would. Watch me, then; enjoy every delicious moment of the show. I can see the hunger in your eyes. Taste it on the air. Are you thinking about my body? My lips? My pussy?"

Naughty. So very naughty to say that word aloud. She'd never dared say it to a lover before. Yet here . . . here she had the courage to do anything she wanted. "Pussy." She said it again.

Claire closed her eyes and let her body take over. The blouse slipped to the floor; her fingers settled on the button at the back of her skirt as her hips rolled; the dance took control of her body and soul. The button eased open; the zipper slid down; her skirt opened enough so that she could push it just over her hips as she turned to face away from his desk.

A sultry smile flickered past her lips as she bent over, presenting her ass to the desk before she eased the skirt down fully. Would he like what he saw? Her bottom confined and presented in the deep red of her panties? They'd been a daring, sexy choice. She'd been turned on by the knowledge that she wore them under her business attire all day; and now she offered them to him for his delight. Did his cock harden beneath his pants? Did his fingers tighten, knuckles whitening as he watched her move, dance, writhe for his entertainment?

He had to enjoy it; she needed to believe that.

Claire turned, swaying her ass. Only her panties, bra, and stockings were left as she danced for him in her heels—heels she had worn for him; she knew he liked a woman in them. It was a small choice that she would pay for later, but right now she didn't care, just as long as he smiled at her.

"Do you want me to touch myself?" Her voice was little more than a low purr. "Should I come around to your side of the desk and show you how I like to be touched? You'd like that, wouldn't you?" She'd never have dared to say that to him if he'd really been there—she just wasn't that type of woman—but this was fantasy, and in fantasy she could be anyone she wanted, do anything her heart desired.

With a provocative, sensual strut, Claire walked around the edge of the desk and settled her ass against it, planting her feet on his chair. She could smell him. His scent lingered in the air, adding to the illusion of his presence. Would he touch her or would he wait?

He'd wait. Watch. Be ready for the moment when she needed his touch.

I need him.

No, she wanted him; he was a desire, an addiction she had to keep under control before it overpowered her.

His eyes . . . She could see them, picture how they flared with his hunger. His lips . . . She could taste them as she bent to offer a kiss. His breathing . . . She could hear the sound it made as it grew heavier with desire.

She slid one hand between her thighs, her skin taut beneath her fingers. Heat radiated from beneath her panties, beckoning her attention. She brushed her fingers over the smooth surface of red satin, and her gaze lowered, desire coloring her cheeks. She wanted to say something, to tease him a little more, but her throat closed. Speech died. She licked nervous lips, trying to find the ability to speak, but her body defied the chance to torment him with words.

His chair, his desk, his presence in the office permeated everything around her. He was here. Even if he wasn't here physically he was here emotionally, and that was all that mattered. Her sex clenched beneath the thin covering of cloth. The urge to slide her finger into her heat grew out of control and she surrendered to it. She eased her hand into her panties, searching for the source of the irresistibly moist warmth.

What would she have done if he really sat there?

He is here. He's right here with me.

Yes, he was. A smile claimed her lips, her inner walls clenched tightly, and her body warmed, hungry for more. She brushed her fingers over her clit. A jolt of pleasure rocked through her core, coating her nether lips with desire.

She groaned and stroked her full labia gently, teasing them, tormenting her clit with soft, light touches.

Yes, touch yourself for me, his voice growled low in the back of her mind, so real, so alive that she could have sworn he was there. *Play for me; I want to hear that slick, hungry cunt of yours. Don't hold back.*

Heat flushed through her cheeks, shame and need combined as she slid one finger deep into her tight center. Her thumb slid over her clit. Claire bit down on her bottom lip, trembling, her panties moist, thighs tight. Her firm bottom pressed against the desk, her heels resting against his chair. It didn't matter that this wasn't allowed, or that the man she was doing this for wasn't here. Her mind was all too willing to fill in the rest of the details.

Hard nipples throbbed against her bra. Her breath came in short, sharp gasps. She groaned. She couldn't hold back much longer. She didn't want to hold back. Her body craved the release that dangled just out of reach. She needed something more. Something that she couldn't have right now.

Why can't you have it?

Yes, why? She had the touch of her fingers, the thick heat that had claimed her inner walls; her body hungered; all she needed now was Simon. He was here, a part of the room, a part of the pleasure she enjoyed. His desk. She sat on his desk. Her thighs parted in front of his chair. His presence filled the room.

Come for me.

"I'm not ready," she whimpered, sweat beading across her

brow. No, she wanted more. For him. For herself. Her hips danced; passion claimed her thoughts and movements. She no longer cared whether there was someone in the hall, someone who might walk back and hear her.

All that mattered was this moment. This stolen pleasure.

Come for me—now.

"No, I need more, please. I'm not ready for this." Tears stung her eyes; she didn't want the moment to end.

Yes, you are; you want it, need it, so come for me—come for me now.

She did feel the need to come, but she'd wanted to draw it out. She hadn't planned on . . . on any of this. She'd entered the room to do some work, file some papers, not play around like this. Yet here she was, a wanton, heated slut begging for his attention, needing it with every fiber of her being, and he . . . he sat there, encouraging her to enjoy it.

She groaned, her hips shuddering. It hurt. Oh, God, it hurt, and she wanted more. Needed more. He'd given her permission to come, even told her to come for him.

So do it, give in to it, enjoy it. Please. For me.

Her thighs clenched; she couldn't prevent it. Not now. Pressure built in the pit of her being. She groaned, hips tipping, her heels pressed into the seat of his chair. Her fingers moved feverishly beneath the soft material of her panties, her nipples ached, her breath burned in her chest. Thought fled.

Yes, that's it; come for me now.

She whimpered, her body no longer her own. Pressure rippled through her body, tore into her. She gasped, her back arching as it hit. Hard. Fast. Without mercy. Not a thought for her sanity as it tipped her into the center of the maelstrom and tossed her out on the other side, a beaten, sated wreck of a woman.

Claire slumped back onto the desk, trembling, sweat coating her skin. The phone beeped. A file was knocked to the floor, spilling the papers in a spray of white. Pencils rolled off the end of the desk, but she didn't move. Not yet, at least.

Her heartbeat slowed, her thoughts settled, and Claire shivered. She'd done it. The impossible. A fantasy that she had kept buried for so long, so deeply, had been played out this once, and only this once. She could not take that risk again; nor would she.

She pulled herself up from desk and took a deep breath.

Time to move. There were things she had to tidy up before she left the office. When he returned to work tomorrow, she couldn't risk his knowing what had happened here. What she had done and how she had behaved.

It didn't take long to put things back into place, and thanks to the private bathroom adjoining his office, Claire was washed, re-dressed, and presentable within ten minutes, with barely a hair askew. She smiled and looked around the room. He'd never know; there wasn't one thing out of place that she could see. The smell of sex had even been covered up with a quick spray of vanilla in the air, and by the time the door was opened again in the morning not a hint of the scent would remain. Or so she hoped.

Claire took one last look throughout the room and walked out of the office, locking the door behind her.

Yet, as careful as she'd been, Claire had missed two small things: matching holes in the leather chair left from the heels of her shoes.

THE SOUND OF REVENGE

by Gwen Masters

"I just called to see how you are."

Adam's voice was cool and careful on my answering machine. "I just wanted to check on you. . . . Where are you, anyway?"

Ignoring the phone, I turned to the man beside me. The man in my bed, on my blue satin sheets, the man who wore nothing but the marks of my hands and one neat mark of my teeth. His hand was firm and demanding on my knee. Opening my thighs. Rolling me under him and probing, thrusting, sinking deep.

"Chris," I groaned.

I knew exactly what I was doing. I was cheating on a man who probably didn't give a damn about me, but would be furious to find himself on the wrong side of the fidelity fence. I was cheating on a man who had asked for some space, and now expected me to wait in the corner like the good little girl who had done something wrong.

But the good little girl was too busy doing all sorts of things right.

"Yes," Chris hissed into my ear. The muscles in his arms tensed and relaxed with every thrust.

I thought of Adam, how he had wanted sex only when it suited him. How he would insist on doing it his way, then sulk when I couldn't come, giving me that look that indicated it was all my fault. We would finish with me sucking him off, doing all the things he liked, and he would fall asleep afterward while I stared at the ceiling, frustrated. Who cared what I wanted?

Neglect, mixed with anger, is a powerful catalyst for revenge.

I bucked up into Chris.

He moved as if my body were a gift, not a right. He whispered my name as if it were a message of praise, not a plea.

Adam probably believed I was looking at the phone, longing for more than the few calls we had shared lately. He would be right about the fact that I was looking at the phone. I watched it as it rang again. Three times. Each time, Chris pushed into me, making the bed rock. Then the answering machine picked up again and Chris slid into me from behind. He already knew I loved to feel him grow longer and thicker while he was inside me.

"Baby?" Adam's voice was hesitant, questioning through the tinny speaker of my answering machine. "I just wanted to say I'm sorry. I know you don't deserve the way I've been treating you. I'll make up for it all. Just give me time to work these things out in my head. This separation will be good for us; I promise. Hey . . . where are you? Are you okay? Call me back."

Chris pushed harder. His hips cradled mine as I sank back against him. I swiveled my hips and he groaned.

"Do you want to talk to him?"

"Does it look like I want to talk to him?"

Chris began to thrust gently and I met him each time.

"Next time he calls, will you fuck me while I talk to him?"

Chris laughed out loud. I looked at him over my shoulder. The sound vibrated through him, and his little belly jumped against the cheeks of my ass. His cock twitched, and I squeezed back until his laughter died down to a smart-ass leer.

"Should I fuck you hard, or should I keep quiet?"

That was another thing: Chris was loud. He was as loud as he wanted to be, without regard to what the neighbors might think. He said things, naughty things, called me names and made me blush. He could whisper an endearment just as quickly and easily as he could slap my ass and call me his "sweet little cock-whore bitch."

Adam was always careful to stay quiet, and admitted he was afraid someone might hear. Afraid, as if sex were a dirty thing that we shouldn't be doing. He never called me names, he never said things that shocked me, and he never, ever made me blush. Adam never lost himself completely in the act with me.

"You don't have to keep quiet," I said.

"How do you know he'll call again?"

"Oh, he'll call," I said. "He can't stand the thought that I might not need him anymore."

I slid up and down on that cock that was longer than Adam's. I made it come, let it flood me, and I'd be damned if I didn't come right along with it.

Adam did call. He called while we were eating lunch. He called while we were taking a walk outside. He called once while we were taking a nap, exhausted from all of that fucking. Chris and I had sampled every position known to man and then some. We had explored every kind of fuck, from the slow and easy to the quick and hard. His dick had been in every hole more than once. Chris and I had done more in a week than Adam and I had done in the last year.

I didn't answer Adam's calls. I didn't even consider it, not until the moment Chris was between my thighs and his tongue was working magic on my clit. When the phone rang out into the darkened bedroom, I smiled and picked it up.

"You naughty thing," Chris whispered.

Adam's voice was almost frantic. "Where have you been? I've been calling all day and I've been worried sick!"

I sighed. "Worried? Why?"

Adam's temper was barely held in check. "Because I know you're taking this really hard. I know you are really upset most of the time. I don't want you to do anything. . . ."

"You don't want me to *do* anything?" I repeated.

"I don't want you to . . . well, you know. You're depressed. I don't want you to hurt yourself. . . ."

I laughed out loud. It was a sudden, glorious sound, thrusting against my throat and making it tickle. How long had it been since Adam had made me laugh?

Chris chuckled from between my thighs as he slid two fingers into my pussy.

"What the hell is so funny?" Adam demanded.

"I wouldn't exactly say I'm depressed," I corrected him, when I could catch my breath. Chris got tired of fooling around and braced himself above me. One long stroke and he impaled me, his dick harder than usual, reaching as deep as he could go. I sucked in a breath.

"What are you doing over there?" Adam asked, his voice wary. Almost disbelieving. On some level, he knew already, though the knowledge hadn't quite sunk in, like knowing someone had just died but not being able to grasp the concept of the person actually being gone. I almost felt sorry for him.

Almost.

"I'm a bit busy, Adam. . . ."

Chris leaned down and nibbled on my neck. I bit my lip to keep from squealing in delight. I reached down between us with my free hand and laid my fingers on my clit. Pushed down a bit lower, so I could touch his dick with my fingertips as he pumped in and out. He was slick, so wet, and hotter than a fever.

"Are you sure you want to talk now?" I asked.

Adam huffed. "Well, I certainly think we should. Don't you?"

Why had I never noticed that nasal, whiny tone before? His words didn't leave room for argument, and, truth be told, I had never really protested much anyway. It was easier to agree than it was to get into a long and tense discussion, after which I would wind up agreeing, regardless. Adam was used to getting his way. Whatever Adam said, went.

At least, that was how it *used* to be.

"Well, it's your choice," I said. "You just tell me what you want, Adam, and you shall have it."

The sarcastic tone of my voice wasn't lost on him. He began to talk about how I needed to lose that chip on my shoulder. Perhaps I should find someone to talk with? Someone to help me through this? Perhaps I should get some counseling. There were good counselors who knew how to deal with the kind of anger and abandonment issues I was having.

Chris gently urged me to roll onto my belly. Once I was where he wanted me, he pushed a pillow under my hips. He spread my legs. When his tongue slipped into my pussy from behind, I had to bite my lip to keep from laughing out loud. Then Chris ran his tongue up, playing the tip around the pink rosebud of my ass, and I lost the urge to laugh. I wanted to scream with ecstasy instead.

Adam was still talking. Wasn't he? I pulled the phone back to my ear and tried to concentrate, even as I pushed against Chris and rolled back over. I spread my legs and then he was in my pussy again, staying there for a moment before slowly pulling out.

Adam was going on and on about what it was like to be dependent on someone, about how it wasn't healthy. "I understand you feel like you have to have me around," he said. "It's a natural feeling. But you can be okay on your own, honey. We'll be stronger for it after our break. You'll see soon enough. . . ."

Chris pushed in again, harder this time, rocking the bed. At the same time, he reached under me and pushed a long, slim finger into my ass. My pussy contracted around the cock that was pumping slowly in and out. I ran my hand up his chest, found his right nipple, and pinched it.

Chris moaned.

Adam's tirade went silent for several long seconds, and then his voice came back in a tortured whisper. "What was that?"

"What?" I bit my lip hard and shook my finger at Chris. *Bad boy.*

"That sound . . ."

"Oh. This?" I ground up against Chris, just the way he liked it, and he pushed his finger deeper into my ass. He moaned again.

Silence rang out on the other end of the line.

"No," Adam finally whispered.

"Oh, yes."

Chris began to move harder now, all that staying power finally slipping. I thrust up to meet him every time he plunged deep, no longer hiding the sounds, not trying to make everything seem normal.

"You slut!" Adam hollered, and hearing the word almost pissed me off. How interesting that he could call me names now, but when he was in bed with me and I wanted it from him, he acted as if there were something wrong with my desires. Son of a bitch never had a fucking clue.

"You idiot," I shot back. "Do you really think you are that much of a catch? I'm not depressed. I'm not suicidal. I'm just the opposite. I'm getting over you. You just said you wanted me to find someone to talk to. Someone to help me through it. I'm one step ahead of you, honey."

"How dare you!" Adam shouted, but his anger now seemed impotent and petty.

"Want to listen?"

I still held on to the phone, but I started talking to Chris instead. I told him to make that cock explode inside my cunt; I asked him to fuck me as hard as he could. I described how it felt when he fucked my ass, how it burned and hurt so damn good. I told him how much I loved the way his come tasted when he shot it into my mouth. I told him how good it felt to have a man who would fuck me whenever I wanted, not just when *he* wanted.

"In fact," I praised him, "it feels good to be able to tell a man what I want and actually *get* it, however I please, whenever I please. I never had that before. Isn't that right, Adam?"

"You whore," he whimpered across the phone line.

I pushed Chris back a bit and rolled over onto my belly again. Pushing my ass up into the air, I looked back over my shoulder and gave Chris a saucy grin. "He says I'm a whore, Chris. You know what whores like, don't you?"

Chris laughed as he grabbed my hips with both hands. With his thumbs, he spread my cheeks until my tight little asshole winked at him. He pushed the head of his cock against my ass, slowly putting more and more pressure against it, until we could both feel the opening of my tight passage.

I sucked in a breath as he slid a little deeper. "Fuck, yeah.

That's it, Chris. Fuck me up the ass. Give it to me like a real man, honey. I've never had one of those before."

"You are not!" Adam blurted, still listening in. What a masochist.

"Oh, Adam, you're still there?"

I pushed back against Chris, and suddenly, everything clicked. He slid into me with a small burst of pain that quickly faded to a sweet, aching stretch. He knew the groan that came from me was more pleasure than pain, and it was also an invitation. He started to fuck me, sliding in and out, his hands on my hips. He pushed as deep as he could go, rested there for a moment, and then pulled slowly out, only to do the whole thing again. I knew he was taking his time, letting me get up to speed so I could come along with him.

Chris really *was* the best of fucks.

"Adam," I hissed into the phone. "It feels so fucking good. I can feel that big dick stretching me open every time he slides in. He's got a big one, sweetheart. Huge, as a matter of fact, and the first time he fucked me up the ass, I was sure he would split me in two. But I learned to take it, didn't I? I learned, like good little whores do. Or is it sluts? I've lost track. Which one am I, Adam?"

"Both," he answered immediately, and I grinned. He had to be so pleased with his ingenuity.

"Oh, aren't you clever?"

But that was almost all I could say, because Chris was getting tired of waiting. He was pushing harder and faster, his moans getting more rhythmic with every thrust. His hands were gripping harder now, his fingertips digging into my hips as he pulled me back to meet his strokes.

"Damn, Chris," I managed. "You're going to come soon, aren't you?"

He thrust so hard I dropped the phone. I fumbled for it, found it with one hand, and reached underneath myself with the other. My fingers touched my clit and I stroked it once. Twice. Pressed hard on it, the orgasm right on the horizon.

"I'm going to come, Adam," I said into the phone. "Want to hear me come for my new stud?"

I could hear the heavy breathing on the other end of the line.

"Are you crying, Adam? Or are you getting off? I can't tell which."

Chris laughed, out of breath, close to the edge. I could hear Adam on the other end of the phone line, saying something incoherent. His voice was tinny and distant, but I didn't miss the note of anger it still held.

"Come for me, Chris. You come right now," I demanded.

Chris pressed me hard into the bed. He roared his orgasm, loud enough to wake the neighbors, loud enough to make my intentions clear over a phone line. I strummed my clit for a moment and then I was there . . . almost there . . . a bit harder . . . and I came with a hard, convulsing shout. I dropped the phone onto the pillows. I pushed back into Chris, taking all he had to give me. He pumped into me until he was drained, then collapsed onto the bed with a resounding sigh.

Turning to rest on my back, I caught my breath and picked

up the phone. I could hear Adam breathing, the sound edged with fury. Why had he stayed on the line? There was a note of something else there, and now I knew it was more than a little bit of excitement. Adam always did like the thought of watching me with someone else. Now he got the next best thing.

Even while being fucked over, Adam still thought it was all about him.

"You slut," he growled again.

"I prefer the term *bitch*," I said sweetly.

"You are! You are a bitch! And a slut and a whore and—"

"Yes, yes, all that, too. Good-bye, Adam."

I hung up on him and looked at Chris. He smiled. "Bitch, huh? I think you've been such a *bad* little bitch. You need another good ass-fucking, don't you?"

Chris rolled me back onto my belly, and I buried my face in the pillow. I clutched the headboard as his fingers started to work their magic. I knew it wouldn't take long before his dick was hard enough. I knew he would push it into me, stretching me and turning me on and making me burn, and he would make me come again and again, just the way I liked it. I knew Chris would not stop until I was satisfied.

While we fucked, the phone rang and rang and rang.

SPANKED ONSTAGE

by Iona Blair

"**S**o what you are, in essence, telling me," Dame Philippa stated, in a voice that could have withered a rose, "is that if I don't submit to a spanking in the last act, I'm out of the play."

"Well," producer Roger Ashton replied hesitantly, "I wouldn't quite put it that way." Then, seeming to gather courage from some invisible source, he added with more confidence, "But that scene *is* an integral part of the story."

It was a bright August morning, and a warm gust of wind blew past the theater door as it opened to admit an athletic-looking man with black hair and bold, blue eyes.

"Hello there, Boyd." The pale little producer greeted the newcomer with obvious relief. Facing down the formidable Dame Philippa by himself had been unnerving indeed.

And, as Boyd Sutton was the actor who would deliver the spanking that was causing all the fuss, his appearance could not have been timelier.

Dame Philippa barely acknowledged the newcomer, choosing instead to continue to focus her attention on the unfortunate producer. She was a distinguished aristocrat of an actress, with aquiline features and a mop of silver hair. Accustomed to always getting her own way, she was determined to beat down the insipid Roger until he bent to her will.

"I will not be upended and spanked by anyone," Dame Philippa declared decisively. "Least of all by a B-movie actor like Boyd Sutton." And with that rude denouement she turned her stony gaze on the hapless Boyd, whom she had always disliked.

The play was entitled *The Dinner*, an upper-class romp of a story about a spoiled woman and the man who ultimately tamed her. An integral part of this disciplinary process was a sound, over-the-knee spanking that took place in front of a roomful of dinner guests.

"There is no reason why I should submit to such an indignity," Dame Philippa insisted, her handsome face obstinate. "That the spanking takes place can be just as effectively alluded to, and it would be in much better taste."

Roger Ashton knew that although Dame Philippa was an actress of the highest caliber, she had, in recent years, declined in popularity. This play was a golden opportunity for her to jump-start a flagging career.

He drew himself up to his full height, drawing strength from Boyd's charismatic presence. "If you're not willing, I have a line of talent who would jump to play this role. I'm sure the young and beautiful Ashley Barnes would be more than willing to bend over Boyd's lap."

The furious actress at last agreed. "Oh, very well then." She haughtily tossed her silver hair as she strode from the theater in a royal huff. Dame Philippa was just as accomplished in making dramatic exits as entrances.

The following morning, the rehearsals began, and the entire cast was on hand for the occasion. Dame Philippa, still rather sulky, but performing like the true professional she was, dazzled the company with her brilliant oratory skills and dramatic flair.

Then it was time to rehearse the spanking scene.

Wearing a thin pair of cotton slacks that emphasized her tall, rather coltish figure, Dame Philippa allowed herself to be dragged over Boyd Sutton's lap and spanked at least a dozen times.

Spank . . . spank . . . spank . . . spank . . . Boyd wielded an enthusiastic hand more heavily than was necessary. He was delighted to warm the ass of one of the snootiest actresses in the business.

Spank . . . spank . . . spank . . . spank . . . He paid her back on the seat of her pants for the many insults, both overt and otherwise, that she had hurled at him over the years.

Spank . . . spank . . . spank . . . spank . . . until the howling, which was part of the script, became more of a personal cry of pain.

"You bastard," she hissed when the brisk spanking was at last over. She longed to rub her smarting backside, but knew how this would delight the rest of the company. She was angry with Boyd, but it was the unsettling quiver of excitement tingling through her genitals that upset Dame Philippa the most. That she should actually become aroused by Boyd's spanking, with all of its humiliating undertones, left her feeling shocked and bewildered.

"You did lay it on a bit hard," Roger Ashton agreed with Dame Philippa's complaint, although his thin lips twitched with approval. "Just ease up a little bit, old man; we don't want the leading lady walking out on the production."

"And with a blistered bum to boot." Boyd laughed uproariously, still feeling his palm tingle from its impact with Dame Philippa's regal behind.

The first and only dress rehearsal was performed for a full house, with the usual contingent of journalists and photographers hogging the front row. In a recent tabloid article about the production, the ongoing animosity between Dame Philippa and Boyd was played to the hilt, followed by a vivid description of the spanking scene that had quickly become the highlight of the play.

The article ran with a lewd sketch of the veteran actress being whapped by a grinning Boyd. Her behind glowed as red as her fine-featured face. *Come and see Dame Philippa get her bottom spanked*, the caption invited with wicked enthusiasm.

The air in the crowded theater was electric with excitement as the curtain finally rose and the play got under way.

Dame Philippa was a scene stealer, and looked magnificent throughout in an expensive wardrobe that had been provided by a local fashion designer. Meanwhile, the surly Boyd looked darkly handsome in finely tailored suits that fit him like the proverbial glove.

But slick though the production was, and despite the excellent acting that went into it, the audience grew restive as they waited with barely concealed impatience for the spanking scene.

"Put her across your knee," one impatient patron called out from somewhere in the back stalls. The impromptu remark was followed by similar suggestions amid much jollity and ribald laughter.

Dame Philippa felt her pale face flush. That she, one of the leading actresses of her time, should be subjected to such vulgarity was insufferable. This was producer Roger Ashton's fault entirely.

"Damn the man," she muttered angrily beneath her breath. Would she ever be able to live down this humiliation?

When the curtain finally rose on the last act, the audience sat on the edges of their seats in anticipation. The photographers stood poised with their cameras to record all the action. They awaited the dinner party scene, which took place in a richly furnished mansion with a small army of liveried servants in attendance.

Dame Philippa's character was obnoxiously haughty, as usual, taunting the Boyd character about his humble beginnings and accusing him of being a fortune hunter.

"If that's what you think of me, I'll leave right now and never return." Boyd threw down his linen napkin on the immaculate tabletop.

"But first," he added ominously, a fiery gleam leaping dangerously in his blue eyes, "I'm going to teach you a humbling lesson that you'll never forget."

Then he dragged the protesting Dame Philippa from her chair at the head of the table over to a low, padded stool that sat flush against a wall by the stage-set window.

The veteran actress screamed and fought as she ended up, due to the proximity of the stool to the floor, on all fours on the carpet, with Boyd's lap merely intercepting this most humiliating of positions.

Dame Philippa wore a long, shimmering gown that clung to her shapely bottom like a gossamer web. As Boyd began to spank her, a cry of approval arose from the audience.

Spank . . . spank . . . spank . . . spank . . . The loud whacks rang out through the pregnant hush of the highly charged theater. They landed directly over the crack of Dame Philippa's handsome bottom and made it bounce and jiggle.

Spank . . . spank . . . spank . . . spank . . . The flashbulbs popped like giant fireflies on a sultry evening.

Dame Philippa was determined not to become aroused by the spanking this time, but her body had other notions. She willed herself not to squirm.

Spank . . . spank . . . spank . . . spank . . . Then finally it was over, and Boyd dumped her unceremoniously on the floor before striding purposefully toward the door.

The morning editions all carried blown-up shots of the spanking. Dame Philippa cringed with embarrassment as she forced herself to look at them.

In one photo she looked as if she weren't wearing anything at all, such was the flimsiness of the gown. In another, Boyd's hand was captured for posterity as it landed flat on the crack of her shapely behind.

My God, it looks as if he's fondling me. Through a scarlet haze of mortification, passion flared within her like an activated air bag. *Stop it*, she willed her disobliging libido. *What is wrong with me that I'm getting off on this horrible spanking scene?* She shuddered, thinking about the dozen or so performances of the play she had yet to get through.

I should never have agreed to the spanking, she castigated herself with relentless severity. Yet, she had to admit that it was catapulting her into the limelight in a way that she hadn't been for years. In fact, her flagging career was enjoying a new lease on life. She had already received offers for other projects when this production was over.

And that happy event couldn't come too soon for her liking. For not only was the spanking scene something that she dreaded with every inch of her being, but at the end of the play her character was reconciled with the odious Boyd character, who kissed her lasciviously as the curtain fell.

"Whoever thought acting was easy," she murmured to herself with wry amusement, "has never been spanked and then kissed by a man whom they could not stand . . . nor suffered from becoming hotter than a firecracker in the whole undignified process."

"I'M HEREBY *FORMALLY* DEMANDING THAT Boyd ceases to spank me so hard." Dame Philippa stared down at producer Roger

Ashton, her face stony with dislike. Her regal bottom was, indeed, beginning to bear the marks from the nightly scourging.

"I'll talk to him about it," Roger replied tactfully, although he already had done so numerous times, to no avail.

"We wouldn't want to compromise the reality of the most popular scene in the play," was Boyd's standard response when Roger approached him. "And if Dame Philippa's bum must bear the brunt of this authenticity, then so be it."

JUST ONE MORE PERFORMANCE AND *I'll be through with this hateful production forever,* Dame Philippa consoled herself as she prepared for the final night of the play. It was a foggy November evening, with a cacophony of ships' horns booming out from the harbor. She powdered her imperious features, peering into the mirror with the intensity of the shortsighted.

A whisper of a melody long forgotten drifted in from another dressing room and brought a fleeting smile of remembrance to Dame Philippa's brightly painted lips. She dabbed at her wrists with an expensive French perfume, which mingled with the scent from the floral tributes that were stacked in every corner of the room.

And there would be even more tonight, for as the final curtain fell, the stage would simply be showered with fragrant bouquets from her adoring fans.

But first there was another spanking scene to endure. Her already tender bottom winced involuntarily at the painful thought, while at the same time, her clit twitched in wicked anticipation. "Damn you," she muttered. "You're supposed to hate this as much as I do." She fortified herself for the ordeal with a couple of stiff gins.

"Five minutes, Dame Philippa."

The curtain call sent her into a flurry of last-minute preparations.

As usual, the theater was packed with a lively, expectant audience that wiggled impatiently for the performance to begin. And, as always, it was the last act with its now-famous spanking scene that had drawn most of them.

Dame Philippa delivered an especially good performance, fueled at least in part by the trusty gin, which had made her feel deliciously mellow and smooth.

Perhaps that was why, she decided later, when she bent herself across Boyd's lap for the final spanking, it was with less reluctance than usual.

In fact, as his firm hand began to whap away at her magnificent butt, she allowed herself to enjoy the ensuing rush of desire that had so galled her before.

Spank . . . spank . . . spank . . . spank . . .

The tumultuous sensations coursed through her excited body. "Five . . . six . . . seven . . ." the audience called out enthusiastically.

Dame Philippa trembled with passion, willing the spanking to continue as long as possible, so that she could explode in a glorious orgasm before it ended.

"Eight . . . nine . . . ten . . . eleven . . ."

Boyd delivered an extra-hard swat on the last one.

"Twelve!"

However, it wasn't quite enough for her to reach her nirvana. So, flush-faced and with a soothingly wet pussy that throbbed like a dynamo, she straightened herself up as best she could and hoped that no one suspected her arousal.

But Boyd had been aware of it from the start. He had noticed the tensing leg muscles, the slight movement of her pelvis against his thigh, and the general bloom of passion on her usually austere face.

So the iron lady of the theater is only human after all, he mused delightedly. His cock jumped to attention at the thought. When it was time for them to embrace as the final curtain fell, he pulled her to him with a desire that raged for release.

"Oh, God," Dame Philippa moaned as Boyd penetrated her hungry mouth with his foraging tongue. Then, pulling her taut against him, he explored her straining body with eager hands until she gasped as if scalded, and ground her throbbing sex vigorously against his.

"Encore . . . Encore . . . Encore . . ." the audience demanded. And before the love scene came to an end, Dame Philippa erupted in a frenzied humdinger of an orgasm that left her gasping, disoriented, and weak.

Boyd, shuddering as one in the grip of an ague, hoped no one would notice the great, telltale come stain that spread like an accusation of guilt across the front of his well-tailored pants.

Loads of floral tributes were tossed onto the stage during a standing ovation. The last performance had not disappointed.

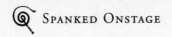

*　　*　　*

THE NEXT MORNING, RAVE REVIEWS popped up all over the newspapers.

But Dame Philippa was in crisis. "Damn that bloody Boyd," she cursed, as her body craved the spanking that had so aroused it during the play.

"You're a bit restless, old girl; anything the matter?" Her henpecked husband, Basil, looked concerned.

Imagine his surprise, Dame Philippa thought grimly, *if I were to tell him I wanted to be spanked.* It was impossible to imagine poor old Basil delivering the kind of brisk, over-the-knee correction she now craved. In fact, it had been quite a long while since they'd been intimate at all, which lent assurance that he wouldn't notice any handprints that might be left behind on her behind.

This new wrinkle in her repertoire was so unlike her stalwart public image, she could scarcely believe it. Dame Philippa appeared far more suited to deliver a spanking than to receive one. But her newly awakened fetish drove her on. The question was, How was she going to satisfy it?

THE DUNGEON WAS AN UPSCALE establishment that catered to sadomasochism in all its forms. "I want to be spanked," explained Dame Philippa to the receptionist. She had disguised her appearance for the occasion and altered her accent, yet the fear of someone recognizing her still persisted.

"Over the knee, bare bottom?" The receptionist wore black leather and bizarre makeup. "Hand, cane, or strap?"

Good lord, you'd think she was talking about a laundry list, marveled Dame Philippa. *She's so matter-of-fact.*

"Over the knee." She mustered as much dignity as possible, considering the circumstances. "A hand spanking, but definitely on a covered bottom."

"Would you like to be spanked by a man or a woman?"

"A man."

The excitement began to pound in Dame Philippa as she was led into a private room. There she was introduced to the Colonel: a tall, distinguished-looking gent with a bushy mustache. He was seated behind a large mahogany desk.

"You've been a naughty girl," he scolded, wagging a finger. "I'm going to give you a spanking. Come here and bend over my lap."

Dame Philippa did as she was told, her heart pounding with anticipation. It was such a submissive position, balanced on her toes and hands, with her bottom raised. The Colonel smelled of tobacco and discreet cologne.

He ran his hand over her bottom experimentally, and thrills shot through her like wildfire. She had deliberately worn a thin dress to better savor the sensations.

She moaned with pleasure. What would Basil and her fans think if they could see her now? she wondered. The ultradignified Dame Philippa about to get her bottom spanked, and not as part of a play. Her face burned scarlet at the thought.

Spank . . . spank . . . spank . . . first on one bottom cheek, then on the other, perfectly timed, and just hard enough to make her behind bounce and sting. Her legs grew taut with sexual tension, and her breathing became labored. An orgasm began to ignite deep in her loins.

She felt suddenly ashamed. Was she expected to go off like this, or hold back until he stopped spanking her and she reached the toilet? She recalled having heard that these sessions were strictly nonsexual.

Oh, to hell with it, she decided. *I'm paying handsomely enough for it, and the customer is king.* She couldn't hold back any longer. Her genitals were on fire. It was torture. She moved her pelvis against his thighs in a desperate fucking motion.

He raised her skirt and spanked her lightly on top of her panties. "Bad girl," he whispered.

"Oh, my good God." Dame Philippa gasped. His hand burned through the flimsy silk, and she experienced sensations so acute they were painful. Yet at the same time, she resented the liberty. Hadn't she stipulated that she wanted the spanking delivered with all her clothes on?

"Pull my skirt back down," she demanded, if weakly. "For decency's sake."

"Now, that's not really what you want," replied the Colonel. "Besides, I'm in charge here." To prove the point he tugged down her panties and told her he was going to give her a bare-bottom spanking.

Dame Philippa squirmed and moaned as he ran his hand slowly over her hot cheeks. It felt cool and wonderfully erotic. He settled his hand directly over the crack, low on the sit spot.

"How dare you . . . ?" Dame Philippa managed to murmur,

desire thick in her throat. "You're fondling my bare bottom. That's way out of line."

"Now I'm going to spank your bare bottom," responded the Colonel, completely nonplussed by her protestations.

She found the sound of the spanking—the sharp *smack, smack* of flesh on flesh—as stimulating as the humiliating position she was in. Her bottom smarted and burned. And she felt shame that the Colonel could see how red he had made it.

But the sheer power of the passion it aroused within her overrode all objections or sense of decency, misplaced or otherwise.

An orgasm pulsed through Dame Philippa, making her feel feverish and disoriented. She bucked and groaned and clenched her feet and hands. She would have toppled off the Colonel's lap if he hadn't held her.

He patted her bottom until she quieted down. Then he pulled up her panties and lowered her skirt. Dame Philippa made no move to get up. She felt so totally satisfied that she could have happily remained there forever.

"I . . . should be going," she murmured.

But the Colonel told her there was no hurry. "Just relax," he said. He placed one hand on the nape of her neck, and the other one rested on her covered behind.

AFTER THAT FIRST SIZZLING EXPERIENCE, which gave her such excitement and relief, the Dungeon became a regular part of Dame Philippa's life. Yet, there was still something missing, and what was more, she knew what it was.

Boyd had spanked her in front of an audience—a full house—and it was the public nature of the humiliation that had added that extra dash of spice.

The Dungeon sought to oblige. The next spanking Dame Philippa received took place in front of a small company of spectators.

Wearing a mask to hide her identity, she lay across the Colonel's lap. He gave her a long, slow spanking, first on top of her dress, then on her panties, then on her bare flesh. Her bottom felt as if it were on fire, and she knew how red it must be.

The Colonel ordered her to bend over a chair. He was going to spank her with a cane. She could feel every eye in the room riveted on her scarlet bottom, and knew that in this vulnerable position her genitals were visible as well. She thrilled at the indignity.

The Colonel laid the cane flat across Dame Philippa's bottom and let it rest there for a while. It increased the humiliating aspect of the punishment. Then he gave it a series of little taps—taking aim—prior to delivering each excruciating stroke.

Thwack . . . tap, tap, tap, tap, tap, tap, tap . . . thwack . . . tap, tap, tap, tap, tap, tap, tap . . . thwack . . .

"The cane is playing with you, teasing you, caressing you," he explained. "Little love pats, and then the agony and ecstasy of the pain . . ."

Dame Philippa moaned and rode a crimson cloud of pleasure that finally crested, a few painful strokes later, into a shuddering explosion. Her audience clapped their approval.

Yet even that failed to satisfy her completely. There was still something missing. The Colonel, excellent spanker though he was, simply wasn't Boyd. She hated to admit it, but damn it, there it was. Bottoms were picky things. Once a certain hand had spanked them to arousal, they wouldn't settle for another. She expected to see the handsome actor at Roger Ashton's Christmas party. It was a lavish affair, held annually at the Hilton. The prospect of seeing Boyd again lent intense excitement to her visits to the Dungeon in the weeks before the holiday.

ROWS OF CHANDELIERS SPARKLED IN the ballroom. A gigantic tree stood by the French windows. Dame Philippa, dressed in yellow silk, browsed the banquet table.

"Can you sit down yet?" Boyd whispered the impertinent question so close to her ear she could feel the warmth of his breath.

"You bastard," she replied. But her eyes were soft and full of promise.

The orchestra struck up the opening bars of "The Tennessee Waltz." Boyd led her onto the dance floor. Dame Philippa trembled at his touch.

"Have you missed me?" he asked boldly.

"Of course not." But when he pulled her closer to feel his erection, she relented. "Yes," she admitted. "Sometimes."

"Like when you feel like getting your bottom spanked?"

She blushed at the directness of the question and refused to reply.

Boyd was undeterred. "I'd like to spank you right now."

"Here on the dance floor?" Dame Philippa was incredulous. Horny, too, and that unsettled her the most.

"Not quite. I have a room upstairs."

The possibilities this offered thrilled her to the marrow. "Basil's with me. I can't disappear for too long."

Boyd nodded. "I'll drift out in about five minutes. Room five oh two."

Dame Philippa shook with anticipation. Her nipples tingled and her pussy throbbed.

Basil was deep in conversation with a group of actors. She slipped out of the hall unnoticed.

Boyd opened his door for her and wasted no time. "You've been a naughty girl, and naughty girls get their bottoms spanked."

Dame Philippa bent eagerly across his lap. He caressed her silk-clad behind. She moaned and ground her pelvis against him. "Ah, yes, you do need a spanking," he declared.

Spank . . . spank . . . spank . . . spank . . . She counted out each delicious swat as if it were manna from heaven. Her bottom trembled with excitement.

Spank . . . spank . . . spank . . . spank . . . Then Boyd raised her skirt and patted her silk panties. Dame Philippa moaned as his hand burned through the thin material to her skin.

Spank . . . spank . . . spank . . . spank . . . first on one cheek, and then on the other.

"Now I'm going to spank you on the bare bottom." He tugged down her panties, rubbed her reddened bottom, and spanked her until she trembled on the brink of orgasm.

"Oh, God." She panted, rubbing her clit against his leg. She exploded against him.

He massaged her back, bottom, and thighs until she calmed down.

"Bend over the bed," he ordered after she caught her breath. She did as she was told. He spread her legs wide apart and entered her with a cock like steel. Dame Philippa's greedy cunt muscles gripped him like thumbscrews. She had never been pounded so vigorously before in her life, and the sensations it aroused in her were acute and unfamiliar. She gasped and groaned and raced toward another planet-tilting climax, with Boyd not far behind.

"God, I wish you could stay all night."

She moaned as he slipped her panties back on and smoothed down her dress. He patted her bottom. "Until the next time," he said, his eyes hot with promise.

THE TASTE OF LOVE

by Alicia Night Orchid

*W*e begin with a canapé—a delicate round of seedless watermelon floating in a ginger-shallot cream sauce, surrounded by emerald green cilantro oil. The watermelon round hosts a spoonful of sashimi tuna marinated in soy, ginger, garlic, and chili, topped by a pale yellow mango crisp.

Wallace observes that he enjoyed a similar dish earlier in the summer. That sauce, however, was an anise emulsion, which he believes offered better balance. You have to respect Wallace, because he's eaten everything and carries the paunch to show it.

Camille complains that her mango crisp isn't really that crisp, having suffered the unfortunate fate of absorbing the tuna's marinade. She finishes her second glass of champagne and prods Wallace for another. She's wearing more jewelry than I own, but is unable to hide the look of someone whose age has caught up with her all at once. There's a looseness to her flesh, as if she's wearing her wrinkled skin as a bodysuit. It's rumored that she once slept with Bill Clinton, or was it Newt Gingrich? Camille can be indelicate, but her palate is unmatched—so long as she remains sober.

It's Laci's reaction that I'm interested in. I watch as the watermelon melts in her mouth. Her warm brown eyes, set wide apart in a tan, boyish face, flutter sensuously.

"They should have sautéed the ginger and shallot in higher-fat butter," she concludes. "The butter they used caused the shallot to caramelize, overwhelming the delicacy of the dish."

She's an ex-chef from a four-star restaurant in Los Angeles and has been the food critic for a major East Coast newspaper for the past ten years. Even Wallace is impressed with her observation, and his loud harrumph confirms it.

"What do you think, Alana?" Laci turns her whole body toward me in a sweeping motion.

I think she's the most self-assured woman I've ever met. I think her taste is impeccable. I think about how wonderful it would be to kiss her, run my tongue across her perfect teeth, smear her red lipstick. It's hard to resist the urge to lick the smudge of cream sauce from the corner of her luscious mouth.

"What makes the dish is the tuna," I say, trying to sound more confident than I am. "Let's face it: This is the most delicious tuna any of us has ever eaten, and each cube is as perfectly diced as its sister."

"No denying the tuna," Wallace agrees.

Laci smiles condescendingly. We both know I'm a token at the table, the food critic for the local paper, while my table companions are international gourmands with a global following.

"This is good tuna," she admits. "Too bad the sauce overwhelms it."

"Yes, I suppose that's true," Camille says, stifling a yawn. "Okay, okay, I'm ready to move on. What's next? Are we having the sauvignon blanc or have we decided on that overpriced pinot grigio?"

Laci winks at me. "I could probably teach you a thing or two."

I wish she would, and I tell her so.

For our first course, Camille and I have selected Pacific prawns on a bed of fire-roasted-tomato risotto. The shrimp is sweet and tender, with a hint of the open sea, the risotto creamy and rich. Fresh peas dot the dish's surface, varying both the appearance and texture. A pinch of microgreens adds interest and a surprising burst of flavor.

"Oh, my God." Camille tilts her head back and stares heavenward theatrically.

"It's wonderful," I say. "I love the peas. Crunchy on the outside. Like velvet on the inside."

"The shrimp is perfect. And there are even bits of lobster in the risotto," Camille reports to the table. "Delicious, just delicious."

Wallace and Laci have opted for scallops. A pan-seared cylinder of flesh resides on a bed of sautéed leeks. A beet-juice reduction, a dazzling crimson concoction, crisscrosses their plates, reminiscent of a Jackson Pollock painting.

"Yes," Wallace says. "Very nice."

Laci nods. "My scallop is slightly overcooked, but otherwise, it's wonderful."

Camille shoots her a glance. "Ah, yes, but you like it pink on the inside, don't you?"

Laci smiles naughtily. "I've been known to."

"I remember only too well."

"Ladies, please," Wallace intervenes. "It's more than an old man can contemplate."

Laci rolls a bite of scallop in the beet reduction, spears a leek round, and offers me a bite.

"How do you like it?"

The scallop is like butter from the sea; the beet and leek are earthy and sweet. I lick lingering juices from my lips. "Incredible," I breathe.

Laci downs the rest of it in one bite. "Scallops should quiver on the inside," she instructs, pointing her fork at me. "Otherwise, this is excellent."

"Next"—Camille waves for the waiter—"It's time for something more robust. We need a white burgundy or a chardonnay."

Wallace fills her glass with the last of the pinot grigio. Camille takes a sip and leans near him, her mouth at his ear. She whispers something while looking directly at me. Wallace stifles a chortle before sliding his arm around her shoulders.

"You are such a vamp," he tells her, to which she merely nods in agreement.

Laci and I choose a butternut squash soup for our next course, while Camille and Wallace settle on the field greens salad augmented with poached quail's egg and lamb's tongue.

The soup, the color of autumn itself, exudes a tangy aroma of star anise, its texture smooth as the underside of a lover's tongue. As the soup coats my throat, I am sated and filled with longing at the same time. I consider discarding my spoon and drinking from the bowl.

Laci's lips close around the spoon as if she's sucking a nipple. She nods approvingly. "Oh, my. Now, that is just right. Simple, elegant, ripe with flavor."

Her shoulders rise up slightly, and under the table, she rests a hand on my knee, as if we are coconspirators in a grand scheme. "Wouldn't this be nice in front of a fire? I just had a wood-burning fireplace installed on my patio, next to the Jacuzzi."

I blink as I see a fantasy image of naked flesh dappled with goose bumps, backlit by a flickering flame. She's a large woman, not obese, just womanly in the classic sense. Her breasts are pendulous, motherly. I imagine her ass—broad, white, and as inviting as an unmade bed.

"Maybe you'd like to try it sometime?" I feel her fingers tighten.

"I'll bring the wine. You make the soup."

"Something like that," she says coyly.

Across from us, Camille and Wallace are increasingly chummy. They've linked arms to share a sip of the California chardonnay Camille settled on. They're laughing heartily at who knows what at this point. Camille quaffs her wine. "Watch out for her, my young friend," she tells me. "When she eats a peach, she doesn't leave the pit."

"Camille!" I feign embarrassment.

Laci is undaunted. "How's the salad, Wallace?" she asks.

"The lamb's tongue," he says thoughtfully, "reminds me of a young man from San Diego."

"He's such a whore," Camille says.

"That's the pot calling the kettle black," Wallace replies.

Laci's touch rides a little higher on my thigh. I adjust the napkin on my lap and stroke the back of her hand with my fingertips.

Between courses, a dollop of lemon sorbet arrives to cleanse our palates. Someone—Wallace, I believe—has ordered a peppery zinfandel. White wine leaves me edgy and wanting more, but the zin warms me, fills me.

Once, in high school, before declaring myself a lesbian, I allowed a boy to fuck me in his car—a used Ford Expedition that smelled of leather and cigarettes. I was on the pill, and because he was a nice boy, I let him come inside, my legs spread wide, feet straining against the back of the front seat. The feeling of red wine hitting bottom reminds me of the sensation of his warm semen bathing the walls of my pussy.

For their main course, Wallace and Camille enjoy a veal loin swimming in a silky demi-glace, accompanied by a parsnip puree and an assortment of wild mushrooms and truffles.

Laci and I have chosen the rack of lamb. The scent of rosemary and garlic rising from the medium-rare chops is like coming home from the woods on a winter evening. The pink of the flesh is like the pucker of a lover's ass.

Wallace raises his glass in a toast. "To the chef."

"To the chef," we all repeat.

We watch as he inhales a bite from the tines of his fork. His expression is pure bliss. He chews once, twice, and then rinses it down with another sip of wine. "Oh, yes. Yes, yes, yes."

"Now, who did that remind you of?" Camille asks. "The young man from New York or that married fellow from Boston you seduced last week?"

Wallace shakes his head. "Neither, my dear. More like the tender loins of other boys I had when I was but a boy myself."

"Tender loins, my ass." Camille waves a hand over her dish, inhaling the fragrance of the mushrooms. "Oysters, porcini, chanterelles. Black truffles. It's fucking sex on a goddamn plate."

The folds of the oyster mushrooms glisten in the dim light, and the entire restaurant is suddenly redolent with the truffles. I can't look away, and Camille reads me for the wanton little slut that I am. She offers a taste from across the table.

"Oh, I can't," I stammer.

"But you must," she says. "Never pass up a chance encounter with a fat black truffle."

Taking the truffle and rolling it through my mouth is like eating a lover's pussy for the third time in the same evening—musky and familiar—and no sooner do the juices release in my mouth than they release in my satin panties. Oh, I'm slippery down there, all right, slippery as an oyster in its shell. An oyster ready to be shucked and swallowed whole.

"This lamb," Laci says, "is outstanding. Domestic, for sure, not gamy, like the Australian lamb Wallace and I had in Philadelphia last week."

Her measured tone belies her surreptitious movements under the table. I'm still recovering from the truffles when her hand takes mine and pulls it deep into the crotch of her wool-blend slacks. "What do you think, Alana? Have you tried the lamb yet?"

Wallace and Camille are too engaged in their tenderloins and truffles to pay us any mind.

"Not yet," I manage, barely able to speak.

"You really should," she says, but when I try to withdraw my hand, she clenches powerful thighs together. "Here, I'll cut it for you."

Laci reaches across to my plate and slices a bite of lamb. As she feeds me, her forearm brushes my nipple through the silk of my blouse, and she might as well have tweaked my clit. I am thankful that she and I are against a wall, and no one can see my hand caressing the fabric between her legs. She's wet, too. I can tell by the way the fabric glides across her slit.

Her eyes are on fire as she watches me devour the lamb. It's strong, chewy, filling.

"You two, you two!" Camille snaps her fingers at us. "You can take the girl out of the bedroom," she confides to Wallace, "but you can't take the bedroom out of the girl. Look at these two lovebirds."

I pull my hand away from Laci. "You have such a dirty mind," I tell Camille.

"You wouldn't have a clue," she replies, "but you can find out anytime you want."

"How's the lamb?" Wallace asks me, saving the moment.

"Luscious, delectable, scrumptious. All these things and more," I say.

"You're drunk, to boot," Camille says, and tilts her wine-glass in my direction. "Short-ball hitter," she concludes contemptuously.

"I'll bet she can go the distance," Laci says.

"But can she take you the distance? That's the question," Camille replies pointedly.

"Bitch," Laci breathes into my ear. "Her, not you."

Dessert arrives in a flourish of waiters and plates and decaf coffee. Laci and I share a chocolate-chocolate raspberry torte decorated with chocolate ganache butterfly wings that remind me of freshly shaven labia. So much fucking chocolate. I want to eat it off of Laci's breasts. I want to melt it on her belly and drink it as it drips from between her legs.

Camille and Wallace are sharing an old standby, the crème brûlée. Camille feeds it to him as if he were a baby. His face has grown heavier, his voice more gravelly over the course of the evening. "The cream," he mumbles between bites. "I love the cream, love it, love it, love it."

"There, there." Camille pats his back, rubs his shoulder. "Of course you do, of course you do."

49

Laci grips my forearm. "We're off to the ladies'," she announces, pulling me after her.

"Sluts," Camille calls after us. "You're both sluts."

It's late and we've overstayed our welcome, even for food critics. The restaurant, including the ladies' room, is deserted. Laci kicks open a stall, towing me along. Once inside, she kisses me, gives me a swirl of tongue, before pushing me against one wall and flattening herself against the opposite.

"Show me your breasts," she demands.

And, of course, there's no denying her now. I fumble with the buttons of my blouse, the front snap on my bra. My tits spill into my hands, white and firm, but no larger than passion fruits.

"Milk them," she orders.

How does she know I'll do anything she asks? I squeeze and pull, gently at first, then more aggressively, watching her watch me. Her mouth is a perfect O, her eyes glassy. I'm dizzy, floating, suspended like an egg about to be poached.

"Feed them to me," she breathes into my ear.

I cup a breast in each hand and offer them up, kneading as if I'm making bread. She graces first one nipple, then the other with her mouth. Sharp teeth nibble and nip.

"Suck me till I bleed," I say in a gasp. My ass thumps the bathroom wall like a pulsating blender.

She steps away, face flushed. "Show it to me. I've been thinking about it all night."

I lift my skirt, push panty hose and panties down, step out of one leg. Below the stripe of curly brown hair, I open myself. I'm ripe and red as a blood orange, oozing juice.

"Fuck," she says. "Turn around."

I face the wall, panting like a bitch.

"Spread your cheeks. Show me everything."

I'm beyond any semblance of modesty. This woman owns me. I thrust out my ass, rotating it, beckoning her. I spread myself for her like a cheap whore. She's down on me that fast, her nose in my butt crack, her tongue in my cunt. While she laps at my opening, I finger my clit. I feel it building, bubbling like a pot about to boil. "Oh, shit," I whisper. I'm almost there already, sooner than I want to be.

It's her clue to withdraw. She leans against the far wall again and wriggles out of slacks and a thong. She takes my hand and guides it between her legs. I love it that she's natural, bristling with fur. The residue of my own syrup shimmers on her cheeks as my fingers find her groove. She's so wet it's like dipping into a finger bowl.

Inside, her pelvic muscles tug and squeeze at my tentative digit. She pulls away and lifts my nectar-coated fingers to my mouth. "Taste me," she says.

She's salty and sweet at the same time, like Junior Mints and popcorn at a movie, and I want more. I drop to my knees, burying my face in the fur, kissing thighs and lips, running a tongue inside her crease. A strong hand on the back of my head pulls me closer.

I penetrate her with two fingers, while the flat of my tongue circles her clit. This girl knows what her lover needs. This girl knows how to get off. She rides my fingers, grinds against my face, whimpers out her fuck noises. I flick her fast and light with the tip of my tongue until a sudden, sharp intake of air tells me that I've got her. Her come starts with a, "Yes, yes, yes," continues with a long spasm of her belly, and ends with the walls of her cunt rhythmically clenching my fingers.

When she's seen it home, I nuzzle my way up to her throat. She holds me, telling me how beautiful I am, what a wonderful lover I am. I sink into her arms, those large, firm breasts. She pushes a thigh between my legs, and I begin to hump while her hands clench my ass. I'm beyond lust, in the fuck-drunk zone where the only way out is to come and come and come.

"Oh, God, oh, God."

She's kissing me and I'm grinding against her. Our nipples duel like swords. Our bodies undulate like batter in a blender. And then I'm there and there and there, my face in her shoulder, my pussy slick and swollen and twitchy against her greasy thigh. When it's over and she's wrung every drop of pleasure from my body, she kisses me hard enough to bruise my lips.

"This is just the beginning," she whispers.

"I want to crawl inside you."

"I'll tell you when."

Camille and Wallace have departed by the time we return. The busboys have cleared the table, and the headwaiter explains that Wallace has paid the tab, courtesy of one of the several periodicals for which he writes.

"Wallace always picks up the tab," Laci says. She pulls a fifty from her wallet. "Our compliments to the chef."

We hold hands on our way to the door. "I can't wait to

make you breakfast," I tell her. Breakfast is something I can do. I've had plenty of practice on myself.

"What did you have in mind?"

"Eggs Benedict, bananas Foster, French toast. Anything you like."

"An omelet with Gruyère cheese and chives works for me."

"Strong, hot coffee."

"Definitely, and maybe a Danish," she says.

"Maybe bagels and lox," I counter.

"With capers, mascarpone, and diced red onion."

"Mmm."

Laci smiles and squeezes my hand. She flags a cab by twirling her panties in the air. We both laugh, giddy with the meal, the wine, the sex. I think this woman is going to like me—at least, as long as the food lasts.

ABROAD

by Chelsea Comeau

I have never felt the flat side of a ruler strike me until this very moment, but I know now that every second of it is entirely enjoyable. I also have never been bent over the edge of an old oak desk in a schoolroom, but they say that there's a first time for everything, and that is certainly true today.

A bouquet of hot dirt and sweat is ever present; I've grown used to it. I live in a small apartment in Johannesburg, South Africa, and even the curtains harbor the aroma of warm earth. The heat is inescapable. I teach English to sweet-faced ten-year-olds in a classroom filled with mosquito nets and ripped-up textbooks, and I feel as though I can always smell the pungent moisture in the crooks of my armpits.

There is another teacher here, Canadian like me. Jacob is a Nova Scotian, while I am from a dry prairie province filled with golden wheat and the smell of tractor exhaust. We might as well be from opposite sides of the world. He has smooth, pale hands that move languidly when he speaks, as if he is never in a rush to do anything at all. The female children are all absolutely in love with him, and as the boys head home after their lessons are over, the girls surround Jacob. They giggle and try to brush him with their hands.

Everything he does is with purpose. I never pegged him for the spanking type, but here he is. He's relinquished the ruler in favor of his open palm, swatting occasionally between the rhythmic bucking of his hips. He is all grunts and calculated squeezing, as if he has been thinking about this for a very long time.

To say I'd never wanted him would be a bold-faced lie. In all honesty, I've often fantasized about his long fingers gripping my breasts, how his tongue might taste in my mouth.

Jesus. I haven't had sex since I was twenty-seven, which was four years ago. The thought saddens me. There is a rivulet of something hot and sticky trickling down the inside of my thigh, and it's surprising to me—I barely remember the minor details of this sort of thing. Jacob's right hand clamps softly over my swinging breast and tugs gently at the nipple. The gasp I hear is coming from my own dry throat, disembodied as it seems.

His arm is suddenly around my midsection, and in one liquid movement he has withdrawn and flipped me over onto my back. The desk beneath me is smooth and polished and squeaks against my flesh. The seconds of emptiness are agonizing. He slides me toward him so that part of my ass hovers off the edge of the desk. Both hands cup my breasts, and he slides seamlessly back inside. My spine arches.

The blood has rushed my ears, buzzing warmly, and I almost do not hear the knocking on the door.

Everything finishes as quickly and suddenly as it began. I am confused when Jacob's shoulders slump and he pulls away, quickly buckling his pants around his waist. But then I hear the persistent rapping on the door, and panic sets in like fog. I hop down from the desk and slide my skirt from the crumpled heap around my hips back to my knees. An administrator has come with an armful of paperwork and questions, and I busy myself with marking while Jacob handles the inquiry.

When I glance at my watch, I realize that it is time to go home and feed my cat. He is probably mewling hungrily at the door, pawing at his empty food dish and hating me. And I'll have to call my mother soon so she doesn't panic. If I haven't picked up the telephone by a certain time, she is sure that I'm dead, and all manner of I-told-you-sos are flying through her head. I am already slinging my purse over my shoulder when Jacob finishes speaking with the administrator.

I HAVE NEVER HAD SEX without discussing it afterward, whether I'm arranging a date for it to happen again, or telling So-and-so that it's probably best we don't see each other anymore. There is always some sort of conversation about it. This time, however, I am scraping tuna out of a tin and into a plastic food dish with my phone cradled between my ear and shoulder, telling my mother that nothing out of the ordinary has happened today.

"I went to my book club this afternoon, and do you know

what?" My mother's book club is literally her life. Since my father passed away, she has filled her empty rooms with books, classics like *Pride and Prejudice*, which she secretly can't stand, and modern marvels like Miranda July's collection of short stories, *No One Belongs Here More Than You*.

"What, Ma?"

"Alice brought *the* most delightful lemon bars, and they were low in fat! Can you imagine? Low in fat and smothered in icing! Splenda, she says she uses."

"That's great, Ma, low-fat."

"'Just write the recipe on a napkin for me,' I told her, and she did. I'm going to send it to you. Not the napkin. I'll write it out again on some paper and send it to you. Can you make lemon bars in Johannesburg?"

"Of course, Ma." My cat is tracing figure eights between my feet, and I stoop to place his food down on the tile floor. "Listen, Ma, I have to go finish making my dinner, okay? I'll give you a call tomorrow."

She wants to tell me more about the lemon squares, but she knows that I'm probably not even listening, so she tells me she loves me, and that's that. I hang up and start digging in the fridge for the raspberry jam. I'll have a sandwich for dinner, and maybe even some fruit. And I'll be thinking of Jacob the entire time.

After I eat, I brush the bread crumbs off the counter and wash my plate in the kitchen sink. I remember the last time I had sex—awkward fumbling in the front seat of a red Honda after one too many bottles of Alexander Keith's pale ale. The phone rings. I think it will be my mother, excited about something she saw on CNN. Or outraged. Either one warrants a long-distance phone call.

"Kerry." It's Jacob.

"Hi." My voice eases into a smooth, velvet tone easily. I'm secretly impressed with myself.

"Things were interrupted, and I feel terrible. Are you busy?"

I pause for dramatic effect, so he thinks that maybe I'm a little preoccupied, that maybe I can't make any plans with him right now. "Not really. Why?"

"Well, I was thinking maybe we could finish what we started earlier."

I can tell without seeing him that he is smiling, and that there's a thin film of sweat on his upper lip. I give him directions to my apartment and then erupt in a flurry of cleaning and changing. I leap out of my skirt and blouse, unhook my bra with one skilled hand, and begin pawing through my dresser drawers for something more acceptable than my everyday garb. Jacob is the sort of man who demands silk and lace without really demanding it. His chiseled bottom jaw and sea foam–flecked eyes say things his mouth doesn't.

When I originally packed my bags for Johannesburg, I didn't think I would ever need my silk teddy, the color of cold cream, but I shoved it in there anyway, between my jeans and a white cotton T-shirt. I wanted pieces of home to travel with me everywhere, in case I felt nostalgic. Now I praise myself for the decision. I wriggle into the teddy, sliding my panties down and off, and unbind my hair so that it hangs down to the middle of my back in what I romantically imagine are chestnut waves. Really, my hair is probably too wild and frizzy from the heavy heat. There isn't time to wash and condition and mousse before he arrives.

I wish momentarily that there were candles to light, but the sun is dipping below the horizon, and an orange-pink glow swathes my living room. Perhaps candles would ruin the effect.

There is a knock on my door, and my heart is suddenly thundering in my chest. It is all I can hear as I grasp the knob in my fist and turn. Jacob has picked a large, vibrant flower from a tree somewhere nearby. I don't know what kind it is, but it's something that would be quite exotic to everyone back home, and I smell it when he hands it to me. He kicks his shoes off, and I shut the door behind him.

"I have wine," I say. "Would you like a glass?"

"Please." He grins, sitting down on the sofa. I go to the kitchen counter and pour two glasses. He hasn't mentioned the teddy, but I know he notices; he's watching the sway of my hips as I come to sit down next to him.

We are suddenly down two glasses apiece, and the room has gone soft and fuzzy. Jacob's fingers twirl strands of my hair, and we talk about the most mundane topics. I am now equipped with the knowledge of Jacob's favorite colors and movies, and how he got that jagged scar on his kneecap. He tells me about the neighborhood in which he grew up, the bully who broke his nose when he was nine. I have no stories for him from my childhood. I was completely average in every way, except for the third-grade spelling bee I won because the kid beside me misspelled *population*. Nothing is more meaningless, or more wonderful, than banter that inevitably leads to sex.

I open a second bottle of wine and pour us each another glass. As I set the bottle down on the coffee table, he catches my face between his palms and presses his mouth against mine. His lips slide warmly open, and his tongue flicks against my own. That smell of dirt and sweat is everywhere, intermingling with his musk, and goddamn it, I want to finish what we started earlier. I press harder into him, and he unbuckles his pants. I am lifted into the air, deposited onto his lap, speared by his cock. His nose rests between my breasts, and I begin moving slowly up and down on his hardness to the rocking of some distant ocean. The Atlantic, maybe, rushing to the Nova Scotian shore.

My head tilts back, hair swaying. His hands slip over my hips to the mossy space between my thighs, and his thumb moves in lazy circles. There is a quiver beginning like a tremor in the very pit of me, a commanding heat. I rail against it, prolong its swell, but it surges on relentlessly until it washes over me and a shudder rocks my entire body.

Jacob exhibits a subtle twinge, and leans forward to capture my mouth in a kiss. He quivers, and a deep groan escapes his throat. Chest heaving, he falls back against the couch, and I loll there for a moment or two before climbing off of him.

I had forgotten about the all-encompassing Johannesburg heat until this very second, and it strikes me like a heavy blow. I am unable to move, every inch of me sodden. I crave cool water, and my thoughts race to the shower only a few feet away from us. Jacob reaches forward and downs his fresh glass of wine.

"Would you like to shower?" I ask him, and he nods, eyes hovering at half-mast in a swoon. I rise and lead him to the bathroom. I can feel my hips swaying as though I am a sated feline who is very pleased with herself.

I run the shower water much cooler than I normally would, and when we step into it together, Jacob squeezes watermelon body scrub into his hand and stirs lather between his palms. His fingers trail a firm path from my shoulders to my breasts, and I am deliciously soapy. He takes my earlobe into his mouth and tugs. He is determined to feel me shake again.

If I had ever considered the act of someone else washing my hair, I would probably have worried they would get shampoo in my eyes, or not rinse properly, or any manner of unfortunate things. But as Jacob begins kneading conditioner against my scalp, I realize that nothing could be more exhilarating than being washed by another. Suds slide down my back, pooling at my feet, and then Jacob takes another handful of body scrub. Over my belly his palms rove, around my back to cup my buttocks. And then the purposeful trail to my front, where his fingers slip between my legs and work my clit rhythmically back and forth. I brace myself against the wall, knees trembling. I feel my orgasm stirring again, slower this time, but deeper.

My fist closes around a clump of fish-print shower curtain,

and as the hot swell rises up over me once more, I am shaken by a spasm and I tug, tearing the curtain from its plastic rings. A shout has escaped from my mouth, and Jacob smiles, holding me firmly around my waist.

I inhale deeply. There is no scent of hot dirt this time, no sweat. There is only clean, slippery skin. And watermelon.

RED UMBRELLA

by Belle Watling

They first fucked on a Monday morning. The sky, a slate gray, scattered pearl drops of wet on the sidewalk. He opened his wide, red umbrella for her; she lifted her skirt for him. His fingers, slick and cold, pressed into her slippery and hot pussy. He drank deeply. Used a long proboscis tongue to reach deep and draw out the sweet nectars. Pressed against the wall, her skin rubbed pink against rough, dripping bricks; he pushed his cock in deep. She rose and fell with his grunts, rose again to grasp a thrumming orgasm, and then fell nose-first into the expansive wool on his shoulder. He smelled of cut oak. Her panties were torn and soaked; she left them behind.

At the office she noticed telltale runs on her stockings; those she tossed in the wastebasket beneath her desk. In the conference room she carefully crossed and uncrossed her thighs, aware of the semen he had left behind.

What was his name? She tried to remember.

At lunch a cherry tomato burst in her mouth, a reminder. She said to her companion, "Cecilia, I think I have a problem."

"Oh, don't worry about it, Vanessa, you know Bob can be a creep."

"I'm not talking about work."

"Then what?" Cecilia tore a muffin between her fingers.

"I had sex with another man."

Intrigued, Cecilia leaned forward, one eyebrow arched. "Who?"

"I don't know his name."

"When did this happen?"

"This morning, before work. He shared his umbrella. Those hands . . ."

"Where? At your house? Was Josh home?"

"No, no. Of course not at the house." Face pink, she leaned forward, whispered, "In the alleyway behind the brewery."

Silence.

Then, "How did this happen, Vanessa? This doesn't sound like you."

"I couldn't help myself. One large hand held the umbrella, and one held mine. His was like an envelope, my hand a love letter."

"I don't understand. I thought you loved Josh. Why did you do this to him? And with a stranger, too!" Cecilia wore a look of reproach, but Vanessa saw something else in her eyes. Envy? Excitement?

"I didn't do anything to Josh. I did this to myself."

The hour was up. They pushed their chairs back, returned to the workday.

Vanessa stared blankly at her computer screen; she could think of nothing else but the stranger in the wool coat. She had seen only his hands and his face swathed in a stretch of unblemished cocoa. He had seen her thighs, her breasts, her pussy. She wondered what his cock looked like. Was it a marble pestle or was it flesh?

Five o'clock. Only a fraction of her article completed. She zipped her laptop and notes up in her bag; work would come home with her tonight. The rain had cleared. She passed by the brewery, the rich scent of hops arousing her senses. She considered going to look for the panties; instead she hailed a cab and rode home.

Josh was there, wearing only an apron and socks. He had made lasagna, her favorite. A shot of regret stung her throat.

"Hi, baby!" He snuggled her tight, kissed her with those familiar lips, his stubble scratching at her tender skin. She hadn't kissed the stranger this morning; she wondered if his kiss would have been as forceful as his thrusts. Would his cheek have been smooth? Josh gripped her bare thigh with one hand. "I see you went without stockings today." His breath was hot on her neck. "Sexy." His hand inched up under her skirt. She was wet despite herself. "No panties either. For me?" He pushed a finger inside and beckoned her to come.

Vanessa gripped her husband's bare shoulders. Bit deep. Josh knew how to touch her; she'd been schooling him for five years. She came wet and hard. She gushed onto his hand, onto the tile. She hoped that Josh didn't notice the scent: the smell of her musk tainted by the seed of a stranger. He bent her over the counter, shoved her skirt up around her waist, and fucked her furiously. Grabbed her hair like reins in his hand and slapped her ass crimson. The granite edge bit into her elbows, and she imagined it wasn't the pink cock of her husband, but the stranger's mysterious cock pounding her into the counter. It was this thought that sent her over for the second time. A freight train resonated in the night.

The lasagna burned; they ate takeout.

TUESDAY. A FOG HAD DESCENDED over the city, but no rain. Vanessa pulled on a lacy pink thong, spent a few extra minutes looking at her reflection in the mirror. Her heart beat quickly; a tingle had erupted in her belly. She couldn't eat the waffles that Josh had made her. She drank black coffee. Remembered his black hair, short, textured hair so unlike Josh's soft blond curls. Josh reminded her she should bring an umbrella. "It might rain," he said. She hoped so.

The driver dropped her at the same street corner he had the day before. She stepped out into the fog. Everyone looked the same. Shadows in the gray. She waited, desolate. A beat passed. She walked slowly. Laughed at herself. What was she thinking? She shrugged off her fantasy, lighter now, her pace quickening.

A hand on her arm.

His hand on her arm.

She looked up. His eyes, black as eternity, looked down at

her. He twisted a lock of her hair around a finger. Fire around a coal.

A smile shared, they knew what was next.

No need for the umbrella this time. Fog shrouded them in ethereal privacy. She sat on iron stairs. He kissed her with ripe mango lips. He enveloped her mouth in his, profited from her breath. His cheek was smooth, his tongue spicy. Her heart clattered and knocked in her chest. His kiss spread downward like paint, rolling up and down her neck in long strokes, then along her chest in short, wet bursts as each button came undone. Those lips imbibed her nipples. They painted slick stripes between her breasts, and varnished her stomach till it shone. They spackled her lower belly with desire and finally rested where skin met skirt.

He spread her open with eager fingers and mashed his face into her scent. He tore her thong in two. A distant guilt sounded like a faraway church bell; the thong was a gift from Josh. Remorse was forgotten in her need to see his cock. She lifted his face away from her pussy, encouraged him to stand. His belt, leather, was undone. She shrugged his pants down. His cock sprang forth, awakened. It was dark brown, long, sheathed in foreskin. She stroked its length; it was big enough to hold in two fistfuls. She opened her mouth, swallowed him halfway. The enormity of the situation began to sink in. How could she live without this cock? How could she be with Josh and his conservative pink dick after this?

She gobbled him up, felt his balls heavy in her hands; then they tightened. He exploded with the flavor of fresh cucumbers, and she swallowed.

He picked her up, set her on the stairs so that her ass was in the air before his face. He tongued her there, a place where Josh had never touched. She squirmed. He pushed the flat of his hand on her lower back and opened her up to him. His long tongue pushed and coaxed until her resistance drifted away into the fog.

She thought it would be impossible. She was wrong. His cock, hard again, pushed between her ass cheeks. He spread her wide with his fingers and worked her juices up and around his shaft. She felt herself relax. Her hands gripped the cold metal of the stairs, and she allowed herself to slide deep and wide on his persistent cock. Her pussy felt empty and wet and wanting. A cry erupted; had it come from her lips? She didn't know, but soon her body quaked. The railings rattled.

It took only a few short thrusts and he expanded inside her. A grunt. A kiss on her soft, round cheeks. He slid out and she wanted him back inside more than anything.

He helped her straighten out her clothes. He pushed an errant strand of hair behind her ear. She watched forlornly as his shadow receded into the fog.

CECILIA LOOKED WORRIED. "WHY ARE you so late?"

"The fog."

Unconvinced, she asked, "Why do you look such a mess, Vanessa? Your mascara is running. Were you crying?"

She tried to remember. Had she cried when the stranger left her? Had she cried when she realized that her husband would never satisfy her again? She remembered. She had cried when his cock had deflowered her asshole. "Yes, I cried," she said.

"Are you okay?"

"No. I'm in love."

"You are lucky."

"No. I'm in love with that stranger."

She went to the bathroom, cleaned her face with a damp towel.

THAT NIGHT JOSH LOOKED AT her with concern. "You seem tired. I hope you aren't getting sick." He made her a cup of tea, changed the bedsheets, and tucked her in with a kiss. When he climbed in bed later, he pulled her to him, opened her legs in the night, and groaned as he came.

She slept.

Wednesday the sun shone. She felt optimistic. Josh handed her a mug of steaming black coffee. "Do you feel better?"

"Yes, much." She kissed him, left for another workday.

The air was warm and smelled clean and fresh. The scent of seawater wafted in from the shore. She inhaled. She smelled oak where sea should be. He was there.

No coat this time. She could see the coil of muscles beneath his shirt. She felt excited; she felt ashamed at her excitement. Her nipples betrayed her.

He held her close. His breath traveled in her hair. "Let's go," he whispered.

She wanted to say no; she wanted to say yes. "It's sunny out," she said.

"We'll find a place," he reassured her.

A door off the alley opened into a utility room. The electric vibrations thrilled her. She could feel her pussy blooming. She wanted him in her. In her mouth. In her pussy. In her ass. She wanted him.

He drew her to him, stripped her bare, and pushed her to her knees. He entreated her to open his zipper to suckle his cock, draw it to hardness. She did; she would do anything for this man.

Her tongue lapped and licked at his length. It stretched to forever. She wanted this forever. Tired of the teasing licks, he held her head in his hands and pushed in deep. Gagged her. He stroked her throat insistently in a rapid and unforgiving rhythm. Her mouth stretched around his girth. Her jaw ached; she smiled up at him with watery eyes. Saw him looking down at her, his lips curled in a grimace of pleasure, his eyes glimmering in the dim light. She saw in those eyes that he wanted her as much as she wanted him. Maybe even more.

He lifted her up in his strong hands, suspended her over his cock, and slid easily inside. No need for preliminaries. She was slippery with need, ready for him. She swung by the strength of his shoulders, pistoned on the thickness of his sex. He pushed her thighs up and down, sliding her along the length of his cock as if she were as light as a marionette. He kissed her neck, suckled her breasts, pulled her nipples in between his teeth, and bit. The electric thrum in the room was contagious. She pulsed and rippled and drew out his seed. A moan erupted from both their mouths, entwined.

He eased her to her feet. He admired her body with avaricious eyes.

"I think I love you," she said, a whisper.

"I'm leaving," he said.

"Where are you going?"

"Home. To Morocco."

"When?" She tried to sound flippant, not forlorn.

"Tonight."

He slid his pants back on. A final zip cleaved the air around them. His eyes, which had been shot through with passion, were now dimensionless. He ushered her out the door and walked west toward the water. She walked east.

Distraught, she phoned work. She was sick, she said. Lovesick, she thought. She wouldn't be in today. Tomorrow, she hoped.

She couldn't go home. Josh was home working. He would see her sadness and ask why. It would hurt.

She sat at a small, round table inside a cafe. The air smelled of baked goods and love. She ruminated on love; what was it? An orgasm? A kiss? An embrace? A man walked in carrying a red umbrella, closed. Her heart leaped. Was that love? It wasn't him. Her heart quieted. She had nowhere to go. She ordered a second coffee, black, and sipped on it slowly until it grew cold in her hands. Her passion cooled. What had been wet now dried.

That evening she returned home. She took her suitcase out of the closet, opened it, and stared at the empty space for some time.

Josh asked, "You leaving?"

"I need a vacation," she said.

"I love you." He smiled. He came up behind her and kissed the nape of her neck, sending frissons down her arms. "I love you, Vanessa. I love everything about you," he whispered, his breath hot in her ear.

She closed the suitcase.

Satisfied.

PLEASE, SIR

by Jordana Winters

The temperature in her apartment was stifling, the air thick and oppressive. She'd sat down for a few minutes, but it proved to be a feeble attempt to soothe her nerves, so she'd resumed her spot on the floor and continued pacing.

She'd chosen her outfit carefully—a black bustier, black panties, red garters with vinyl platform boots, and a submissive collar.

She kept glancing at the time, but the hands on the clock didn't seem to be moving. She felt panicky, scared, and yet, at the same time, she was giddy with excitement.

Getting Cole to her place had been easy. She'd called him, feigned boredom, and told him she wanted to do something. He agreed, and she knew he assumed they would do the usual—go out for coffee, drinks, catch a movie, or just sit around shooting the shit.

They'd met in college and had been best friends ever since.

If neither of them had been in a relationship when they'd met, she would have pursued him. Their story was so clichéd it would be the perfect tale on which to base a romantic comedy—best friends in love with each other, neither of them wanting to admit it. Or at least, Jenna was in love with him, a fact that she could no longer deny. She was wickedly attracted to him—his charm, wit, and intellect, not to mention his physical presence, which, as the years progressed, she found more and more difficult to resist.

In three years, they had come to know each other better than anyone else could. He'd comforted her through every breakup and vice versa. Why theirs had never progressed to a romantic relationship, she didn't know. Together, she knew they would be unstoppable.

They'd fucked once. He had been Jenna's date for her employee Christmas party. They drank too much and ended up having sex on her couch. It was awkward and unexpected. Afterward, neither one of them mentioned it. It might as well not have happened. But it had. She'd had a taste of something she liked, and she wanted more.

The truth was, he had drunk too much. He'd been flirtatious, making sexual innuendos, and he'd touched her in more than a friendly manner over the course of the evening. She couldn't resist his attentions and so went along with his game. She ended up bent over the back of her couch; he grabbed at her hips roughly and bit into her neck and back.

Her pussy twitched at the memory. She liked it hard and she liked it rough. Evidently, so did he.

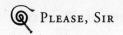

She'd liked how he'd kissed, soft yet forceful, sensual and teasing. He'd undressed her quickly, all but torn her clothes off. With or without the slight buzz of alcohol, she had been powerless to stop him.

Jenna thought he would make a killer dom, and told him as much. He had an aggressive and arrogant manner about him—one that commanded attention. She had managed to drag him to a fetish party once. He liked the scene, but he wasn't much into clubs and said he would rather "play at home" if he were to play at all. That had been the end of the conversation, until now.

Jenna was tired of their constant flirting and sexual tension. She supposed she could have seduced him in a more vanilla manner, but she had a fantasy in mind that had ahold of her, inspired by the night at the fetish party, and she couldn't let it go. Now, pacing her living room floor, she was still surprised she had gone this far.

Her collar was attached to a thin leash that tapped lightly against her belly with each movement. Her boots weren't meant for pacing, and she felt a tingle in her toes as her feet began to lose sensation. She couldn't wait much longer. She might lose her nerve.

She stopped midstride upon hearing the doorbell. Without hesitation she pressed the button, allowing him entrance to her building. Positioning herself in the center of the room, she took a deep breath and exhaled loudly just as he rapped on the door.

"Come in."

"Hey, girl . . ." he said, his voice trailing off upon seeing her. "Shit. That's hot. Where are we going?"

"Nowhere. Please say nothing, sir."

In an instant, she recognized a look of understanding on his face.

She pushed away the flutter of fear that she felt course through her and settle in her stomach. The worst thing that could happen likely wouldn't: He would leave and never speak to her again.

She approached him with trepidation, took his hand, and gently kissed his cheek. She pulled away, leaving their lips inches apart. She slid herself down his body, pressed tightly into him, and stopped when her face was eye level with his waist.

"Please, sir. You know what I want. Will you indulge me?"

She held the leash handle up for him to take. Staring at the floor, she trembled in anticipation, waiting for his answer.

"Tell me what you want," he ordered, his voice loud and strong.

"You know."

"Do I?"

"You do. I want you to spank me. To dominate me," she hissed.

Silently, he took the leash from her and pulled roughly on it.

She glanced up at him. He fixed his eyes on a chair sitting in the center of the room, clearly out of place.

"Over the chair."

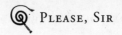

She stood and moved toward the chair, forgetting the length of leash restricting her. He tugged on it, hard, pulling her to him. Placing both hands around her neck and cupping her face, he whispered in her ear, "Are you sure this is what you want?"

"Yes, sir. I'm certain."

"Go, then," he barked, and released the leash.

Backing away from him, she knelt over the chair. Her stomach and breasts pressed hard into the wood.

"I've got some toys over there on the couch, if you're interested," she whispered.

"I noticed."

She wondered what he was thinking. He didn't play this way, after all, and wasn't that familiar with riding crops and floggers. Even so, she could tell he was intrigued. If he was uneasy he was covering it very well.

"Your eyes. I want them closed."

"Yes, sir."

She heard him shuffling by the couch, and she wondered if he looked at her as she lay bent and helpless over the chair. She wondered if he would have second thoughts and leave her there. Seconds passed like minutes.

"Relax." His voice soothed her. She felt a blindfold come down over her eyes; the soft velvet kissed her skin.

Then, in an instant, he had a handful of her hair, pulling on it hard enough that he forced her head to lift from the chair. Delicious. Her clit was tightening, her lips moistening.

His other hand slowly trailed down her back. He tugged

her hair again, and then down came his hand, hard on her ass. The loud smack of skin on skin filled the room.

"Thank you, sir."

Again she felt the sting of his hand, harder this time, on her other cheek.

"Thank you, sir. Again, please. I want your handprints left on me," she whispered.

His assault on her ass continued—several quick and very hard slaps. For someone who had never done this before, he seemed to take to it naturally. Each swat was placed precisely where it needed to be, and in quick succession.

Biting into her lip, she felt tears building behind her closed lids. Her ass cheeks stung; every nerve ending felt as though it had come to life. Yet with each new swat, the swell of pleasure in her sex increased. She'd allowed a girlfriend to spank her once, at a fetish party, more for fun than anything else. This wasn't even comparable. The intensity of his assault was exactly what she had been coveting.

"What do you say?" he snarled in her ear as his hands roamed over her ass and gently grazed her stinging skin.

"Thank you, sir."

"Good girl."

She felt his hand slither up her thigh and settle on her sex, where he rubbed her gently as his other hand kneaded the skin of her ass.

"You're wet."

"Yes, sir," she said, panting.

Thrusting her ass back, she pushed her sex harder onto his

hand and ground her hips, hoping to get off. He abruptly removed his hand from her pussy and grabbed another handful of hair while giving her ass another firm swat.

"Get up."

Unsteady on her feet, she stumbled as she stood, leaning her body into his. Cole grabbed her around her elbows and pulled her to him. Then his hand moved possessively over her breast, squeezing and kneading it through the material of the bustier.

She moved to kiss him, her kiss landing on his cheek, still in the dark because of the blindfold. He kissed back, hard and quick, but just enough to tease.

"Into the bedroom," he ordered. Swatting her ass hard, he took her by the leash and led the way.

"Your clothes. Off," he barked, and she heard his footsteps retreat.

She stepped out of her underwear and released herself from the restrictive bustier while still listening for him in the next room. She felt vulnerable, now nearly nude save for her stockings and boots.

He returned. She felt him twist rope around her wrists as he bound her arms tightly together behind her back.

"Turn around."

He grabbed her by the waist and pushed her roughly until she felt her legs collide with her bed.

"Over," he demanded.

Down on her knees, she moved her body so her stomach lay over the bed, leaving her ass exposed. She shifted herself slightly, awkwardly, hands bound, in an attempt to rub her sex against the bed.

A loud crack echoed in the room. She felt what could only be her riding crop as it came down hard on her ass.

"Stop that!" he commanded.

More hard smacks rained down, moving from her right to her left cheek consecutively. She anticipated each blow, and attempted to push herself closer to the bed in a useless move to escape the sting of the crop.

Fuck. She was so turned on. Her pussy lips were engorged, her clit was tight, and she felt an increasing slickness between her thighs.

He stopped just as suddenly as he had started. Behind her again, he pressed tightly against her, his hands on her back, caressing her skin. His nails scratched hard down her back. She felt his hardness against her ass; she was happy at its size, having forgotten he was as large as he now felt.

He wrapped his arm around her waist and pulled her body away from the bed and closer to him. His other hand roamed over her thighs; his lips kissed the small of her back, then her ass cheeks. His kiss was tender, but it still stung her burning skin.

His hand at her waist moved down; the one on her thighs moved up. Connecting together, his fingers slipped into her from behind, and played her clit from the front. Humping his fingers, she came hard and fast, grunting, moaning, and crying out in ecstasy.

When her orgasm subsided, he helped her up and turned

her around. He pushed her down on the bed, landing on top of her.

"Thank you," she whimpered.

"I'm not done."

He pushed her legs apart and buried his face in her sex. He suckled at her, licked and bit, nipped and fingered.

Jenna was never a woman who had multiple orgasms. Getting off once was all she could usually ever hope for. Coming twice had only ever happened once before. But now Cole did it with little effort.

"Fuck," she growled, bucking her hips as she humped his face.

Reaching down, she pressed her nails hard into his scalp.

"Jesus. Stop!"

Insistent, he ignored her and stopped only when she dug her nails harder into his scalp firmly enough to elicit his full attention.

"Please, Cole," she pleaded, "I've had enough. Lie with me."

She leaned into him, kissed him tenderly, smelled and tasted herself on his lips. Spooning, he snuggled behind her and nuzzled at her neck. He deftly removed her blindfold.

"Was that a mistake?" she asked quietly, hoping she wasn't about to spoil the mood.

"No, Jenna. Not at all," he said, and propped himself up on his elbow. His fingers lazily stroked her cheek. He leaned in to kiss her, teased her with a peck, backed up, and kissed her again.

"You're a tease," she whispered, and pressed her lips to his.

"I like your lips, Jenna. This wasn't a mistake. I want this. I've wanted it for a long time," he said quietly, looking her in the eyes before kissing her again.

"Good," she whispered, and snuggled in closer. She turned around so they were facing each other, and she buried her face in his chest.

So, I did it, she mused, *submitted . . . but only once with such obedience.*

She chuckled and purred quietly, thinking ahead to the next time, and imagining what a little brat she would be.

"What's so funny?" he asked.

"You'll see."

DARK GIRLS

by P. Alanna Roethle

Her eyes are dark, rimmed in black, and reflecting pinpoints from the red lamps in the corners of the dusky, holelike room. We're sweating, a thin sheen that raises musk, sprawled over the twin bed, death metal raging under its breath from the boom box.

She doesn't have much: posters scattered over dingy walls—posters of Amy Lee, Jolie, typical rocker girls; lights from Spencer's, a black light, a red stoplight, and one of those spider lights that crackles when you touch the globe.

The room feels smoky, the smell of incense caught in the drapes and bedsheets. I roll over onto my back in the heat, trying to feel the spin of the fan blades across my skin. I feel like my body is dripping off my bones. The night feels unreal, a little too hot, a little too black. One of the curtains is pushed slightly aside, and the clouds build in a bank that looks unnatural. Like something from a horror flick, it floats, menacing and angry, over the city lights. There are flickers of lightning far off, and I wish it had rained earlier, when we were sweating in the mass of people rocking out at the concert.

We're both high, a little—leftovers from the concert—spent from being on the dance floor all night, jammed against each other or reaching for each other's hands in the press of bodies, the tightness of all of us together, swaying, jumping, fighting for air or just to be noticed in the pack. My ears ring, and I feel the bass still reverberating through my chest.

I reach for her back, sliding a hand up the black satin, down her arm with the half sleeves and spiked jewelry. Her curly black hair is wild, stiff with sweat and gel, and her tattoos glow in the black light over the bed. Her skin is alive, mottled with colors, dragons, images of death.

I watch her, the breath catching in my throat, under my tongue. So beautiful, even though she tries so hard to hide it. Every time I look at her, I almost expect her to disappear. She's like a dream I had, a bad dream, but one I want to come back every night just so I can feel like something more than normal. Until I met her, I'd been too normal to pay attention to, even for myself. I needed someone to notice me, and she does.

She turns to look at me. I start. She catches me looking, and I blush and am glad it's so dark in here. I never like to admit she makes me blush, but she gets to me. I think she knows it. She has to know it.

"That fucking bitch in front of me kept pushing me away from the rail." She hisses it, heat escaping from her lips. She rolls to sit up, lights a cigarette, lets the smoke drip from her nostrils and curl into the fan, scattering like sheep before the wolf. Her eyes slide down my body—my midriff exposed to the fan, baggy pants, black boots—and back up to my face. My body tingles. I'm not sure if it's the X still in my nerve endings, the serotonin surging through me, or the sly glint under her long lashes. She stands up, rocking to the music, sliding a hand under her dog collar jingling with chains and piercings. I breathe in her smoke, liking the taste of it.

"Why didn't you kick her ass?" she asks, a hint of danger under her words. She doesn't make sense when she's high, flies over the world with wings spread above reality, doesn't look down. She knows I'm not the type to kick anyone's ass, but a thrill starts through me as I imagine that she might think I am. She moves to the bed, between my legs, throws my long, tangled hair out of the way, feels the rings in my navel, slides a hand to my crotch too soon. It's always like this with her, unexpected, surreal, suddenly about sex when sex is the last thing in the air.

"You want me?" she asks, standing there, swaying with the drugs, with the metal, rocking her head, eyes shiny.

"I'm fucking tired," I say, teasing her. I always want her. She has a choke hold on my libido, and I have no control over it. I move up farther on the bed, sliding toward the wall, pulling her with me. "Just lie here for a minute."

She pulls back, disgusted. "I hate you sometimes. Such a bitch." She spits smoke, stubs the cigarette out on the dresser. While she's turned, I slip my half shirt over my head, slide my hands over my breasts, wiping sweat away. My hands trail down my stomach and I hook my fingers into my belt. I'm open to her, muscles tense and excited, waiting for her to turn around.

Her eyes narrow when she sees me. "Tease." She leans against the wall, walking eyes like fingers over every bare inch of my flesh. I'm already wet for her, barely moving my hips against the rough fabric of the jeans, flesh on denim, no panties.

"Now you want me to fuck you, bitch?" She laughs, throaty, flinging her hair, snakes blending with the tats. "You can wait. Never can make up your mind. Typical girl." Like she isn't, but I don't say anything. She slides out of her pants, undoing the belt, letting them drop to the floor. She wears guy's pants—black, of course. Her tattooed legs are bruised from the mosh pit, and there's the shine of metal in her crotch.

She's watching me, looking for a reaction, seeing my skin flush and my lips part as my hands move under my jeans, feeling my own slickness and heat. I put a finger to my mouth, licking it, tongue ring clicking against the rings on my finger. She moves backward, not taking her eyes from me. Her hand disappears into the dresser, and she pulls out a dildo—a black one, a big one; it looks strange in her hand. She has delicate hands, matching the feminine bones of her face, a physical contrast to the front she puts on—that she's tough, that she's mean, that no one hurts her. It's a lie; everyone hurts her. I can see it, see her push it away, only to drip silent agony into the pillow at night.

She's grinning now, baring her teeth, sharp like a night dweller's. She pulls the chair to her, naked legs and pussy. She's still wearing her shirt, and she looks like a paper doll someone hasn't finished dressing. She licks the dildo, slides her mouth over the top, sucks on it. It's a game, like she's playing with someone else, making me watch. I am almost jealous; I feel the emotional stirrings separate from the physical stirrings. I touch myself, sliding fingers up and down over my hard clit, then deeper inside.

She holds the dildo on the seat of the chair and straddles it, facing me. Slowly, she slides over it, gasping as it enters her, sitting all the way onto it, taking its length inside her.

I moan, imagining the pressure she feels as I watch, straining toward her from the bed, lifting my hips and moving them as she moves hers. She closes her eyes, biting her lip, acting it out, head thrown back as she slides up and down, so slowly, one hand wrapped around the dildo and the other on the back of the chair, steadying herself.

My eyes close for a second, being her, feeling it, and when I open them she is there, dark eyes hovering over me, tongue licking her lips. Her hands are on my pants and she takes them off. The dildo is warm and wet, and it slides into me easily. It fills me with smells of her and warmth from her body.

"This is my cock," she whispers in my ear. Our naked legs come together, and she holds it to her pelvis, just at the place where it would jut out if it were her own. "Do you want it? Do you want me?"

I moan, trembling inside as she slides the dildo out, too slow, then barely back in, turning the tip in small circles, and teasing me. Suddenly, she thrusts it into the base, her body pressing tight against me as her hips push it. She holds me down with both hands, and I see the other end is rounded, too. For her.

She moves her pussy over the dildo, sliding it into herself, and our lips come together wetly, below and above, both of us filled with it and with each other. We start to move, hot air in ears and lips, this thing between us alive and throbbing, sliding in and out with the movements of our hips. We're so wet, we can barely stay together, and suddenly she starts to pump, fast and short, against me. The slap fills the room, and the sweat and smell are unbearable. We are both crying; it hurts, but the pain is sweet, and there's no way to stop it. We want it, slamming into each other like the people in the crowd, sweat and dirt and straining.

I feel myself start to come, my muscles spasming inside, around the hot rubber, and it gets stronger and stronger until I'm screaming aloud from the pain, the absolute joy. The X in my system is making it last, stretching the orgasm out like cotton candy, and the sensation amplifies until I can't take it anymore. I twist away, but she holds me down, tight to the bed.

"I'm gonna come, too," she whimpers. "Hold still." My insides are swelling, tight, and the pleasure is almost too much, but I don't want it to stop. She slams into me again and again, her face twisted in pain and ecstasy.

We rise together, our sweat and wetness running down our legs, hands grasping hair and sheets, bucking against each other. The neighbor bangs on the wall as we scream each other's names, as the headboard cracks the paint, breasts slapping against one another, her against the wall now, holding me up, coming over and over, tied into each other like strings of pearls, my dark girl and me.

HUMAN

by Jeremy Edwards

*I*t was like a clumsy form of synesthesia. Naomi's presence flooded me with an emotion, or a consciousness, or an appetite. I couldn't tell them apart anymore, and maybe it didn't matter. What difference did it make whether I was hungering for her scent, or yearning for her reassurance, or conceiving of a way that I could connect with her?

What was significant was that the workweek had just begun, and already I was jerking off in the bathroom because the woman I worshipped from an interoffice distance overwhelmed me as flesh, or as laughter, or as an idea to cream for.

These days, I hardly even had to fantasize to bring myself off to the thought of Naomi. I vaguely imagined looking at her face, listening to her voice, feeling her jaunty breasts, and tasting the fresh skin of her ass cheeks. But these images were peripheral to my experience, mere breezes at the edge of my erotic storm. I was so immersed in my infatuation that it was almost enough simply to close my eyes and say her name.

My orgasm was effortless, and it arrived ridiculously fast. Alone in a tiny room, trousers at my ankles, I lived, breathed, and ejaculated for Naomi. And she had no idea.

While I dabbed the head of my cock clean, I resolved that I would come up with some excuse to visit her in her wing of the building. As a technical artist, I had little idea what they did in her department—a mysterious group known as "reconcilers." It had something to do with accounting.

"Yep, I'll be right with you," she said peremptorily as I entered. She didn't even glance up from her desk.

I noticed the shimmer of the fluorescent lights on the sculpted, soft waves of her brown hair.

"Okay," I said timidly, taking a seat.

Naomi looked up. "You're not the man I thought you were."

That didn't take long, I told myself. Five seconds into our relationship, and I'd disappointed her. "I'm sorry," I said aloud.

She waved a hand dismissively. "Don't be. He's a nuisance."

I looked around. "Who's a nuisance?"

"The guy who I thought was here when I heard you come in. Jim fucking Johnson from bookkeeping. He shows up almost every day at around this time to fetch reports, and he always finds something to complain about regarding how I've assembled them. I must have assembled them in all possible permutations at this point, and he's objected to every one. Bastard." Her face opened into a cataclysm of refreshing laughter as she spit out the last word. I felt privileged to be in on this outburst.

Naomi collected herself, but mirth still danced pleasantly in her brilliant eyes. It may have been at that moment that I realized how deeply in love I was.

"I apologize for having ignored you, Hector. What brings you down here?"

I'd known this would be the inevitable question, and yet I hadn't properly prepared an answer. The real answer—that I wanted to take Naomi to bed with me forever—was, of course, my little secret. So I had to say something businessy and plausible; and the major obstacle here, as hinted, was that I really didn't have a clue as to what the hell they did in the reconciliation department. So I tried to reconcile myself to the fact that I would most likely end up looking like a fool, and I just plunged in.

Jim "fucking" Johnson came to them for reports, I had learned. I reasoned that what was good enough for Jim F. Johnson would be good enough for me.

"We, um, need a report."

She seemed surprised. "Oh. Okay. For the . . . art department?"

"Yes. That's right." I could feel the back of my neck turning crimson.

"What detail?"

"Sorry?"

"What *type* of report are we assembling for you?"

"Well . . ." I faltered. "What types have you got?"

"Aggregate accounts. Bulk accounts. Special accounts . . ."

"Yes," I said hastily. "That will be fine."

She looked puzzled. "Which one?"

Naomi was the first person I'd met in a long time whom it mattered to me to please. I'd been drifting along for a while, comfortable in my skin, not worrying too much about anything. However, in these past few months, with the awareness that this astounding woman was in the building—a woman who seemed to embody everything that appealed to me in women—I had become very conscious of my own inadequacies. My clothes never looked right on me. I was glaringly ignorant about matters outside my field—like what went on in a reconciliation department, for instance. I had a habit of revising my thoughts in midsentence, causing me to break off or stammer. I was always misplacing things.

How could I hope that she would take any interest in me when I wasn't perfect, like she so obviously was? Her face was the ideal of beautiful intelligence, with eyes at once sharpened by common sense and softened by compassion. Her body was statuesque; the subtle curves and understated smooth lines might not epitomize feminine loveliness for all beholders, but they certainly did for me. She spoke with a gentle efficiency that was conducive to her being both respected and well liked in the workplace. She listened to what people said, and she laughed at their jokes.

I felt like a teenager with a hopeless crush on a movie star.

But hope springs eternal, as they say, and here I was, sitting in her office, because hope had brought me here. If I wasn't careful, I feared that my idiocy might get me thrown right back out.

"Oh," I finally said. "I guess I'll have to check on that."

"All right." Naomi smiled. I was pretty sure she was onto me. She studied me for a moment—curiously, kindly.

I stood up, but I didn't leave. "So . . ." I ventured, "how's it going?"

"It's going okay, Hector." Her voice sounded a little strained—not like I was irritating her, which would probably have sent me scurrying to the safety of my workstation, if not all the way home to hide under my bed, but like things were possibly not so "okay," in fact.

I really was a mess. Five minutes back, I'd been consumed with the desire to fuck Naomi. Now I wanted to wrap her in my arms, kiss the top of her head, and gently ask her what was wrong. As if we'd been married for ten years. As if she weren't just a casual workplace acquaintance who hadn't even known me four months ago.

"Sorry it's not better," I said.

My tone must have revealed some of the turmoil inside me, because she put her pen down and gazed at me as though she were touched—and perhaps a bit concerned. The corners of her mouth crinkled up. "Don't worry, Hector," she said soothingly. "I'm fine. Just another grumpy yuppie on a Monday."

She was *grumpy*. That made her seem more human. But, in essence, I still suspected she was perfect. And I still wanted to kiss her delicately on the head, for good measure. And, yeah, fuck her.

"Did you need anything else from me?"

No, I didn't need anything else from Naomi. I needed *everything* else from Naomi. But I didn't tell her that. Not yet.

Despite my complete goofiness, I was proud of myself. I'd actually gotten my foolish ass into Naomi's office, and I'd managed to establish a slightly more intimate rapport with her. Granted, it was mostly thanks to the generosity of her friendliness. Nevertheless, I felt like I'd put in a good day's work.

I thanked her and drifted back to my part of the building, wondering how and when I could engineer another encounter. I was grateful for the built-in excuse of getting back to her with the requirements of that essential, nonexistent report I allegedly needed. No reason I couldn't follow up tomorrow, I reflected cheerfully. In theory, I could even return later that same day, but I didn't want to push it. Moreover, I felt that my nerves had taken all they could for one day.

What my nerves weren't counting on was the accident of my ending up alone in the elevator with Naomi for the 5:05 flight south. And, in the same way that I'd clocked out as a commercial artist at five—and would therefore have been unwilling to deal with any further job-related problems until tomorrow—my nerves seemed to be looking at their watches, shrugging apologetically, and saying, "You're on your own, buddy."

Without the luxury of nervous deliberation, I was forced to go on impulse. "I know it's only Monday," I said, "but how about a drink?"

She decompressed into a smile, as if the forthcoming drink had already begun to refresh her. "What do you mean, '*only*

Monday'?" She laughed. "As far as I'm concerned, Mondays *invite* drinking."

She even had a favorite place. And within ten minutes, there we were. My nerves, at this point, decided to clock back in for an overtime shift.

"Relax," she said with an indulgent grin.

It was easy for Naomi to sit there and say, *Relax*. Naomi wasn't out for a drink with Naomi. Naomi was just out for a drink with me. *Yeah, right*, I wanted to say. You *try relaxing when you're sitting across the table from you, staring into your magical eyes.* But I didn't say that—I didn't want to sound completely nuts.

The moment when I'd invited her to come out with me for a drink seemed like a dream, and I felt deeply indebted to the improbable reserves of courage and savoir faire that had jumped to the surface of my personality and enabled me to seize that crucial moment.

Now I was terrified that I would let the opportunity afforded by those reserves somehow slip away. I was desperately afraid of letting Naomi down, and of letting myself down. I guess she could tell.

"You're funny," she said.

"I am?"

"Sitting there like a handsome little field mouse on his first date."

Any ambivalence I felt about being a field mouse was far outweighed by the thrill of being a handsome one, in her estimation.

"You make me feel as if I'm frightening," she said pleasantly.

"I'm sorry."

"Chill, Hector. I take it as a compliment. But, for the record . . . I'm not frightening. In fact, I'm pretty damn cuddly, once you get to know me."

"I'd like that." Another unexpected flash of courage to the rescue.

"So would I, Hector."

And now I thought I was going to pass out. So much for courage.

"I'm sentimental," she confessed. "And I'm demonstrative. I don't know why I'm telling you this. Don't let me scare you off."

Fat fucking chance, I thought. I might be cowardly, but I wasn't crazy.

"I know a lot of men are threatened by vulnerability. And by honesty. They can't handle it."

Vulnerability? Naomi? I couldn't process this.

"You'll take me home, and I might kiss you so hard you'll be afraid I won't let go." She chuckled. "I might cry in your bed from sheer emotional exuberance."

My mind felt like someone had poured warm brandy into it. Here we were, still on our first round of drinks, and somehow, as far as Naomi's predictions for the evening were concerned, she had already wound up in my bed. Believe me, I wasn't complaining, but I was finding it a trifle hard to keep up.

"I'm speaking hypothetically, of course," she added, touching my right hand, the one that gripped my pint glass as if it were the only anchor in a gravity-free world.

She continued speaking hypothetically for the following hour. It wasn't all about her demonstrativeness (which I couldn't wait to see more evidence of) or her supposed vulnerability (which I still didn't fully believe in). Over the next pint, she got on a roll discussing G-rated, hypothetical things we could do together—*we*. "I should show you my favorite Postimpressionist gallery sometime"; "You *have* to let me buy you lunch at the amazing falafel place on my block"; "Remind me to point out the weird old building my great-grandfather owned for about a year, until the market crashed in 'twenty-nine." Naomi seemed enthusiastic about all sorts of things, once rescued from the mysterious drudgery of the reconciliation department. Or maybe, I realized with a shock, her enthusiasm was not so much about these hypothetical projects as it was about *me*.

Her conversation may have been largely hypothetical, but when we left the bar, her actions were as real as the fingers that briefly, but meaningfully, stroked my shoulder.

"Where to, Hector?" She was so natural, and so in control of the situation. And I was so thankful that she didn't seem to notice my clumsiness as I sputtered an answer.

"I don't know. . . . We could . . . I mean . . . if you want to . . ."

A big red letter A, for *awkward*, seemed to float in the sky, as seen so many times in the margins of essays handed back to me by my high school English teachers. But Naomi didn't see it.

"Thank you." She seemed to sparkle, a knowing glimmer in her eye. "That sounds wonderful."

I babbled anxiously, but revealingly, as we walked toward my building. I told her about my pet theory that holds that most of us spend the first third of our lives figuring out who we are, and the second third of our lives learning to accept who we are. She giggled when I concluded by speculating that someday I'd spend the final third of my life clinging to who I was, to die a stubborn but self-confident old man of ninety-nine, like my grandfather.

A short time later, I found myself admiring Naomi's skirt-perfect ass as she preceded me into my apartment. The dream-like quality of the whole evening was intensifying, and a wave of disorientation hit me as we passed through the door.

I knew at this point I had to stop thinking, lest I freak out or freeze up. On a sort of basic bachelor autopilot, I created an ad hoc conversation nest using one couch, one floor lamp with a cozy beige shade, and a couple of glasses of red zinfandel.

We sat down, and she kissed me. And she'd been right—it did feel as if she might never let go. But I liked that.

It felt soft but urgent, nurturing but intensely sexual. I was not, in actuality, a field mouse on a first date, but Naomi's kiss did make me question whether I'd ever been kissed before.

Wasn't it remarkable, I reflected, that somebody could make a kiss feel that good, instead of just a little bit good?

Don't examine it, I told myself. *Just experience it.*

What happened when we finally pulled apart took me by surprise.

"Oh, fuck, I feel so inadequate sometimes," said Naomi.

She looked into my eyes with something like anxiety. She was tearing up.

I was aware that I had just learned a lesson I'd never forget: She was as human as I was. "Naomi." My voice was deep. "You're perfect."

She stood up and began to pace restless but elegant strides in front of me. I could smell her womanhood, and in this way Naomi engaged the vital fifth sense that my workplace fantasies had neglected when I'd imagined tasting and feeling and looking and listening.

I stood, too, so that I could pull her back onto the couch. And, all too typically for me, my smooth move turned into a clumsy fall when we got halfway down. Together we collapsed—then collapsed with laughter. While we were cracking up, I kissed Naomi's face. The feeling of her laughing body in my arms gave me an incredible hard-on.

Now she kissed me even harder than before, while bringing my fingers up to the buttons on her blouse.

"I'm sorry if I'm awkward," she said while I undid her, speaking half to herself and half to me. She was letting me eavesdrop on her insecurities, and again I felt privileged.

I cupped her left breast in my hand. "You're as graceful as good poetry," I informed her. Fifteen minutes before, I would have doubted I'd have the confidence to say something like that to this goddess.

But she wasn't a goddess, I reminded myself, no matter how much she looked and acted like one. She was tender and fragile, kind of like me.

"Sweet man," she whispered in my ear. And then we stopped talking.

Her skirt slipped off as if someone had greased it. She embodied a different sort of perfection now, vividly raunchy rather than elegantly poised. Her blouse was two-thirds unbuttoned, and her black panties and creamy thighs told a story of female sensuality that her stockings had only hinted at.

In my bed, her panties were all that needed to be removed. I wanted to fuck Naomi while she was half-undressed and half-undone. I wanted to plunge my face into her raw, wet juncture while she still wore some of the trappings of her businesslike allure. I wanted to feel the heat of her tender humanity around my cock while still enjoying the glittering exterior that had made me idolize her.

I flipped her over and admired the hilly landscape of her bottom, bisected into eastern and western regions by a river of black fabric. I hesitated briefly, holding my breath. Then I ripped that thong off as quickly as I could.

I kissed and kissed the divine cheeks. Then she turned herself faceup again, and my adoring kisses sought various locations above her hip bones, around her navel, and along the deepest territory of her inner thighs. Each spasmodic touch of my lips seemed to find a direct contact point for her sensuality; she moaned and writhed for me like no woman had before.

Tasting her sex was such a heady experience, and I worried that I might bring myself to orgasm before I took Naomi there. The flavor of her soft folds triggered a carnival of light, music, and motion in my mind: My consciousness reeled with kinetic harmonies of color, and a sound like that of a vibra-phone lighter than air, tickling every receptor on my person. The savor of Naomi's nectar appeared to encapsulate a universe of superlatives, as her pulsating cunt seemed to surround not just my tongue but my entire self, containing me in a spinning capsule of delirious bliss that was frozen in time and infinite in space.

When it came, her climax bled joy into my face and saturated my senses. Her thighs hugged my ears as if it were for keeps, and I wasn't sure whether the muffled words I heard amid her gurgles of ecstasy were, "Thank you," or, "I love you."

I felt that my life could end right there—that I could die not even having been inside her yet.

But I didn't die. I clambered onto Naomi's living flesh and became part of her for a while.

As she absorbed me, I felt rigid in a way that was magnificently novel. Rather than being possessed of an ordinary erection, I felt as if I were possessed *by* an intangible energy that clung to me in the form of the hot, wet embrace of her cunt, and soaked through to my core. Thus I, the penetrator, was myself penetrated by a potent feminine presence that intoxicated me through osmosis. My cock slithered, pulsed, and pounded like a separate entity, some organic cluster of maleness that had been brought to life by the magic powers of Naomi's pussy, which charged my dick with electricity and guided its every twitch and stroke as if it were an obedient, well-oiled machine.

The rest of my body could only follow the lead of my prick:

My balls slapped against Naomi in applause, and my hands molded her breasts into foothills for the mountainous event taking place in her snatch. My cock, leaping with joy, was a performing animal in her control, and my other physical attributes could only endeavor to keep pace with it.

I watched her eyes the whole time. They were wide with unanticipated delight. Even more than the impossibly lush sensation of her cunt squeezing me into my own crazy paradise, I remember Naomi's eyes that first time.

When I lost control and sent my fingers, just in time, on a mad dash for her clit, her eyes lit up a notch further. She screamed intimately in my face as I emptied my soul into her.

I drifted toward sleep in Naomi's arms. The sheets smelled like her pleasure, the wood of the bed frame smelled like security, and the room smelled like trust.

CHERRIES

by Alice Sturdivant

*S*he'd been seated in a corner, the hostess purs-
ing her lips coolly before showing her to a little
two-person banquette tucked away from the
more desirable tables. A table where no one would be dis-
turbed by the sight of a thirty-ish (a lady never tells) woman
eating alone. Nestling her suit-skirted rump and hips into the
leather seat was comforting. She sighed, closing her eyes momentarily, savoring the conclusion of another week's business
away from home, and the subsequent self-indulgent ritual of
enjoying dessert at an unfamiliar, posh restaurant.

She opened her eyes to the polite question, "Miss?"

Despite the smooth baritone of his voice, what truly captured her attention were his hands. They were the suggestive
reddish brown usually found on intimate places on the body—
the lower lip, a flushed cheek, a nipple. His fingers were long,
at their tips nails bluntly trimmed. Gentle-looking hands.
Elegant. They folded almost delicately around the leather of

the menu. His espresso eyes were playful, though small, the nose a little large. The mustache and goatee that perched above and below his lips would have been effete had the mouth they framed not been so wide and blatantly provocative. Sharp, high cheekbones were swathed in cherry-wood skin. He was young. Younger than she, certainly.

Something about the way his hands looked against the thin leather . . . She'd have bought him a fortune in gloves. Or fine leather straps with which to torment her. Fine leather anything, as long as he would use his hands on her. His voice would be steady as he delivered stinging blows to her sensitive ass cheeks and then rubbed them gently, or as he tweaked her nipples. *I wonder, miss, if I can make you come from just flicking your nipples. Do you think I can do that, miss?*

"Sweetened iced tea, and dessert, please." Her voice was cool, a little condescending. Up here, you had to tell them you wanted the tea both sweet and iced. Sweet tea, decent public transportation . . . apparently it was a trade-off.

"What sort of dessert, miss?" His mouth quirked up at one corner: not condescending, but amused. One was not usually vague in one's choices at a place like this. The chefs did not appreciate it.

But this was part of the game, to see what she'd be brought. The surprise, the implications of which dessert was offered. Pie: plain, homey. Chocolate: decadent, but typical—depending on the dessert. Cake: traditional. Fruit, any number of things: smooth, tart, sweet. She preferred pastry: light, adventurous, maybe hiding a secret. The patron leaned forward in

her seat, let him get a peek of cleavage, and stage-whispered conspiratorially, letting her Southern-girl drawl run over the half smile of her lips, "Surprise me."

His eyebrows rose a moment, lowered, and he let his gaze travel over her: the café-au-lait skin (rare enough in this part of town, much less this restaurant), the full lips, the twists of hair tied back into a businesslike bun, the expensive but boring black blazer and white top. The collarbone above the tiny mole right where her fingers traced over the delicate skin. The platinum band (no diamonds) around her fourth finger. A warning? A challenge? He nodded, lifted the corner of his mouth in a deferential smile, and tapped his index finger against the menu. "Absolutely, miss."

He pivoted, turned, and faded into the plush ambience of the other staff and patrons.

Suddenly, she decided his were not the hands of a man who learned about sex from pornography. She laughed at her own conjecture. Usually the waiters were not so openly curious; neither was she.

Hands so unlike her husband's, whose own digits were stocky, also blunt. But she'd mistaken his dexterity with the small instruments of his career for the promise of skill in other areas. They were honest hands, forthright and plain. They handled things like the remote, the garden shovel—and, heavily, her breasts, even when she ached for a subtler, teasing touch.

She'd had enough experience with elegantly tapered, artistic fingers, which could play a woman's clit as well as any instrument, to tally the potential of his in a single glance.

They were smooth; his skin hadn't the slight roughness of a man in his thirties, or that of a man used to manual labor or hours in the sun. A student, maybe? The blunt edges of his nails were clipped, but not manicured: He was not able to afford—or more likely, too typically male to see the point in—manicures, but nevertheless took care of his appearance.

The hint of red (as opposed to the pink that infused her lighter brown hands) was intriguing. But steam and warmth could account for that. Still, the notion of that color generated flickers of thought about other areas: Would a hard suck on the inside of his thigh turn his skin the same color? The head of his cock? Perhaps it grew a dark, juicy purple? Or a more succulent, bright red, like a pomegranate?

The graphic designer in her briefly mused about the Pantone color necessary to re-create his flesh into art. A stark photograph, just a crisp, cream linen cloth clasped in his palm, draped around his wrist. The light would fall across hand and cloth just enough to suggest either a utilitarian task (perhaps he was shaking out a tablecloth?) or the flex of muscle before tightening in pleasure (his hand grasping at the sheets? Or—even better—grasping the crisp linen that covered the table in front of her?).

The iced tea arrived quickly, and she kept her gaze demurely lowered to the cream tablecloth where he set the crystal, so that only his hand would enter into her field of vision. A bead of moisture rested upon the inside of his wrist, surprisingly delicate and pale compared to the other side of his hand. Her tongue wanted to taste it, to see if the liquid was sweet or plain.

His palm cupped the goblet. Her nipples tingled. Did he cup a breast the same sure way? His own balls?

"Your sweetened tea, miss," he intoned softly, a note of intimacy in his voice that suggested she meet his eyes, lest she be considered rude or, worse, not up to the challenge.

The small smile again, the same flare of amusement in his eyes. "Thank you." She couldn't very well ignore him.

"You are quite welcome, miss." His answering nod was practiced and detached, the pivot and turn completely polished by rote. She wondered at the strange warmth in her breasts—and cheeks. It had been years since she'd blushed! She bit her lip to keep from smiling at his retreating figure. She pressed the palm of her manicured right hand into the napkin draped across her lap, as if to forcibly stifle the building pressure of arousal.

It wasn't just his voice, though his voice was part of the allure. There was no telltale twang or dropped consonants to announce his origins, only the almost-British crispness of the word he used to address her: *miss*, not the more politically correct *Ms.* or the ubiquitous Southern *ma'am* she was used to hearing at home, nor the deferential and possibly offensive *madam*.

Anyone looking at her in the tiny banquette meant for two could see her, poised and waiting in her seat, her hand in her lap, the very image of urban disinterest. She was imagining the waiter's hands splayed out beside her temples, his wrists twin posts beside her ears, his body angled above hers as he politely asked, *Would you like me to fuck you harder, miss? More cock, miss?* She licked her lips at the thought, felt another flicker of pleasurable amusement between her thighs. She crossed her legs beneath the fine linen tablecloth and squeezed them together gently, tilting her hips just enough to tamp down the urgent bulb of her clit.

Not just the voice. Nor his eyes, which were dark, nearly black in the dim light. They had looked directly into hers. He wasn't shy. He was fully aware of his appeal. And for some reason (maybe his youth, maybe his politesse, maybe his complete lack of creepy smarminess as he wordlessly flirted, appraising her warmly but discreetly), it only made her appreciate him all the more.

No, the thing that made her actually have to squirm in her seat to alleviate the slow pulsing in her pussy was his patience with the uncomfortably warm plate he balanced on his fingers.

Such a cliché, flirting with a waiter, but those hands . . . She would cast him in her next fantasy as a master violin maker, or a magician, perhaps, with the strength and power in his fingers to make women come with a flick of his wrist. Or to fill her with just his middle and ring fingers.

"Take care, sir; the plate is very warm," the waiter murmured to a patron at the table in front of her as he gracefully eased the plate from his fingers to the tabletop. A sip of lemony but weak iced tea did nothing to cool the heat rising from the region between her breasts. He didn't let the plate clatter to the table; nor did he try to avoid the center of the plate by letting his fingers clasp only the edges of the dish. When he delivered it to the tablecloth, it made no sound. In truth, she wanted to

cheer. He didn't even blow on his fingers; he merely brushed them with the crisp cloth he'd tucked into his waistband, as if they'd been merely moist, not scalded. Perfect presentation; his attention was for only the diner, who nodded approvingly at his dish.

Was he hurt? Did his fingers burn? She'd have paid dearly for the chance to put his fingers into her cool tea, then into her mouth. She could feel the whorls of his finger pads against her tongue. Not biting; his tips would be too sensitive for the tease of her teeth. Just soothing laps with the flat of her tongue; maybe she could blow on them after that—just to make sure they'd cooled down. Complete altruism. And how, exactly, could he show his thanks?

Eyes met hers, knowing. She was caught and pinned like being fucked against a wall. That little quirk again, as if he knew exactly what she was thinking. A quick, businesslike step brought him back to her table, where she blandly met his gaze and tried to deny it with a bored look. He left again, and she was not convinced he hadn't read her completely.

More tea, mostly cool, citrus-sharp water. She gave up try-ing to cross her legs against the needy coiling between them, and tried to shame it down instead: He wasn't flirting with her, just doing his job, and wasn't she the worst kind of stupid, countrified tourist for thinking otherwise? She was a grown woman, married. Just because she hadn't had an orgasm in eleven—had it really been that many?—days, and it felt so good to be finished with work, and he had promising hands, and her pussy was basically throbbing now, and nobody could tell what she was thinking, and she was grown, right? And the waiter *was* cute. . . .

Damn, who was she kidding? That young man was fine. She set her feet and calves apart, spreading her legs the few inches the knee-length business skirt would allow, let her hips tilt under just a fraction more, pressed the bend of her thumb into the need, looked out into the restaurant, saw nothing. Hoped her face didn't give anything away.

"Miss."

Caught again, and this time she couldn't cover her expression. Her eyes were too far away, her lips parted by anything but boredom, her chin raised just a fraction too far, her cheeks and temples infused with the same heated red that she'd seen in his skin. He bent closer to her than necessary, as if she were speaking too softly for him to hear. The plate was set noiselessly before her, unseen. The waiter's eyes slid from hers to the line of her neck, across her collarbone and the bit of caramel-colored cleavage, the tiny mole like a peppercorn, and followed her right hand beneath the tablecloth. He straightened, and this time the smile reached both ends of his wide, plush mouth. "It looks delicious, miss; I sincerely hope you enjoy it."

Years of Carolina upbringing, auntie advice (*We Marks women may know we've lost, but we never show it, honey,*), and the possibility of upending the table if she jerked her hand away from her crotch made her keep her face and body schooled into a portrait of urbane good behavior.

"I'm sure I will, thank you." Damn training; she put a little extra laziness in it, just because. A dimple appeared at the cor-

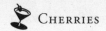

ner of the mustache. Step, pivot, and he was gone again. She still didn't move her hand.

The plate was so black against the tablecloth; at first glance it seemed a hole had opened up in the table. Alone, in the midst of the dark, were three bright red oversize cherries, like neon lights. Interesting, if a little disappointing. She frowned, unsure what to think. Her arousal dimmed a bit; her thumb eased the pressure while her left hand plucked up one of the stems. Her mouth opened, her brain expecting the familiar glassy taste of maraschino.

The rum hit her nose before her tongue, the heat flooding her mouth before her teeth burst the delicate skin. And then an explosion of sweet, almost sharp cherry, compounded with a hint of almond, that made her close her eyes and emit a blissful moan. A tiny bit of thick cream burst across her tongue, and it reminded her of . . . *Oh, God.*

Her eyes blinked open and locked on his espresso gaze from across the dining room. He stood there, coolly appraising her reaction. She wriggled in her seat, her core suddenly liquid at the thought of him watching her, while reaching determinedly for another of the cherries. Now that she knew what to expect, she made a little show for him, letting the pink cup of her tongue dart out to catch the cherry before it disappeared between her lips. She closed her eyes again. It was hard to concentrate on the flavor and also the tight coiling of pleasure that her right hand was discreetly producing beneath the table.

She took a moment to regain her composure. She sought his eyes again, finding them, and, at his nod of acknowledgment, made a desperate, lucky grab at the last cherry and popped it in her mouth to cover the fact that she was gritting her teeth as she came.

The muffled groan of release, her bowed neck, the slight sag of her back against the banquette, made the diner next to her smile with concern when she opened her eyes and glanced around the room. Had he understood what happened? Did he suspect? No, he calmly averted his eyes to his plate of half-finished pasta. Expensive flatware and conversation tinkled and murmured around and over her like a stream around a stone. Nothing was untoward; no one knew. She allowed herself a sigh of relief and smelled the rum on her breath. It made her smile.

"Miss," the waiter said with a slight throatiness that made her squeeze the napkin in her lap. She instead raised it to her lips and dabbed while she elevated her gaze to meet his. "I trust you enjoyed your dessert?" Such an attentive man.

"It was absolutely delicious." Her tongue lingered over the Ls a beat, drawing them out as she tasted the cherry and rum on the point of her upper lip where it touched.

"So glad you were pleased, miss." He slipped the black receipt wallet onto the linen. The dimple was deeper this time. And this time he did not pivot and turn, but stepped back from her table a few paces, as if he didn't want to turn his back on her.

"Me, too." She dabbed her lips one last time, then turned her attention to the receipt wallet. When she looked up again, he was gone.

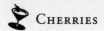

No one in the restaurant took notice of the average-looking black woman who sauntered out of the dining room. The figure-eight swivel of her buttocks in the skirt suit garnered no remark. But the obscenely generous tip she left was the talk of the waitstaff later that evening. When pressed, the young man shrugged and said he'd merely been polite.

DAISY: THE COOK,
THE HOUSEKEEPER, AND THE MAID

by Kay Jaybee

"How long has she been here like this?"

Cold, lust-filled eyes flicked across the tethered body.

"Two hours."

The reply was sharp and clipped. Mrs. Alborough, the estate housekeeper, never wasted her words.

The kitchen was large. Huge pine dressers covered with the paraphernalia of domestic life lined the walls, and the range pumped out a fierce heat that made the room hot and stuffy.

Daisy lay faceup and spread-eagled on the massive wooden kitchen table she frequently had to scrub clean. Naked, with wrists and ankles bound to each table leg, the maid's pale, rounded body was stretched to its limits with tight ropes. Her back ached against the unyielding oak, her long mess of blond hair hung off the tabletop, and her wide blue eyes stung from the tears of humiliation, anger, and frustration that had dried tightly against her face.

It was the feeling of frustration that dominated Daisy's thoughts now as Mr. George, the cook, continued to stare, his tall, thickset frame towering over her. "Why is she being punished this time?"

"She dropped a bag of flour across the larder floor."

The cook nodded solemnly, his eyebrows knitting together into a fake frown. "And how has the punishment been administered so far?"

"Attention has been given every ten minutes, for one minute only, with this . . ." The housekeeper, her slightly graying hair pulled back from her slim, angular face into a short, tight ponytail, held up a pastry brush. Its pale cream bristles glimmered and shone with the maid's syrupy juices.

Daisy's insides contracted as she saw the innocent-looking object. So soft a brush was an essential tool in a busy kitchen, but when it was stroked against the tender flesh between her outstretched legs it became an implement of torture. The bristles felt exquisitely delicious as they danced over her clit, building an intense knot in her stomach and taking her to the very edge of orgasm before they were cruelly withdrawn when each carefully timed sixty seconds was up, thus plunging Daisy into the hell of having to endure neglect for an incredibly long ten minutes. Then Mrs. Alborough would begin the cycle again, keeping the recalcitrant maid forever on the brink of pleasure.

"Any attention to the tits?" Mr. George leaned close enough to the maid's large, milky-white breasts for her to smell his newly washed short brown hair. Daisy couldn't help but shiver as he deliberately blew warm breath against her restrained flesh.

"None." The housekeeper began to search through a nearby drawer. "These?" She held up two yellow rubber cones, normally used to help loosen tight jar lids.

"Excellent. You are most inventive, Mrs. Alborough."

The housekeeper's usually ashen cheeks blushed into life under her handsome counterpart's praise as she passed him the flexible cones.

Daisy whimpered as the rubber encased her firm breasts and instantly irritated her nipples. Her whimpers quickly turned to yelps as Mr. George pushed the cones hard, twisting them back and forth as if he were trying to unscrew her luscious tits from her body. Pain shot through Daisy, a dark, hot hurt that suddenly mingled with pleasure as the housekeeper began to circle the soft head of the pastry brush up and down her legs.

The maid fought to hold back a fresh wave of tears. Two hours she had endured; her longest period of chastisement to date in this unusual stately home, where the rules of discipline were unlike anything she'd ever known before. Daisy's arms and legs felt numb from being pulled at the sockets for so long, and there wasn't a part of her that didn't ache. She bit her bottom lip hard, trying with all her might not to do what they wanted her to do; she was determined to stop herself from begging for release.

Mr. George recognized the fortitude in Daisy's glistening eyes as he continued to roughly knead her tits. "You've learned much self-control since you've been here, girl. I confess, I'm impressed." He turned to the housekeeper. "You've taught her well."

Mrs. Alborough inclined her head in recognition of the compliment, her sharp gray eyes blazing with shameless desire. "Thank you, but I think a further level of instruction is still required."

Daisy's mind raced. How could she possibly take any more? Yet she couldn't help feeling a small surge of pride. She had come so far, and, for the first time since she'd started experiencing these disciplines over a year ago, she hadn't broken down with the pain, the wait for satisfaction, or the shame of the growing realization that a secret part of her had begun to look forward to these situations.

Leaving the yellow cones in place, but withdrawing the brush, her employers retreated to the other side of the kitchen. Perspiration prickled across Daisy's forehead and ran between her tits. The rubber guardians pinched and suckled at her breasts as the room's warmth made them stick to her pert flesh. More than anything, Daisy wanted to knock them off and have a cooling tongue soothe her, and to feel a thick cock between her legs. She sighed, waggling her imprisoned fingers pointlessly as she faced the reality of her situation: She was at their mercy, again.

Daisy couldn't see her tormentors anymore, but she could hear the rumble of their voices coming from the larder. Her mind could focus only on what she wanted them to do to her, *needed* them to do to her. She would not allow herself to think that she'd been abandoned permanently, for sometimes they never did let her come, but simply left her there, tied and untouched, until all her wasted desire seeped away, and only discomfort and embarrassment remained.

A few minutes later her superiors returned, carrying a basket of vegetables that Daisy had previously sorted to be used in the evening stew. "Time to start preparing supper, my girl." Mrs. Alborough spoke calmly, although Daisy could see that her face was even more flushed than it had been, leaving the maid to helplessly speculate about what the cook had done to her while they were out of sight.

The laden basket was placed between Daisy's outstretched legs. Taking a short knife each, the cook and the housekeeper began to peel potatoes over her bound frame.

Daisy watched, holding her breath in disbelief, as strings of vegetable skin dangled over her body. The first piece broke away, landing with a small slap on her clammy flesh. Its chilled, smooth texture made Daisy flinch. As strand after strand of cold peel followed, the slow buildup of their touch against her stomach felt as erotic to her desperate body as the lapping tongue she'd been longing for.

Mr. George stopped his work and, much to Daisy's relief, removed the rubber cones from her chest. Then he picked up a carrot and carefully began to cut away its orange coat. Long, curling strands teased at her tight tits. The cool shavings tickled her nipples as they dropped to her chest, making Daisy quiver and moan. Her hips rose slightly from the table, threatening to destroy all the self-control she'd been so anxious to preserve. As Mrs. Alborough snaked coarser parsnip skins across her chest, Daisy closed her eyes tightly in a last-ditch bid to concentrate.

Mr. George snapped at her, "Open your eyes."

Sensible of further punishment, Daisy obeyed instantly, but kept her mouth shut and her teeth tightly gritted.

"See here, girl!" He grabbed a handful of Daisy's yellow hair and yanked her head up so that she had no choice but to look at what he was holding. "Look at the width and shape of this carrot—or maybe you'd prefer to glance at this parsnip? Wouldn't you just love to feel one of them inside you? You're very wet, girl; you've soaked this table. Perhaps a plug is required?"

Trussed and vulnerable, Daisy licked her dry lips as the cook continued.

"You want to feel better, don't you? I think you want something stuck up inside you *very* badly indeed."

Mrs. Alborough began to trail a long string of carrot skin around Daisy's tense stomach. The maid had been so determined not to beg, but her body had been left on the edge of satisfaction for too long—pure desire was taking over.

"Daisy," Mr. George continued, "you *would* like that, *wouldn't you?*"

"Yes, sir." Daisy felt the final vestiges of her resolve crumble. "Yes, sir, I would, I really would."

The cook instantly adopted a harsher tone. "Are you *begging,* girl?"

Daisy cowered beneath his victorious gaze, yet she couldn't help being privately excited by the bulge in his trousers that her presence had created. She took a gulp of air and answered, "Yes, sir. Please fill me, sir." Silently, she hoped he'd do the job himself, but he never had yet, so the parsnip would just have to do. In fact, Daisy was so eager to be shafted that anything remotely dick-shaped would do.

"Mrs. Alborough." The cook looked grave as he addressed his counterpart, and, speaking with mock pity, he said, "This girl has reached an all-time low; surely she has no pride left. She is actually pleading with me to fill her with a vegetable."

"It's a sad thing, Mr. George, a sad thing." The housekeeper shook her head from side to side, but her hands were quaking, and the blush of desire that had tinted her cheeks was turning a deeper, beetroot red.

"Should we?" The cook looked directly at the housekeeper, who didn't reply, but returned his gaze hungrily.

Daisy stared up at them, powerless as her employers reached over her body and kissed each other passionately. She could hear their mouths clash together in their urgency, and felt their bodies press hard against her sides as they leaned in, arms outstretched. Leaving their maid temporarily forgotten, they moved to the foot of the table, where they made short work of removing each other's work garments in a sudden frenzy of pent-up longing.

Craning her neck to see, Daisy felt her mouth begin to drool uncontrollably as she observed the spectacle unfolding before her. For a few seconds, Mr. George and Mrs. Alborough broke away to stare at each other, chests heaving deeply as each admired the other's naked form. Then the cook launched himself forward, attaching his mouth to the housekeeper's dark, chocolate-colored nipples and surrounding cream flesh, suckling hard and fast until she was mewling like a cat.

As the housekeeper ran her work-blunted fingernails through her lover's cropped hair, Daisy could only listen with envy as Mrs. Alborough's climax built, and watch her body rock against Mr. George's.

The moment the housekeeper had regained her composure, she was on her knees. Daisy couldn't see what she was doing, but from the self-satisfied look on the cook's face as he stared back at the maid, she assumed that Mrs. Alborough's lips were working up and down his shaft. Daisy began to wonder if the housekeeper had also thrust one of her long, thin fingers up his arse. . . . It was a thought too far.

This was so unfair! Daisy had begged. She'd done what they wanted—let them humiliate her for hours for the most minor of crimes—and now her aching, lust-racked body was being ignored while they took out their own carnal wants on each other. It was too much. Something in Daisy snapped. Normally she would never have dared complain, not about anything, but her overwhelming need for attention had stripped away the final vestiges of her self-control.

"Please!" Her unexpected shout echoed around the kitchen. "Fuck me!"

They instantly stopped. The housekeeper's head popped into view and they both glared at the maid. Daisy had expected them to shout back at her, or maybe beat her with the wooden spoon that they occasionally spanked her with, but she was totally unprepared for what actually happened next. In an obviously preplanned move, they broke away from each other and walked toward her.

Mr. George helped his colleague up onto the large table. Mrs. Alborough lay faceup, her bum lying on the wood of the table right below Daisy's. Her hips were framed by Daisy's open, bound legs, and she stretched her own legs against either side of Daisy's torso. Her head, which the cook gently supported with a dishrag, rested between Daisy's rope-harnessed feet.

The cook stood at the side of the kitchen table and reached his hands toward the two cunts that lay open before him, both equally hungry for his attention. The women groaned simultaneously as he slowly circled their hard clits with his calloused fingers.

Tears prickled afresh against Daisy's eyes as the release she badly needed felt so close, and yet still so far from her grasp. Daisy attempted to rub against the older woman to create some friction, seeking anything that might provide some additional stimulation, but in this position, it was impossible. The cook's right palm swiftly slapped down against Daisy's left thigh, making her cry out in agony as he barked, "No moving, girl," but his temper was swiftly forgotten as Mrs. Alborough made a plea of her own, appealing for him to quickly move on to the next part of their plan.

Mr. George moved toward the counter to collect the suitably shaped vegetables he intended to use as makeshift dildos, and then, his hand hovering above the parsnips, he stopped.

There was suddenly one more thing he wanted to do to his lover before he granted her satisfaction.

Bending the housekeeper's legs up at the knee, so that if Daisy lifted her head, she had an intimate view of Mrs. Alborough's arse, Mr. George began to finger-fuck her puckered anus. Slowly, he built up a rhythm that made Mrs. Alborough moan out deep, guttural words of want, as Daisy watched her receive the most personal of examinations.

Daisy felt the other woman's body stiffen against her own. The cook withdrew his finger and lowered Mrs. Alborough's legs so that she now lay against Daisy's left side, the women's hips pressing together. Without further hesitation, he inserted one of the freshly peeled carrots into his lover's pussy, turning her cries to croons of pleasure. Then, as Daisy's breath snagged in anticipation, he wedged a blissfully wide parsnip between her slick clit lips.

Daisy sighed deeply as she felt herself filled at last, only to gasp in surprise as the large man joined them on the table. Straddling both women, the cook coaxed his dick into Mrs. Alborough's open mouth and stroked himself between her lips. He leaned forward and pushed his face against Daisy's soft mound, licking greedily at her tiny clit. He pumped the parsnip in and out of Daisy's pulsating cunt.

Daisy could hear Mrs. Alborough moaning and slurping around Mr. George's cock. Groaning, sweat dotting her chest and gluing her back to the table, Daisy accepted the cook's thrusts willingly, her muscles clamping around the perfectly shaped vegetable. Bright colors popped inside her head as his tongue worked its magic, and she finally howled out her long-pent-up orgasm.

Mr. George looked up from between Daisy's legs. "I hope you won't be spilling any more flour, Daisy."

"I'll do my best, sir, but I can't promise." Daisy's reply was a mere murmur as her body continued to explode, trapped by the table, the cook, and the housekeeper.

IN THE DENTIST'S CHAIR

by Aimee Herman

*S*tarts out in the waiting room. Expired magazine sits on my lap. Cover story spotlights how to get rid of cellulite from back of thighs by relocating to front of lips. I skip story and focus on photographs. Lick my lips over image of bent women with airbrush-tight limbs and breasts microwaved on high, popping out from lace-infused wire bras.

Drip.

My name is called. I look up. Place magazine to my side and straighten legs. I walk toward voice. Voice with lips just like the ones the magazine boasted about. Occupied by fullness. Dyed deep red as though marinated in distilled cherry juice. Her left breast bears the stitched name Dr. Diane Barrio. Doctor Diane. White coat. Hair pushed back against wall of scalp, handcuffed by elastic band.

Dr. Diane places a blue bib around my neck. Metal clasp scrapes against my ear as she pulls it across to fasten. I shiver. She notices, smiles.

I lie down in blue chair, oversize palm pressing me down. She touches one of my blond dreadlocks. Accidentally? My hair is dead, but I am not. I feel her fingerprints impress themselves into my knots.

Drip.

I cross my legs as she crosses her body against me to fill the tiny plastic cup with water. "Gargle and rinse," she whispers. I grab the small cup from her long, painted nails. Press plastic between lips, taking in stream of cold water. I leave it there. Rinsing, removing, relieving my mouth of any unnecessary particles. Liquid slides down thick tongue, down throat. I swallow. She watches.

Drip.

"Just relax," Dr. Diane advises.

Fingers glide in and out and explore as I stretch and shift around her. Suddenly, I wish I had cleaned up a bit more, unaware she would go so far into me. I would have neatened up. Baked something special to offer her. Something sweet and drippy held beneath my tongue. A surprise she'd find and thank me by remaining inside longer.

My teeth wake up. They feel the need to bite out of habit as she pushes further. I feel her extend. She is wet between her fingers from my accidental sucking. She tastes like rubber. Elastic breath. Metallic fillings. Tongue sap.

In and out, she hides inside me. Vibrating gloves feel each taste bud stiffly standing in an upright position. Sensory receptors signal her to keep going. Pause. Yes. Back there. To the right.

Drip.

"There may be a cavity," I say when she removes her finger. Hollow area somewhere a bit lower down. A crack or cleft of skin pulled apart. She will have to get in there. Look around a bit. Take her time to find where opening begins so she can fill it properly and fully.

Dr. Diane. White coat. Bronze skin. Firm hair. Long legs. Straddling me. Bib around neck remains tied to catch falling lips and pulled-out tongue. Or it feels that way. Mouth is left stretched open, satisfied and sweaty as padded fingers move. Elsewhere. Down.

Drip.

There is no transition from upright to parallel. Or maybe I am too preoccupied with the sound of fabric unclasping to notice. Too engaged in the temperature changing from air-conditioned to heatstroke. Her weight is above me, turning my bones into a long slide of metallic moaning. Gloves pulled off as the weave of lines on her fingers gets caught in mine. She touches my neck as though it is a tree trunk hiding gallons of sap. She squeezes and scratches, tearing her way toward my contents. I begin to think maybe I *am* made of sap, when she sucks so hard I almost feel myself drilled open.

There are no parts left untouched. She moves from my neck to the pillowy flesh of my earlobes. Dr. Diane has a tongue like a drill, gyrating behind my ear as the rest of my body rattles along.

We communicate through moans and the breath burning through our lungs. There is a moment where she looks at me, pausing just above my face. My neck feels as though it has been swimming inside her mouth. Her lips whisper, "Yes?" I smile. Without asking her to clarify the question, I nod.

Dr. Diane caresses my breasts with hers, unwrapped from her dark blue bra that clasps from the front, which she allows me to snap open. She smiles, pulling her breasts off of me like a reverse raindrop dripping back into the sky. She replaces it with her mouth. She sucks with the same passion she bestowed on my neck. My nipple is a button she wants to pull off with her manicured teeth. She searches for the thread to unstitch it. I harden inside her. She takes a bite, though I remain fully intact.

Toward belly—a wave of breaths that move up and down as she wets the skin normally hidden beneath cotton. My hips rock, summoning her attention. When my zipper finally breaks from too much pressure, my two bent thighs part like the earth. She mumbles something into my navel, and I swear my entire body has an erection as skin hardens and swells.

My cunt feels like it has been dieting for months. Years. It feels like it has cooked up something really warm and rich, waiting for someone to come along with proper utensils (stainless-steel fingers welcome) and be devoured.

No underwear. I feel my petals widen. She whispers something into them. I melt into her mouth. She gargles me.

Does. Not. Swallow. Yet.

There is a discovery made, like a newly found country. Untouched land. Wet ocean of depth. She explores. Dr. Diane does not use any instruments down there besides fingers and tongue, uncompressed. I fall back farther into chair and use fingers to unclasp handcuff holding her hair into place. Dark roots run free past shoulders. I push her head down, almost swallowing her. She does not mind.

My cunt contains no cavities. This does not stop her from using sharpened tongue to navigate every corner and crevice of moist parts. There is no getting lost when every direction is investigated. Sometimes she lingers. Licking the same spot over and over.

Drip. Drip. Drip. Driiiiiiiiiiip.

She sucks on my clit as though it offers an elixir. As though my come contains enhanced particles of heightened pleasure. She sucks so hard I fear it will tear off. Then she will either gargle or spit, depending upon her desire or preference. Mixing breath and moisture from her lungs with my erect organ, which is swelling and doubling in size.

I harden in her mouth like fully cooked cuisine. I become numb. Curving back from the chair that my sweat has stuck me to, I peel myself away as my limbs tremble from Dr. Diane's heavy and thorough probing.

She. Finds. My. Cavity. And. She. Fills. It. In. With. Her. Tongue.

I am no longer vacant. I am no longer empty. I am no longer able to breathe.

In the dentist's chair, my arms and limbs become like cut-down trees, tired and limp. All of my nutrients flood out from within their tightened container. There is no time for sipping. She gulps me down, never choking. Dr. Diane is proficient and precise.

She lifts head. Looks up. Hazel eyes become shovels digging into my glazed-over pupils. Hands push her up from between thighs to against my chest. Our faces are parallel. She spreads her cherry-juice lips into mine. I taste me on her face. On her tongue. Between her teeth. Tastes bitter. Salty. A little like chamomile tea dunked into sour cream. Tastes good.

Slowly, Dr. Diane peels herself off of me. I remain still as she unclasps metal from bib and leaves my neck bare. If I stand, I worry I will slip within the puddle rushing from between my thighs. I do not move. She stands above me, smiling.

"I'll need to see you once more," she says to me. "We have run out of time, but there is still more that needs to be done."

I look deep into her. Her lips have grown, smeared color drifting past her mouth from heavy kissing.

"And next time," she adds, "I will wear the bib."

ALL SHE NEEDS

by Heather Monaco

*L*ily stood naked by the edge of the bed, staring down on her sleeping lover. His tanned
skin shone in stark contrast to her white cot-
ton sheets, which were tangled through his runner's legs. The
morning sun coated the room in white light, making it easy for
her to observe the smallest details about the man who slept before her, curled on his side, one hand tucked beneath his cheek.
Details such as the fine dark hair that feathered his arms, the
mole on his hip, the childlike pout of his lips.

Her gaze was not one of adoration, but of annoyance.
Hadn't she told him explicitly last night—just before she had
passed out into her down-filled pillow—that he was not welcome to stay the night? He was more recalcitrant toddler than
angel lying there in her bed, unwelcome.

"Wake up," she said, arms crossed against her small, round
breasts. He didn't stir. "Hey," she said, reaching out to shake

his shoulder, "Hey, you, Mike, or Mark, or whatever the fuck your name is. Wake up."

He cracked an eye and raised his eyebrow quizzically. "Good morning, sunshine. And it's Mitch."

"Whatever. Get up. I said no sleepovers." She yanked the sheets back, exposing his morning hard-on. He grinned.

"You didn't seem to want me to go around three a.m." He grasped his cock with one hand and reached for her with the other. "Looks like I *am* up. Wanna fuck?"

He pulled her on top of him, pinning her there. She felt his cock pressing into her belly, and her pussy dampened. Yes, he had been pretty damn good last night—good and hard. Once they'd made it to the bed, he had flipped her onto her back, pulled her ass to the edge, and wrapped his muscular arms around her legs, lifting her up. She'd come almost instantly, shouting out loud enough that she wondered if the neighbors heard her.

"Do not make me scream, jackass," she growled, pushing herself up and stepping away from the bed. "Now get . . . the fuck . . . out."

Mitch sighed and sat up, stretched lazily, cracked his knuckles. He looked around the room. "One problem, sweetheart. Where are my clothes?"

Lily paused for a second, her mind racing through a thick, bourbon-induced morning fog to the night before. They'd stumbled in around midnight, creating a yard sale as they stripped on the way to her bedroom, tongues entangled, hands exploring unknown territory. Before they made it through her compact living–dining room combination, he was clad in a condom, pushing her against the wall and entering her from behind. His strong hand pinned her neck against the cool glass of a family photo while he rammed his cock as deep into her pussy as he could. The marble top of her antique console table cut into her thighs, making them burn, but she didn't protest. It felt too good to be fucked, hard, by a stranger—a dark, handsome stranger at that. She needed it. She deserved it, actually.

That was last night; this was a new day, and she was finished with him.

"God," she said, rolling her eyes. "In the living room. You can pick them up on the way out. Now get out!" She stalked into the adjoining bathroom and slammed the door shut.

"Aren't you even going to offer me a cup of coffee?" Mitch called. He heard the shower turn on in reply.

Lily let the warm water sluice down her breasts, her smooth tummy, the trimmed curls of her pubic hair, and watched it swirl around her manicured toes. She scrubbed herself with a loofah, removing every trace of Mitch from her skin. She wasn't ashamed of her need to get laid once in a while, or of her desire for no-strings-attached sex.

Most of her girlfriends didn't get it. Her sisters didn't get it. Lord knew her mother didn't get it. "What kind of girl are you, Lily?" her mom would croon across the miles. "Aren't you lonely? Don't you want children?"

Lily turned the hot water up to drown her mother's voice from her head. For Lily, her event-planning company was her child. Her father would have gotten that. He died when she was fifteen—car accident. He had traveled most of the time before that, showing up for important occasions like school plays and birthdays. She hadn't really known him, and that made her sad. A shrink once suggested that her lack of intimate relationships with men—emotionally intimate relationships, because yes, there was sex, and lots of it—had something to do with her distant father. Lily blew it off as so much bullshit.

That brief time of introspection came after a particularly troublesome relationship with a guy who brought her down fast and hard, like a lion on a gazelle. Lily massaged the mint-scented shampoo into her hair as she remembered the man who had eaten her alive. When he had left her carcass along the side of the road one night, she stepped away from her life for a few weeks to get a grip. Her best friend suggested that her therapist might be helpful. At a loss for anything else, Lily saw the guy a few times before coming to the conclusion that she could get just as much healing on the beach, sipping a beer.

So she had gone to Mexico instead.

She stayed at a little hotel on a hidden inlet south of Playa del Carmen. Her room was a thatch-roofed bungalow with its own front porch and hammock. Only a small stand of palms came between her and the azure Caribbean. Lily closed her eyes, letting the suds of shampoo run down her face. She could see the beauty of the beach even now.

Over the first several days of her trip, she took yoga classes in the hotel's circular palapa, its palm-leaf roof soaring twenty feet above the red clay floor. She felt the toxicity of her crazed life leach out of her bones under the Mayan sun. By day five, she was luxuriating topless on the beach most mornings after a luscious breakfast of eggs, white beans, fruit smoothies, and hand-ground coffee in the small restaurant filled with plastic tables. In the early afternoon she'd move to her hammock to read and drift off for a siesta. Later, she'd ride into Tulum or Playa to shop. When she'd return to the hotel by taxi, the sun would have set long before, and she would walk along the surf, hearing but not seeing it crash against the shore. With the sky open above her, she would take off her clothes and lie naked on the damp sand to watch for shooting stars.

By day twelve, she was getting antsy. She'd brought along her favorite vibrator, but a girl could masturbate only so much. She needed to be touched by a human. On one of her walks down the beach, she'd noticed a small white tent with a hand-lettered sign: *Massage, $20 U.S., 1 hour.*

When she arrived at midmorning, a portly man was on the table, being rubbed down by a dark-skinned man. From behind, the masseur looked wiry and strong.

Lily sighed in the shower, goose bumps rising on her skin as she remembered the way his black hair looked, pulled back in a band and cascading to the top of his shoulders.

He had glanced over his shoulder and smiled at her. "*Quince minutos, señorita. Entonces yo le atenderé a usted.*"

She smiled and nodded at him, thinking, *Of course I need servicing from you.* "*Tomaré una caminata y regresaré en un poco,*" she said.

She walked down the curve of the beach, imagining the

masseur's strong hands sliding down her back and along her ass, digging into her hamstrings. The thought of a sexy man touching her started her tingling in her softest places, and she laughed at herself.

And when she was finally naked on the table, facedown under a sheet, she started tingling again.

"*¿Cómo se llama usted?*" she asked.

"Juan-Julio," he said. "I speak English if you prefer."

"I prefer no talking, just touching."

"*Sí, señorita,*" he said, and began slowly rolling the balls of her feet under his oiled thumbs.

He paused briefly with his thumbs lightly pressing on a spot just above her arches. "I also do reflexology and Reiki. It costs a little extra, but it is worth it. Your energy is very scattered. I can help you settle it down."

She groaned her approval and he got to work. Juan-Julio smoothed his hands over her body, touching certain points for a while, digging into knots. She tried to keep her hips from pulsing up as he worked her inner thighs. Her pussy was burning to be touched, and she could almost feel him slipping his thumbs along her lips, opening her, exposing her need like the juiciest fruit. She felt every ounce of her remaining negative energy drain out the top of her head. When she rolled onto her back, she didn't care that he looked at her body as he lifted the sheet. The delicious glow of the massage made her feel effervescent and aroused.

"Now I work on your chakras. I will not touch you, but you will feel me," he said. He methodically moved his hands down her body, requesting that she breathe deeply or shallowly at certain points. Even though his hands never touched her, she could feel his heat on her.

Lily turned under the showerhead, slowly sliding the bubbly loofah up one arm. She had itched to reach up and feel his muscled chest, to pull him down into a kiss, to see what was beneath his linen drawstring pants. But she tempered herself, barely, because if she were to touch him, he would stop doing those wonderful things to her body.

"I will awaken the sleeping snake now, the kundalini," he said. "You may feel much pleasure. Just let it be."

"Okay," she said skeptically. When his hands came to her pubic bone, she opened her eyes in surprise. She instantly felt an orgasm beginning to pulse deep inside her, the energy pulling up from her pussy into the top of her head as it simultaneously rushed down her legs. In one burst, she came, crying out and arching her back. The orgasm seemed to go on for minutes—hours, even. When it stopped she was depleted and more sexually satisfied than she'd felt in her life.

"Do it again!" she said. It had been the best orgasm of her life.

He laughed. "No, you go sleep now. You will be very tired. But if you want, I can come to your room and do more tomorrow."

Lily turned off the shower. Her breath came quickly and her skin felt alive. Perhaps it was time to visit Mexico again. She was due for a vacation, and she certainly wouldn't mind doing Juan-Julio again. She toweled off, donned her black silk bathrobe, and headed to the kitchen to finish her morning ritual: soy latte made with her professional-grade espresso machine, chocolate-banana protein shake, handful of vitamins, and then back to the bedroom to get dressed.

But when she opened the bedroom door, the scent of brewing coffee overwhelmed the small space.

"Feel better?" she heard a baritone voice call across the room. "Forgive me for helping myself, but I'm just no good until I have my coffee."

Mitch emerged from the kitchen holding a steaming mug—her favorite piece of Louis Mulcahy pottery. He was dressed in yesterday's clothes, the white dress shirt slightly wrinkled from its slumber on her living room floor. His dark suit coat and green-striped tie lay over the back of the love seat.

"Well, don't just stand there and gawk at me like you've never seen a clothed man before," he said. "How do you take your coffee?"

Lily realized she'd been rooted to the spot, mouth open, still clutching her white towel to her damp head. She pulled back her shoulders, flipped the towel back onto the unmade bed, and stalked past him into the kitchen.

"I'm calling the cops."

"And you're going to tell them what?"

"I'm going to tell them that you broke in."

"And that I stole a cup of coffee?"

She grabbed a heavy cookbook off the counter and raised it at him, trying to look menacing. He put his hands up and started laughing.

"Hey, there, little missy, no need to get violent. Tell you what I'm gonna do. I'm going to put this mug down real slow-like and back out of here like the coward I am."

She waved the book his way again. "Do it, then."

He grabbed his jacket and tie, then opened the front door.

"See you around, gorgeous," he said, still laughing. "Gotta love a feisty woman."

The door clicked shut behind him, and Lily let out a fierce growl. "God, what is that guy's problem?"

She pushed the power button on her espresso machine, her hands still shaking. She didn't like feeling out of control, and this guy—this Mitch—had certainly done his best to take her control away.

LILY WAS EXHAUSTED WHEN SHE shut her door behind herself twelve hours later. Her day had been grueling. A new client had unreasonable expectations about what she could do for his budget and got belligerent. Another called in a panic because the company president's wife didn't like the theme they'd been working on for months. It seemed Lily had hit every red light possible, and even the line at the local coffee shop had been double its usual queue. She kicked off her pumps and wiggled her toes in the plush carpeting. She poured herself a twelve-year-old scotch from the small bar off the kitchen and collapsed onto her couch.

The lit skyline view from her full-height window reminded her that Denver was still a small town. She felt grateful she had been able to keep herself together, especially in front of clients.

The scotch's warmth trickled through her shoulders and arms and she sighed, lying back into the couch's microsuede cushions, closing her eyes.

Not for the first time that day, Mitch's face crossed her mind. Damn, he was gorgeous. That smile. She felt ire creeping into her throat. But what was his deal? He thought he could push her around.

She sat up and glanced across the room at the picture frame that had left a slight mark on her neck. Her skin prickled instantly as she remembered the feel of his hands on her shoulders, her breasts. He had known how to kiss: lots of lip, with enough tongue to keep it interesting, but not to overwhelm. And, right on cue, there went her pussy. It was so predictable that, the day after a big romp, and especially a drunken one, she'd be hornier than she'd been before the man of the evening.

That pissed her off. She did not want to crave a guy like him. She didn't want to know a guy like him. She turned on the TV and flipped the channels, hoping to find something to distract her from her throbbing pussy. It ached insistently. Her panties were damp. She sighed and turned off the tube.

Lily took her glass to her bedroom and, without turning on the light, stripped and climbed in between the sheets. She reached under the bed and retrieved her Hitachi Magic Wand, then her favorite glass dildo and a bottle of Slippery Kitty from the bedside table drawer. She poured several drops of the lube on the smooth skin above her clit. Her index finger and thumb pinched the skin, and she began rubbing her fingers together.

She settled into her pillow and turned her mind back to Mitch, to his long, muscular legs. To his cock. It curved just slightly up and to the left, she'd noticed when she slid him into her mouth as she knelt before him next to her bed. That had been the start of round two.

She dipped her glass dildo into her scotch and slid the head, a two-inch-diameter ball, into the opening of her pussy. The alcohol burned pleasantly as she slowly slid it in and out. She turned her vibrator on low, pressed it against her clit, and found her rhythm: in slowly, pull up, out slowly, letting each one of the dildo's knobs push against her G-spot. She gasped and her hips bucked involuntarily as the second bulb hit that sensitive spot. She still felt warm and raw from Mitch's dick. She remembered how he somehow knew to pause for a nano-second after its head rubbed across that spot, how closely he watched her reaction, how he smiled at her when she gasped. But after several minutes of slow warm-up, he roughly flipped her on her belly and pulled her, his hands gripping her hips, to the edge of the bed.

"Get on your knees and sit back," he said. She hesitated, glancing at him, his tone cutting through her bourbon haze. "Do it, you dirty bitch."

He twined his hand through her red, shoulder-length hair and pulled her back.

"Hey! Not cool!" she yelled. He responded by planting her face into the mattress and pinning her wrists behind her back. She felt his breath against her neck.

"Are you a good girl, or are you a bad girl?" he'd demanded, voice low and close. He wrapped his hand tighter into her hair and pulled. "Answer me, Lily. Good? Or bad?"

Lily's heart had pounded in her mouth, and she realized she was holding her breath. She let it out in a shudder that surprised her. She usually wasn't frightened by men, but by the way the tide had changed, she was beginning to feel terrified.

"Do you want more of my cock?" he asked.

She felt his lips brush the tiny hairs on the edge of her ear, and her pussy responded with a throb. The combination of adrenaline and desire made her head buzz. She wanted him to leave, but she was so ready for him she wanted him to stay. She nodded slightly.

"Was that a yes?"

Her mouth was watering for him. Her pussy was dripping for him. "Yes."

"Are you a bad girl, Lily?"

In her mind, Lily rolled her eyes. She tried to laugh at him, but she was beginning to lose feeling in her left fingers. His tight grip reminded her that this might not be a game. Anxiety surged again.

"Yes," she whispered, and her mind had flooded with memories of men she'd fucked. Was she a bad girl? Or was she good?

Lily's vibrator continued its sweet, slow rhythm just above her clit.

Juan-Julio came to mind. That second massage, in her hotel room, when his hands caressed her belly and she impulsively reached over and stroked his thigh, slowly, stopping her hand on his cock. To her surprise, he had been rock-hard. She grinned up at him and he didn't flinch. She stroked his member slowly through his pants. He moved his hands over her pussy.

"Juan-Julio, I believe you've done enough for me. I have something I want to do for you," she had said, and pulled the drawstring on his pants. They dropped to the ground and his cock sprang forward. It was not too large, straight and protruding from a nest of soft curls. He was a specimen, and between what she was seeing and what he was doing with his hands—or not doing—she knew that she had to have him right now.

She slid off the table and withdrew a condom from her suitcase. Handing it to him, she knelt in front of him and sucked the head of his dick into her mouth. His precome was sweet, tasting slightly of pineapple. He pulled her up and kissed her. His full lips brushed hers softly, his tongue following along to tease hers out. He kept one hand on her tailbone and one on her pubic bone, and she barely recognized what was happening before it happened. As she began to come, he turned her around, bent her over the table, and slid inside her drenched pussy.

Unexpectedly, Mitch flooded her thoughts, interrupting her Mexican memory. "Say it," he said.

"I'm a bad girl," she whispered.

He let go of her wrist. "Say it again. Louder." Mitch put the tip of his cock into her pussy. Her muscles gripped it, tried to pull it in. Every hair on her body stood on end with need.

"I'm a bad girl." She groaned, shoving herself back against

him. He grabbed her hip with his left hand and pulled her hair—*yank*—with the right.

"Ow!" she said, her free hand grabbing his.

"Hold still." He pulled his cock out of her abruptly and she gasped. He laughed. "Oh, you are a bad girl. You want my hard cock inside you, don't you?" He slammed it deep inside her.

"Now say it!" *Slam, slam, slam.* Her pussy lips tingled.

"I'm a bad girl." She felt a hot sting against her right butt cheek. "I'm a bad girl!" Another spank. "I'm a fucking dirty whore. Is that what you want to hear?" she screamed.

"Yes." He kissed her neck. "Now shut the fuck up." He released her hair and grabbed both hips, pushing himself deep into her while pulling her back. He reached around and pinched her clit between his fingers, rubbed. Lily pushed back against him, matching each thrust, fucking him back. Every inch of her skin burned and tingled. She opened her eyes and watched their shadows moving against the curtained windows.

When she closed her eyes again, it was Juan-Julio between her legs. Each stroke of his cock seemed to push her orgasm deeper into her body, deeper and deeper until all she felt was the reverberations of pleasure—a bass drum echoing in every cell of her body. She didn't know if she was sitting or standing. She didn't care if she was quiet or screaming. She did not want it to end, yet the feeling was so intense she needed it to end now. Still, Juan-Julio kept his hands in place, and her orgasm pulsed around them in vibrant colors behind her eyes. Just when she thought it couldn't become any more ecstatic, she felt all of her emotions and thoughts leave her body through the top of her head so that she was nothing but physical sensations of bliss. Slowly, slowly, the ride came to a stop. Only then did she realize that her highest point had been Juan-Julio's as well. She had felt him come with every ounce of her being.

Mitch thrust hard, repeatedly, violently pushing her ever closer to orgasm. She felt that telltale urge to pee, and she tightened her PC muscle until she couldn't stand it anymore. It was as if she were pulling her orgasm out of his cock, into her pussy, and up her spine. As the hot energy pulsed up toward her head, she relaxed against him and felt herself squirt down her clenched legs. Then her head exploded.

Lily felt the glass dildo push out of her pussy as her orgasm crested at the memory of last night's *petite mort*, layered over the soaring orgasms she had left behind in Mexico. She dropped the vibrator and gasped for breath. Her pink nipples were drawn into knots as she arched her back, the orgasm still pulsing into her extremities. Her right hand combed back her hair as she felt the stress of the past twenty-four hours pour out of her.

She closed her eyes, and there was Mitch again, this time grinning at her, coffee steaming in her favorite mug. All the good feelings stopped short. *Asshole!* The man was a first-class prick. She couldn't believe she'd let him affect her at all. For someone who knew how to rub her, he rubbed her the wrong way otherwise.

Juan-Julio had known how to rub her, too, although she hadn't seen the masseur again. When she had walked down the beach to find him that last day, his tent was gone. It was probably for the best; she might have never left Mexico if he hadn't disappeared.

She rolled onto her sleep side of the bed and reached out to set her alarm clock. She heard something hit the floor. She pulled the chain on her mahogany lamp and discovered—eyes squinting in the sudden brightness—a piece of her turquoise monogrammed stationery, folded in half. She reached down and picked it up.

Lily,
Next time you're a bad girl, give me a call. I know just how
you like to be punished.
M

Inside the folded paper: his business card. She looked at it for a moment. It read: *Mitchell Nevin, Partner. Sunderland, Nevin, & Walsh, PC, Attorneys-at-Law.*

Of course he's a lawyer, she thought, then tossed the paper and card onto her nightstand and turned off the light.

Her last thought before she fell asleep: *No way in hell, buddy. I have all I need of you right here in my head.*

THE WINDOW

by Brian K. Crawford

*S*he fumbled with the lock, twisting the key impatiently, for that familiar sensation was pounding through her body again. Tingling thrills writhed in her belly, causing her to squeeze her thighs together with an involuntary shudder. She knew well what it meant, and what had caused it this time.

It had started just a moment before as she was approaching her building; she glanced up and saw a young postman coming toward her, a bulging mailbag over his shoulder. He was tall and blond, with long hair worn in a ponytail. He wore the pin-striped shorts and dark knee socks of the postal service, emphasizing his well-muscled thighs.

He was already eyeing her appreciatively as she caught sight of him, taking in her long, tanned legs striding along below her short skirt, the provocative swaying of her hips, the gentle bobbing of her breasts beneath the thin blouse. She saw desire and lust in his eyes as he stared at the front of her skirt. He was imagining her nude, she was convinced.

The idea instantly excited her. She imagined he could see her body, as if her clothes were suddenly transparent and he was seeing her breasts thrust out toward him, nipples pert and rosy and begging to be kissed, her triangle of pubic hair rocking as she walked toward him. A rush of excitement started in her cunt, flowed up across her stomach, and warmed her breasts, causing her buttocks to tighten in a spasm of desire. She felt her nipples rise up hard and wondered if he could see them.

She glanced down at his crotch and saw his cock bulging down the leg of his shorts. My God, it was nearly hanging out. She had a quick image of herself opening his shorts and tugging them down, his penis lunging out toward her, the big, shiny knob of it yearning toward her cunt. Then she was seeing him completely naked, walking toward her proud and unashamed, his strong thighs and taut stomach flexing as he walked, his rampant cock bobbing and waving before him.

She stared, hypnotized by the delicious vision, then came to herself and glanced at his face. Their eyes met, and something was communicated between them. He had a curious half smile that said he had seen her gaze and understood exactly what she had been thinking. She quickly averted her eyes, but felt her face burning. Then they were nearly face-to-face.

She twisted her shoulders to pass between him and a lamppost, but he leaned slightly closer as they passed, and his bare arm brushed across the tips of both her breasts. She gasped at the sudden contact, and felt an electric spark on each nipple. Then he was past.

She stared after him as he continued up the street with a swagger she was sure hadn't been there before. She knew damn well that touch had been no accident. She should have been outraged at his impudence, but she couldn't take offense. As she watched, he turned up the steps of a building, swung the mailbag from his shoulder, and started filling the bank of mailboxes. He glanced once toward her, and she realized she was staring at him. She quickly turned and walked to her own building.

Finally she got the door unlocked and swung it open. She glanced back up the street and saw that he was one apartment closer now, working his way back toward her building. Closing the door behind her, she dumped her bags in a chair and slumped against the frame of the entryway. Her body was flooded with sexual need; her nerves were wire-taut, her breath short, her heart pounding. She felt sexy, naughty, and a bit shaky in the knees. She kicked her shoes off with abandon.

She loved this feeling, when her body's desires welled up in an erotic frenzy, overwhelming all other concerns. This was when she felt the most alive. She had long ago learned that when she felt like this the only release was to give in to her urges and do something wild, something daring, even dirty.

Ever since her body had awakened at puberty, these spells had been coming over her—when she could think of nothing else but gratifying her desires as quickly as possible. Usually she could just slip away someplace private and feverishly give herself some relief with her hands. But occasionally, it hit her in a public place and could not be resisted. More than once she had masturbated sitting at a table in a restaurant or driving in her car. One time she'd jerked off while leaning on a bar talking to a very handsome young bartender.

Her most memorable adventure, by far, was one hot summer day when it had hit her on a city bus. She'd been wearing a diaphanously thin dress and no underwear in that sultry heat. The bus was packed and she'd had to stand. Seated right in front of her, his knees nearly brushing hers, was the most incredibly attractive Mediterranean man. She knew he was staring at her body, and she grew wet at the fact. She found herself standing next to him, her hip an inch from his hand. The back of his hand touched her leg. At first it was so light she might not have noticed—if every nerve in her body hadn't been so finely attuned to him. She could have shifted away from him, but it was so deliciously exciting, she simply stood there with her eyes closed. Then he became bolder. His hand slid under her dress and between her thighs. Nearly swooning with desire, she shifted her weight to open her legs and give him access. Neither of them spoke, and never once did their eyes meet, but there on that crowded bus, with people standing all around her, he brought her to orgasm.

That had been the best time of all—she could still bring herself off just by thinking about that one. She wanted that thrill again. But what could she do?

She glanced around the room. Her gaze went to the window, and she walked over and looked out. Her flat was on the first floor, the windowsill perhaps eight feet above the side-walk. People strolled past, their heads only two or three feet below, but they never glanced up at her.

Their proximity gave her a daring idea: She could do some-thing shamelessly sexy right here in the window, just over the heads of dozens of complete strangers. The risk of being seen would add the sexy spice she so desperately needed right now.

People wandered by, oblivious to her standing there watch-ing them. But she wanted to be even closer. She turned the latch and raised the sash. A warm breeze wafted into the room, the filmy lace curtains billowing around her head. The sounds and smells of the street enveloped her, exactly as if she were out on the sidewalk.

Resting her weight on her hands, she leaned out, pressing her tingling crotch hard against the wooden sill.

An elderly couple walked slowly by, close to the wall. She could have easily leaned down and tapped the man on the head. Traffic moved past; a woman ambled along, her eyes on the lights at the corner. Two teenage boys burst out of her building and ran down the street. No one ever looked up to see her standing at the window.

It was a perfect spot. The window was set back slightly into the building, so she could see only twenty feet or so of sidewalk. She couldn't do anything too wild or the people in the building across the street could see her. She had an idea. She lowered the venetian blinds and tilted them down toward the street. She could see nothing beyond the near curb, but the view of the sidewalk was completely unobstructed. Now she could be seen only if someone on the sidewalk directly below the window turned and looked up at her. She could do whatever she wanted, with only a moderate risk of being discovered.

The thought of actually standing nude in the window instantly raised her arousal to fever pitch. She squirmed in excitement, hugging her breasts with her arms. She wanted to do it very much, but would she have the nerve? She decided she would just make herself do it. She made a solemn promise to herself, the serious kind that she always kept: She would stand right up against the blinds, as close as possible to the wide-open window. Then she would strip herself completely bare and stand fully exposed to anyone who passed by on the sidewalk. She would stand there like that, making no effort to cover herself, for, say, five full minutes. If she did that, she knew she could then masturbate herself to orgasm in seconds, if she hadn't come already by simply standing naked in the window.

She was positively quivering with excitement and fear. The danger of what she was about to do made it so much more exciting. She had often dreamed about exposing herself in public, but always ended up just fingering herself, her mind full of outrageous fantasies.

One of her favorites involved wearing a dress that could be whipped open in a second. Of course, she would wear nothing underneath—or maybe something outrageous, like crotchless panties and a shelf bra. She imagined herself wandering around town and, when she encountered an attractive man in the proper situation, giving him a show that would knock him over.

Another fantasy had her making love in a room with the walls and ceiling entirely covered with mirrors, where she and her nameless but incredibly gorgeous lover could be as wild as they wanted, reveling in the thousands of images of themselves fucking in every imaginable position. The best part was what she knew and her lover didn't—that the mirrors were one-way mirrors, and all around them people were watching their every move. Better yet, the room was in the center of a huge auditorium and thousands of people were watching them. That one got her off every time.

But this was no mere fantasy. This time she was really going to do it. She had sworn it to herself.

She stepped forward until her breasts were nearly touching the blinds. She watched the people hurrying past. They were so close! She could see and hear them perfectly, as if they were right in the room with her. Face after face went by, not one turning to look up at her. She gulped and took a deep breath. Now to do it!

She stood very still and straight for a moment, then closed her eyes and began slowly unbuttoning her blouse. Refusing to peep to see if anyone was looking, she shrugged out of the blouse and let it drop down her arms to the floor. She waited for a few seconds to see how it felt. Suddenly she was sure there was a man standing just outside her window, staring up at her.

Popping her eyes open in a rush of shame, she saw a woman walking by with a shopping bag swinging from her arm. A man with a briefcase appeared, sauntering slowly along not five feet away. The sight of him made her instinctively want to cover up, to throw her hands across her breasts, but she fought the urge with a conscious effort.

With shaking fingers, she unbuckled her belt and unzipped her skirt. She held it until a teenage boy went slouching past, his hands in his pockets. Then, keeping her eyes straight ahead and her face impassive, she let it fall. It rushed down her legs, and the belt buckle clunked loudly on the floor. Her heart jumped when the boy's head suddenly turned at the sound, but he never looked up to where she stood in only her bra and panties.

My God, she thought, *what would I have done if he had seen me? What would he have done?* Her blood was pounding. The boy's reaction made her realize again how close she really was to the people on the street. She thought of closing the blinds, getting dressed, forgetting the whole thing. But she had never broken one of her promises. And besides, she was enjoying herself immensely. Never had she felt so sexy and feminine, or so aroused. Scared or not, she wanted to go through with it.

Slowly, deliberately, she slid the bra straps over her shoulders and slipped her arms out. She paused as an old woman shuffled past. A young man approached, and she reached behind her back and unhooked the bra, holding the ends of the straps until he was nearly to the window. Just as he passed beneath her, she let the straps go and dropped her hands to her sides. The bra slipped from her breasts and fluttered to the floor. Looking down at herself, she saw her breasts bounce as they sprang free. Framed right between them was the young man's head. He was so close she could see the stubble on his cheeks.

The cool air on her bare skin accentuated the sensation of being naked in public. She trembled with excitement, causing the tips of her breasts to quiver. Her nipples were so hard that the skin around them puckered.

The young man strolled on, oblivious. He was deep in thought, his eyes distant. She wondered if he might be thinking of sex, perhaps fantasizing about some pretty woman taking off her clothes for him. And here she was right next to him. If he turned, she imagined he could reach up and fondle her breasts as they dangled above his head. The mental image was so exciting she wished he would do it.

This was even better than she had hoped. Her blood felt hot and pounded in her temples. Her body was aflame with lust. But she had not yet fulfilled her promise to be completely naked. A part of her wanted to weasel out of the promise; she was naked enough as it was. It was silly to go any further. But she knew that was rationalizing. Her vow had been specific. She had to do it.

Exposing her pussy would be the turning point, she realized. Once she had done that, there would be no turning back. She wasn't sure she could do it. She didn't feel as if she were safe in her own room; she felt as if she were right out on the street with all these people. She waited, trying to gather her nerve. Several more people strolled by without seeing her.

She tried to imagine how it would feel to actually be naked; how she would look if someone saw her. On a sudden impulse she took off her watch and the fine gold necklace she always wore and placed them on a table beside the window. Perhaps it was only to delay the next fateful step, but she didn't really want to stop. She knew she would go through with it.

She hooked her thumbs in her panties and began to ease them down. When the elastic band reached her pubic hair, she paused again. Just then, a distinguished-looking older man in a tweed suit strolled into view. She rolled her panties down her legs to the floor and pushed her bare cunt out toward him like an offering as he passed. His eyes lit up and he tipped his head up toward her and smiled. Her heart froze in her chest. He had seen her!

Her hand flashed toward the blind to tilt it closed, but she missed the control rod and her hand hit the blinds instead, making a clatter. Now she'd really done it. She looked down at the man's face in terror.

Amazingly, he wasn't looking at her at all. He had seen a friend coming the other way, and was smiling in greeting. The friend's head appeared close to the wall, and he stopped directly beneath her window to exchange a few words. Looking down at him, she saw a flat blue cap and, just above it, her naked pussy. The brilliant sun shone full on it, bringing out gleaming coppery highlights in the hair. The pouting lips stood out boldly, conspicuous through the thin skein of hair.

The older man nodded and smiled pleasantly. If he raised his eyes enough, he couldn't miss seeing her standing there. Then he raised his hand in a wave and walked on. She realized she had been holding her breath, and let it out in a grateful rush.

Then she remembered that the other man was still there beneath her window. He might have heard her sigh. But the man in the hat moved away toward the steps of her building. As he walked away from the window she could see the blond ponytail extending beneath the hat, and she realized that it was the postman whom she had seen on the street, the one who had started this delicious madness in the first place.

The image of his cock pushing through those shorts flashed through her mind again. She couldn't resist leaning out a little to peep at him. The tips of her breasts brushed against the sharp edge of the blinds, startling her so she nearly lost her balance. For one terrible second she thought she was about to fall out of the window, but she caught herself. Talk about an embarrassing situation! What would she do if she tumbled out onto the sidewalk? Run around to the stairs and rush past the postman? Hell, she didn't even have her key on her.

Her terrified imaginings were shattered by a loud buzz. The intercom! What? Who . . . ? She pulled herself together and hurried over to the intercom, nearly stumbling over the clothes at her feet. She thumbed the button.

"Yes?" she asked in a gasp. "Who is it?"

"Postman, ma'am," came a warm, masculine voice. "I have a package for you, but it's too big to go in your box. If you'll buzz me in, I'll be glad to bring it up."

"Oh, of course. Just a minute." She pressed the door release and stood waiting. She couldn't get her fantasy out of her mind. She imagined him standing nude out there, silhouetted against the sun as he opened the door, the hair outlining his body like a golden halo as he walked down the hall to her door.

She stood staring at the door, wondering what to do when he knocked. She was still so hot she felt about to explode. She wanted to throw the door open and pull him in on top of her. But that happened only in the movies. She didn't know this guy from Adam. She was horny, but she wasn't crazy.

But no knock came. She could hear him walking around in the hall, pausing, moving on. Oh, damn, the door numbers had been taken off this week for the painters; he couldn't know which apartment was hers. She opened the door as far as the chain allowed and peeped out. There he was, two doors down, looking confused and scrumptious. Keeping her bare shoulders behind the door, she stuck her head out.

"Hello. I'm down here."

He turned and saw her, smiled. "Oh. Hello," he replied, with a slight accent on the last syllable, expressing . . . what . . . appreciation? He came to her door and held out a package. Here. I'm afraid it's got fifty cents due."

"Oh. Well," she stammered, too flustered to think clearly. "Well, I'll have to get my purse."

He nodded and stood looking at her, a smile still on his lips. Their faces were only inches apart. She was acutely aware of standing there stark naked behind the door as she talked to this incredibly attractive man. The sensation was so exquisite she wanted to make it last as long as possible.

"I'm sorry about the numbers," she said, straining for small talk. His eyes were wonderful, full of interest in her, but also with a hint of amusement, as if he were keeping a delicious secret. She found him so sexy she couldn't resist touching herself. She stretched one leg out and rested it on the table next to the door. Her fingers slid down her belly and cupped her pubis. It was still warm from the sunlight.

His eyebrows rose. "The numbers, ma'am?"

"On the doors," she mumbled, as her middle finger wriggled up into her juicy slot. She imagined his smooth, tanned fingers exploring her.

He nodded again, still smiling. She tried to keep her mind on the conversation, keep him at the door another few minutes.

"They've been painting the hall and entryway," she said. She leaned closer, and her nipples brushed against the molding on the door. Her fingers circled her clitoris, stroking and pinching it gently.

"Looks nice," he replied after a moment. "This neighborhood is really getting fixed up."

"Um, yes." She sighed. Her hand smoothed up her belly to lift and squeeze her breast, her wet fingers leaving her skin slick. "Three of the apartments in this building have just been remodeled."

"Oh?" he asked. She didn't know how long she could keep him here, but he didn't seem to be in a hurry to make his appointed rounds.

She struggled to keep her voice even as her hand worked faster and faster. She alternated between rolling her breasts in big circles and steadily rubbing up and down between her legs.

"Yes, including mine. I had the whole place done over just last month."

"Really? You must enjoy it."

"Oh!" She gasped, with too much emphasis. "Yes, I do. I'm loving it right now. That is . . . I mean . . ."

"I'd like to see it," he said, still with that warm smile. Her fingers froze.

"No, um, not at the moment, that is. I'm not dre— I mean, it's not quite there yet."

"Well, maybe when you're done with it, then."

"Yes, let's do that. Stop by anytime." Jesus, she sounded as if she were talking to an old friend: *Let's do lunch.* But it was hard to keep her mind on social niceties while she was twiddling her clitoris.

She wondered why he was just standing there smiling. Then she realized: Shit, he was waiting for the money!

"Oh, let me get you that money," she stammered. "Just a moment." She withdrew behind the door and closed her eyes as delirious ecstasy swept over her. Maybe a few minutes alone with both hands was just what she needed right now.

She stood with her back almost touching the door, holding her breath so he wouldn't know she was still there.

Stretching her legs apart, she used one hand to spread her lips wide open, and with the other she worked fiercely at herself, rubbing her clitoris. It was only seconds before she started to come harder than she ever had in her life.

Biting her lip to keep from crying out, she pounded her hand into her crotch. She was jogging herself up and down to meet her hand, her breasts bouncing wildly. The orgasm rushed through her body like a blast of steam. Her knees weakened and she almost fell.

But he was still waiting on the other side of the door. She reached for her purse and took out the change. She leaned carefully around the door and dropped it into his hand. It felt strange, as if she were tipping him for giving her such a wonderful orgasm. She wondered if it showed on her face. She felt terribly flushed.

"Thanks," he said. "And I hope you meant it about showing me your place sometime. I'd really like to do that. I'm into antiques, too. Bye, now."

She watched him walk down the hall with that swagger she'd first noticed. Dazed, she pressed the door closed with her hip and flopped back against it, the molding pressing into her bottom. She smiled to herself. She was covered in sweat, and her breasts and belly were streaked with her juices. What an incredible experience! What a hunk! He seemed really nice, too. And he said he was into antiques.

She was just wondering how he knew she had done the apartment in antiques when she caught sight of herself in the mirror on the wall opposite. Of course. It was an early Eastlake mirror, full-length. He knew a good piece when he saw one.

HIS BELT

by Callie Byrne

"*T*hank you, Delia."

His voice is butterscotch, rolling from those full lips with the dips and bumps of the Southern cadence.

I press my thighs together.

Delia pours a fresh batch of gin fizz into the tall, narrow glasses and the ice cubes click together. I smile and nod, taking my glass, the sweat on the outside cooling my palms. Delia returns to the old plantation house. She'll see to the early dinner dishes we left in the dining room before she goes home for the evening.

We're seated outside under a large, white canopy. The sun is slowly setting, and the air around us is aglow with soft orange and peach tones. A far cry from the stark and stunningly bright sunsets I know from my home in New York, the Georgian sun gently caresses the evening sky as it takes a soft bow below the horizon.

My husband puts his hand over my knee, squeezing once. He takes a long drink from his glass before he chuckles in a conspiratorial way and says, "Steven, that was a great game of golf today. We sure don't have beer girls like that back home."

Steven gives him a slow smile and glances at his wife, Sarah. "Well, David, they can't really hold a candle to our present company, now, can they?"

Sarah giggles. "You think you can sweet-talk your way out of anything, don't you? I told you—no more ogling the beer girls on the course!" Her perfect, bouncy blond hair sways and she pinches his arm.

Oh, God. That arm. The crisp line of his white T-shirt presses against his tanned, muscular biceps. Without my looking directly at his arm the shape of it gets caught in my peripheral vision. The ripple of soft movement in that arm and the bound strength under the skin causes my breath to hitch.

I squeeze my husband's hand.

Steven changes the subject. "So, Catie, it's obvious you've got some Irish blood in you."

I blush; I don't know why. "Why, yes, you could say that. Both of my parents are first generation."

"One of my new favorite pastimes is writing limericks," says Steven.

Sarah rolls her eyes.

"Really?" Now it's not just my body that's interested in Steven—I have a soft spot for anything Irish.

Steven takes a drink from his glass and sets it down. He recites:

"There once was a lassie named Catie,
Who had a cute sister named Sadie,
They came down to the farm,
And raised such an alarm,
Folks couldn't decide on th' prettier lady."

We all laugh; my blush deepens.

Steven looks conspiratorial. "Now you."

I'm slightly caught off guard, and any ability I may have to think on my feet is arrested by Steven's flirtatious wink. I glance at David, and he's grinning at me.

"Honestly, Steven, my grandfather holds that the only good limerick is a dirty one," I say, pausing. "And the one that comes to mind right now isn't appropriate to repeat in such decent company. However, I will tell you that it begins: 'There once was a woman named Alice . . .'"

David laughs hard. His share of family dinners ensures that he's heard this one, probably more than he ever would want to.

Steven leans forward over the table. "Oh, now, you must share it," he insists.

Steven's words kiss my ears with that panty-melting accent, and as I look into those dark caramel eyes, I can't help but wonder if there is some kind of wild, kinky, crazy man in there, held in check by good breeding and better manners.

And even as I wonder this, another, slightly more surprising thought arises: Can he see the same in me? Can he see that under this sweet facade of blue eyes and freckled skin, my inner

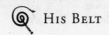

slut waits, ready for any manner of sexual debasement and exploitation? Inappropriate thoughts for such a genteel evening, and yet, I can't help myself.

Sarah's syrupy voice interrupts, liquid and charming. "Honey, don't bother her—can't you see? She's blushing like a bloomin' begonia on a summer's day."

Steven flicks his hand at her, as if brushing away a bug. His eyes continue to prod.

David comes to my rescue.

> *"There once was a woman named Alice,*
> *Who fucked with a dynamite phallus.*
> *They found her vagina in North Carolina,*
> *And part of her asshole in Dallas."*

David and Steven laugh so hard they almost fall out of their chairs. Sarah demurely looks away.

After our drinks on the veranda we retire to our rooms to unpack and get ready for bed. David is in the shower, and I take the moment to berate myself.

Good God, girl, get ahold of yourself! He's one of your husband's best boyhood friends. I shake my head and slap my cheeks. *And he's married, too!*

I place a few of my dresses in the large wardrobe and catch my image in the old, speckled mirror that hangs on the inside door. I can't help but note that, even if the boundaries of the present situation didn't exist, I am most definitely not Steven's type. I look nothing like Sarah, with her perfect suntanned skin, almond eyes, and fake breasts. The mirror reflects the wispy brown hair and thin frame that have stared back at me these twenty-nine years.

I close the door, and David comes into the room with a towel around his waist. His wet blond hair is a messy, damp mop on his head. He catches my wrist and pulls me to his still-moist body. He smells fresh.

"Well, my dear, what do you think of it down here?" He uses his fake Sean Connery accent. David's quite good at it; he's mastered the sexy Scottish lisp that blends smoothly with that rich voice. I laugh at him, and he slides his hands down my back and grabs my ass.

"It's pretty amazing," I say.

"Yesh, yesh, it is. And now, I think it's time for shome pretty amazing shex with my wife," David replies, still in character. He turns and his long, lanky body gracefully falls onto the gorgeous burgundy duvet, pulling me along on top of him. "Kish me, my dear, kish me."

I laugh again into his mouth as his lips part. We kiss, and I run my hands lightly down his neck and over his shoulders. I press firmly and rise up, pretending to pin him down, my legs coming around to rest on either side of his waist.

"I thought you were planning on going down for another drink," I say, lightly circling his nipple with the tip of one forefinger.

"I don't think we'll be missed. Steven and Sarah have already gone to bed."

"Good," I say, and wonder if Steven and Sarah are kissing

and talking to each other in silly voices. Somehow, I can't picture it. I lean down and kiss my husband.

David takes me in his arms and easily rolls me over. He pulls my clothes off with practiced, even motions and throws them to the floor. His towel has come undone, and he's nude as he shimmies down and pushes my legs open and up.

"What are you doing?" I ask, pretending to be surprised.

"I must taste you," he says matter-of-factly, and I let my head fall back. It's a well-practiced dance that we share. He will make me orgasm quickly this way. I will grab onto the tops of his arms as his tongue sweetly circles my clit, lightly swirling and flicking. One finger will find its way to my asshole and will press, oh so slightly, and the combination will make me shudder and gasp until I come into his mouth, my body shaking.

After, he will rise over me, his cock hard, and he will push it into my still-trembling pussy. He will bite into my neck and stroke me. I will wrap my arms and legs around him and pull him deeper, and he will moan into my skin, "I'm going to come, honey, I'm going to come," and I will tell him, "Yes, yes, come inside of me, baby. Fuck me, baby, fuck me."

"Oh, God," he'll say, louder, and then I'll feel his cock pulse inside of me, and his body will shudder, and he'll collapse in my arms.

And so it is this time, as well.

THE NEXT DAY IS SOFT and warm, and we ride through the picturesque country on bicycles. We pedal our way down orchard paths and around quiet lanes. We skim by countless rows of peach trees growing in single-file lines that stretch into forever. The visual symmetry of the planted columns is in striking contrast to the natural beauty of the trees themselves—their fresh leaves trembling along the tips of the dark, gnarled-looking branches. As the forced symmetry of trees flip by, I become delightfully dizzy. I can smell the dirt and fragrance of the plants growing around me; it's a heady experience.

Steven leads us down a dirt road that is nicely packed, and the bike tires glide effortlessly forward. The orchards break up and the natural trees of Georgia take their places. Steven points out yellow poplars and cherrybark oaks. There are a few varieties of pines, as well as dogwoods, crabapple trees, bald cypress, and more. The Georgian natives grow intermingled and randomly, free from the bondage inflicted on the peach trees, and they shade our way.

We break off of the road and come out into a field of sweetgrass. The sky has clouded up a little, shielding us from the heat of the afternoon sun. We lay our bikes down, and I help Sarah unpack a picnic blanket and set out the lunch dishes. Steven uncorks a white Spanish wine and we all lounge and eat and drink. I feel like we're characters from a Fitzgerald novel, in which our greatest concern is whose party we'll attend that evening for a game of croquet.

After we eat, Sarah leads David into the tall grass to help him spot the local fauna for capturing with his Nikon. I can hear her flirtatious giggle fade away in the breeze. I relax onto my back with my book held straight above me, another glass of wine waiting at my side. I'm aware of Steven reclining on the other side of the picnic blanket, his hands folded behind his head, one foot crossed over the other knee.

"Did you like the ride?" he asks lazily. His eyes are closed and he doesn't turn his head. I do. My gaze slides down his profile, pausing on those lips again. They're almost too big to properly fit on a man's face—almost. I wonder what they would feel like on my flesh, wrapped around a finger, a nipple, playing down my navel, between my thighs.

"It was amazing. It's so beautiful down here," I say. "Do things always go at this slower pace? It feels so . . . luxuriant."

"They do." He picks a piece of grass and chews on the end. "Some of us work very hard, but we don't forget the importance of leisure time."

Now he rolls over onto his side, his head propped up by that gorgeous arm of his. He's a little shorter than David, but he's bigger. He's not overly muscular, but I get the overwhelming impression of graceful power.

"Are you still working?" he asks.

I lower my book onto my belly and my knees come up slightly so that my legs are bent. The breeze rustles delicately under my skirt and up my thighs, and I suddenly feel sexy and vulnerable. Steven's attention makes my nipples grow hard, and there's a subtle, sweet clip in my clit. I can't believe the effect that this man has on my body—it's like nothing I've ever experienced before.

"Yes . . ."

He takes a deep drink of his wine. "We all know that David makes enough money that you don't have to."

"I know. But I love my job. Honestly, I don't know if I'd stop working even if David and I had children."

He pauses. I get a glimpse of his tongue as it laps an errant drop of wine from the corner of his mouth. *Dear God.*

"Seems to me, Catie, that you're the type of woman who should be kept home."

I only look at him. I'm speechless, surprised.

"Kept home nude and waiting, with a nice little collar around your neck."

A sharp intake of breath; I bite my lower lip. My panties are suddenly wet—I can't help it. I gaze into his eyes, feeling a little thrilled and a little afraid. His pupils are enormous, and there's a flirtatious grin on his face. I smile back—again, I can't help it.

David's laughter announces his return.

My husband helps me up, and we pack up the remnants of our feast. The ride back is just as nice. The wine slows the pedaling of my legs, and I'm distracted. I laugh halfheartedly with the rest of the group, and sometimes entirely miss the banter that goes back and forth.

When we get back to the house, I'm actually feeling a little sleepy. David can tell. We have only a few minutes to freshen up before we head to town to meet a larger group for dinner and drinks.

I tie up my hair and hop in the shower, turning the water to cool in the hopes that it will revive me. It doesn't help. I dry off, feeling the sleepiness in my bones.

"Oh, Catie, you look awful," David says, taking my elbows

in his hands and looking at me with a mock pout. Even in my fatigue, I notice that with each passing moment, his Southern accent is thickening.

"Thanks, thanks a lot—that's just what a girl likes to hear," I say with a drowsy smile.

He laughs. "Honey, why don't you stay here? Take a rest and I'll send a cab for you in a couple of hours." Yes, even the pace of his conversation is slowing.

I shake my head no, but my body is tingling at the idea.

"Yes," he insists. "Please. We're on vacation—I want you to relax."

"God, I love you," I say. David smiles and pulls down the covers for me.

"Just call when you're ready, okay? Have a good sleep."

I think I'm out before he even shuts the door.

I WAKE UP TO THE sound of a light patter against the windowpane. It's raining. Goose bumps rise up on my flesh and they feel delicious. I smile, stretch.

I get out of bed and wrap myself in one of the plush, knee-length robes that Sarah left for us. It's made from a thin, velvety material that feels amazing against my skin. I look in the mirror briefly—my hair is tousled and a little curly from being tied up in the shower. I feel like a lady of leisure; it feels nice.

I open the door and listen. The house is quiet except for the sound of the rain on the roof and the palatial decks. I didn't sleep as long as I had thought I would, so I step out for a little private time in the house.

I wander through the halls and down the grandiose main staircase. I wonder about the many people who have lived in this home—perhaps hundreds, including the families and servants and, probably at one time, slaves. I wonder how I would feel living in a place with so many ghosts.

Downstairs, there's an enormous room that Steven had referred to as "the old boys' room." He explained that, in the past, it was used during parties and get-togethers as the place where the men would retire for cigars and cards and manly banter when they grew tired of their female company. I walk into it, and the goose bumps on my skin refresh themselves. A delightful shiver runs up my spine.

The windows run ceiling-high along the two far walls of the room, and they are glazed in the rain. A black grand piano sits toward the back apex of the space, obviously the focal point, and there are tables and velvet high-backed chairs perfectly placed for entertaining. Paintings of old men hang on the walls, with the exception of a few landscapes, obviously inspired by the surrounding Georgian hills. There is even a painting of the house.

I run my hand along the piano, thinking again of what events may have passed in this room. What did the men do in here? Did they talk of business, women, war? Did the master and mistress of the house ever retire here together? Did they perhaps indulge in marital relations on that chair over there? Or here by the piano—leaving a sweet, private memory for him to remember later when he met with "the boys"?

A voice behind me knocks me from my private reverie.

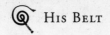

"And what, my dear, are you doing in here?"

I stop suddenly, frightened. It's an unfamiliar voice, the fluid Southern accent thick. I had thought I was alone.

Steven?

I turn around, and I'm sure I'm as pale as a ghost.

David.

I exhale in relief. I step toward him. "Oh, David, you scared—"

"Don't move."

I stop, smile. I go to move to him again. "David, what are you—"

"I said, don't move." His voice is low, the Georgian drawl in full bloom between his lips. But there's something else, too. A warning.

I stand still, my hands at my sides.

"Now, I asked you, what are you doing in here?"

I'm confused. He sounds so strange—threatening. Nothing like the husband I know, the laughing man I married. I feel like a child, small, caught doing something I shouldn't.

I step forward, reaching out to him. Like some wild, ferocious cat, he's on me. It takes him two strides, I swear, to get from the arched doorway to where I stand at the other side of the room. In one movement he takes my right wrist and pulls my body against his, and his other hand snags into my hair at the back of my skull.

"Ow! David, what are you doing?" I cry. I'm frightened and a little bit angry. "What's gotten into you?"

He tightens his grip and pulls my hair hard so that my head

comes back and my spine arches, my throat exposed. Tears spring to my eyes and I shut them—they are more the tears of wounded feelings than of real pain.

"Don't speak. I asked you a question and you refuse to answer it. So now you will just . . ."

He kisses my neck, once, softly.

". . . shut up . . ."

Another tender kiss, his lips wet against my skin.

". . . my dear."

His kiss sizzles down my throat and into my pelvis. I try to press into him.

"No." He yanks back on my hair again, and his voice is chilled. Mean. I open my eyes and look into his. His hazel eyes are cold, and he looks angry.

Again, I feel fear. A sudden swing of panic rises. Whatever I've done, I will do anything to make it better.

"You will do as I say, and only as I say. Do you understand?" I can smell the semisweet odor of good bourbon on his lips, but he's not drunk.

I bite my bottom lip and nod; it's barely noticeable because his fingers are still pressed to my skull.

"I've been watching you, Catie." His gaze holds mine; his grip on my right wrist tightens painfully. "Since we got here, I've been watching. Don't you think I notice? The way he looks at you? The way you blush under his attention?"

Oh, God. My panic surges. He knows.

More tears—they run down my cheeks. I want to turn away, but David forces me to look at him as he speaks.

"I heard what he said to you today. And I saw you smile. Such a flirtatious little slut."

The word stings, and I understand him—he overheard what Steven had said about the collar. He had been witness to my reaction.

"Is that what you want, Catie? A collar?"

I only look at him.

"Answer me," he growls, and I know that he's not playing with me. He is angry.

"Yes." It's merely a breath—but he hears it.

He smiles, but it is only a turning up of the lips. There is no joy behind it.

He pulls my head toward him and forces me onto my toes—his face, those eyes, are inches away. I can barely fathom the strength it takes to hold me up by one arm, but he seems to do it effortlessly. "And would you have fucked him, Catie? If he had asked? If he had been here instead of me, found you in this room, walking around in that slutty little robe? If he had come over to you, put his hands around your neck, told you to suck his cock, would you have done it?"

I am truly crying now—silently. The guilt I feel is excruciating.

But there's something else there, too. With every word he says, my nipples tighten and my clit throbs.

"I asked you a question, Catie."

He's so close to me, so close. If only he would kiss me. If only he would forgive me and release me and fuck me right here. Steven would.

"I don't know," I whisper.

"Yes, you do, you little bitch. Answer me." His hand pulls again, and now I am on the very tips of my toes. My scalp aches. I grimace.

"Would you have fucked him?"

"Ye-Yes," I moan, and close my eyes against the rush of new tears.

Suddenly his mouth is on mine. It is not David's sensual, probing kiss; it is hard, hungry. He claims me, biting my lips, stealing my breath. He releases my wrist and his arm comes around my waist, lifting me off of the floor.

Then, just as suddenly, he releases me. He lets go of my hair; he lets go of my body. The absence of his touch is painful. My legs feel weak, and I crumple to my knees before him. I look up, my eyes pleading for his forgiveness.

"Stay."

I do.

"Take off that robe."

I lower my eyes and look down at his feet as I slowly remove the robe. The air against my naked skin is cool, and though I've been nude in front of this man countless times before, I feel sharply vulnerable. I look up again and hold the robe up to him, hoping to see a softening in his face. There is none.

He takes the robe and smoothly whips the soft belt from the loops. He casually tosses the robe and fondles the belt, pulling it through one hand and then the other.

"You're beautiful when you're scared, Catie," he says.

I don't smile. I am scared. There is no love behind his

compliment—his eyes look at me as if I'm an object, a thing to be played with. I have no idea what he's going to do, and worst of all, I have no idea if he'll ever forgive me.

"Lift your arms."

I do as I'm told, looking down again.

He holds my wrists together over my head and ties them sharply with the belt. He pulls the velvet fabric so severely that it cuts into my skin. It hurts, but the pain is thrilling. I hear the sound of his belt buckle coming undone and then the zipper. I look up to see him free his cock from his pants. He's hard, and he looks bigger than I've ever seen him. His right hand circles it and he strokes himself, once, twice. My clit pulses with an urgency I've never felt before. Oh, Christ, he's beautiful. I've never seen him touch himself before—he's so self-assured, so casual about it. He strokes his cock again, and I can smell the sweet sweat of his balls. My lips part slightly. I so badly want to reach out and place my tongue on the tip, but I don't dare.

Without a word, he takes my bound wrists with his left arm and yanks up, so that I feel stretched. My breasts lift with the pull.

"Suck my cock."

Those words rolling through the reclaimed Southern drawl light my pussy on fire. I open my lips wide and he slams his cock into my mouth in one even motion. He hits the back of my throat and slides down. I gag, try to pull away, but his hand is on the back of my head, holding me firmly in place.

"Hold still, sweet pea, my little slut. You wanted this—now I'm going to enjoy every moment of it."

I can't help but continue to struggle a little—I can barely breathe around his pulsing, thick dick. He holds me against him, and with my hands tied above my head the way they are, I have very little leverage.

At last, when I think I might faint from lack of air, he pulls his cock away, only to thrust it back into my throat again. He fucks my mouth slowly, setting his own pace. His balls slap against my chin and I hear him moan. I sense his legs trembling slightly.

"Oh, fuck, Catie, your mouth feels fucking good."

I can't help but smile around his cock as it slides out.

He stops, wrenches my arms painfully back.

"Don't you dare."

I look up at him, pleading.

"If you think you're getting off easy, you have underestimated me, my dear wife."

The last word is a snarl. He pulls me to my feet by my forearms. For a moment, I think he might kiss me—his face comes close to mine, and again I smell the bourbon on his breath. My nipples are hard and exposed, aching to be touched. I try to brush them against his shirt. Again I see the faint smile on his lips, paired with those hazel, unfeeling eyes. He can control my every leaning by manipulating my bound hands overhead, and he does so, keeping my naked body just out of reach so that not even the softest brush of his clothing will touch my sensitive skin.

He pulls up on my wrists and twirls them to face the other way, and my body follows like a marionette. On my toes again, I turn, and he leads me to the grand piano.

I am brutally pushed forward onto the instrument. My back is flat as my breasts and left cheek press firmly into the satin ebony finish. My cunt and thighs hug the backside of the piano. The contact of my skin against the cool finish makes me shiver.

I can feel David behind me; his body radiates heat. I hear the scraping sound of his leather belt as he pulls it from its constraints. I freeze.

Oh, God.

He smacks the leather together. I jump. I imagine him, the belt folded in half between his large hands, his long, strong legs parted in a predatory stance, a smirk on his face as he eyes my bare ass, turned up for his pleasure.

The leather smacks again.

Oh, fuck. I can't do this. I'm terrified. I've never been slapped in my entire life, let alone whipped with a belt.

"David," I whisper.

He doesn't respond.

"David!" My voice is small, but I know he hears me, can hear my fear.

A palm presses into my lower back. It's gentle, reassuring. Fingertips lightly stroke my skin.

"Hush, my pet."

My arms and legs tremble, but for a moment, I feel relief.

Then his voice again, cool and raw. "Steven may have had some mercy on you, my love, but I will not."

My breath leaves me when the leather of his belt first cracks against my ass. It makes a loud, shocking sound, and feels like a singular, intense strike of white lightning that cuts into my flesh. There's a pause and I bite my lip, clench my eyes shut. My skin burns.

Another crack on the other cheek, just as hard, a pause, and then a series of slightly softer slaps dance along the flesh of my entire backside. Each smack is a reminder of my adulterous thoughts. It fucking hurts, and the pain builds in a crescendo that I'm not sure I'll survive.

I sob, the tears pooling on the shiny surface of the piano as the humiliation of the spanking envelops me. I have never felt so vulnerable or so dirty in my entire life—my hands helplessly bound, my fingers tingling and shoulders stretched, my pussy exposed in the enormity of a strange room, my ass beaten with a leather belt.

And yet my cunt throbs and my back arches slightly, tilting my butt up just a bit more. A glow starts behind my eyes and fills my head. It buzzes and spreads down the nerves in the back of my neck. David delivers another hard crack, right under my left ass cheek where my thigh begins. The pain sears into me, and the glow races down my spine to meet it. Somehow, the pain turns into a desperate pleasure unlike anything I've ever experienced. With the next crack of his belt on my other thigh, my entire body is consumed by a raw, carnal sensation. I rub my pussy against the cold surface; my breasts flatten against the top of the piano, deliciously crushing my nipples. David spanks me again and again with softer slaps, and they smear together until the edges of my consciousness become fuzzy and I simply revel in the pain and humiliation. With a final, brutal strike laid vertically against the crack of my ass, I cry out.

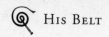

The belting stops.

"Fuck. Your skin. It's so pink and gorgeous."

My body shakes. Part of me hears him strip his clothes off. David pulls my hips and my body slides away from the piano. The absence of pressure against my cunt is agonizing. David pushes his cock into my hungry pussy. He pushes hard until he's filled me to the hilt. His pelvis and legs solidly touch me, and my newly awakened skin is alive and tingling with the contact. He thrusts into me, again and again, deep. His pelvis smarts against my ass and his hands run down my back to my hips, hold there, fingers digging into my flesh. He fucks me harder.

"You like that, don't you, my pet?" he growls. One hand finds my hair again, wraps, pulls. My back arches even more sharply. "Tell me. You like being spanked. Being fucked."

"Yes!" I gasp. His cock strokes in and out of me, and when his other hand comes around and violently twists my left nipple, my cunt explodes. I come so hard my voice leaves me, my body rocking against the piano and around David's cock. With each pump of his dick deep inside me, the orgasm smashes through me until I am delirious.

David slows.

He pulls out, turns me around, and effortlessly lifts me up into his arms.

"I'm not done with you yet, my little slut," he says. His voice is low, but the edge is still there, and it brings me back to attention. Standing, he hugs me close to his body and his cock easily slides into me again; I wrap my legs around him, and his eyes are locked onto mine. In three steps we collide against a wall, and I am breathless. My spine is flat against the stucco, and as David fucks me, slowly at first, then faster, my back rubs up and down, the wall scratching and scathing my skin.

The cold has left his eyes—his pupils are so dilated I can barely see any color. They have become large, dark pools. His mouth, at last, meets mine again, and I feel like I'm melting into him as we kiss and fuck. My knee haphazardly knocks something from a table. My arms come down around his neck, my bound hands sealing our embrace. I gyrate in his arms, pulling him urgently into me. His cock strokes me at such a deep, intimate angle, I come again. It feels sweeter, more complete, and as I gush around him, I moan into his lips: "David."

He growls back and slams into me harder, and I feel his cock pulse and explode.

He lets me down to the floor and joins me to lie on the plush carpet, panting. Our slick bodies are tangled together, and the sound of the rain is the perfect denouement. After a while, reality begins to settle in, and I lift my head. I notice that nothing is out of place in the room except for the one object I had bumped into with my leg. It lies on the floor, the surface of the glass cracked.

It's a framed picture of Steven.

CHOPSTICKS

by Sarah Carter

I have my fingers inside you as I watch your lips close around my cock. It doesn't need the wetness of your tongue to make it ready for you—you are wet already—but your eyes are closed in pleasure, and as the tip touches the back of your throat, you spasm around my fingers. This part is always about you.

The first time my cock slipped between your lips, it shocked me a little. No one had ever done that before. Now I love to watch the stretch of your mouth, your hollowed cheeks, bright eyes flashing from under your eyelashes, and I love the way it makes you shiver and clench your thighs.

Since that first time, you've sucked my dick while it was strapped or held against my thigh, my cunt, my stomach, my chest, and even my lips. But I love it best like this, when you hold it in your hands and I can lie close beside you, touching your wetness, kissing your throat as you swallow. Okay, maybe it's not all about you anymore.

I curl my fingers deeper and close my teeth on your nipple, and wonder if I could come just from watching you. I don't get the chance to find out, because you show me how the heat of your mouth warms the toy. Spreading my legs, you slide it into me, fucking me. You suck on my tongue and grind on my palm, and I think, *This is perfect.*

I want to take you out tonight, to the restaurant where we met. The one in Chinatown where everyone sits at long tables and it's so loud we can hardly hear each other. Where, that afternoon, the stranger across the table—you—gazed at me with those eyes that never stop smiling, and I peeked shyly back at that stranger licking her chopsticks. Caught between watching your practiced fingers and the pink of your tongue as you captured each grain of rice, I was amazed I managed to get any food past my lips. You finished lunch before me and winked as you slid your card under the edge of my plate. The card was simple. It read: *Catriona Wells, Graphic Design,* and it had a phone number.

I walked back to work thinking of the red of your lips, of the way they curved in a smile and slid against the faux-ivory chopsticks. I got back to my desk and sat looking at your card, doing nothing. When I finally picked up the phone and dialed, you answered, "Catriona, graphics."

I almost hung up, but instead, said, "Hi, it's me, the—"

You interrupted; your low laugh was thrilling. "I know. Hi, I hope you enjoyed the rest of your lunch."

I said something inane about the food. You laughed again, said, "Call me Kit. And you are?"

I laughed as well, said, "I'm Evie," and accepted your invitation to a reception at the Museum of Modern Art that evening.

"Eight o'clock, I'll meet you out front. Oh, and wear something black. Gotta get back to work." You hung up before I could say good-bye.

I was useless for the rest of the day, but the phone hardly rang, so I made it through. Despite being sure I'd be late, I arrived at the museum early, only to find you standing near the doors in an emerald dress and shoes so tall they made me dizzy. You said my name as if it were a secret we shared, and ushered me inside.

We drank champagne and ate canapés before going upstairs, where I fell a little in love with some photographs of Sunset Boulevard taken the year I was born. In one room, you explained why Paul Klee was a genius, and in the next, I wondered aloud if you thought rusting car parts were art. It was years since I'd been there, and I was glad to have so much to look at so I wouldn't embarrass myself just staring at you.

When we'd admired our fill of art, you drove me home, where you made sure I liked Elvis before you kissed me. I asked if you were allergic to goldfish and took you upstairs to my apartment.

You followed me to bed, whispering, "A little less conversation, a little more action," in my ear as you slipped off your shoes. "That's better." You sighed, and stretched a toe toward the drawers next to my bed. "Anything in there you want to show me?"

I half shrugged, shy, but giddy with champagne and your

company. You took it as the invitation it was. As I stepped out of my dress, you found what you wanted. Then you turned to meet my lips with kisses that were rich and deep and seemed to make promises. Your dress was laced up the back with a ribbon. Reluctant to leave your mouth, but keen to have you out of your garment, I untied it and kissed the pale pink mark the knot left on your skin. You draped your dress over mine on the back of a chair before pulling me down onto the bed.

The way you kissed me, like you wanted to know every way my lips could feel against yours, made me breathless. Slick with sweat and wanting, I felt our legs slip past and between one another, tangling until we hit that perfect spot to rock together. I was close just from that when you flipped me onto my back and reached over to where you'd dropped my thigh harness and dildo. I tried to catch my breath while I waited for you to don the dildo yourself. You surprised me by strapping the harness on the thigh you'd been riding and looking hungrily at the cock jutting upward.

The look sent a stab of want shivering through my belly, and I was desperate for you to fuck me, fingers thrusting, thumb on my clit, while you rocked against me. When you moved closer, I thought you'd spread your legs, lower yourself slowly, or maybe tease the head of my dick against your clit. I didn't expect you to bow your head.

You looked at me with a question—*Is this okay?*—as you ran your tongue up the length of silicone. I could tell by the glitter in your gaze that you knew I wouldn't say no. Head propped on my fist so I could see you better, I caught my lower lip between my teeth and nodded. My breath, already ragged, came faster and faster as I watched you fill your mouth, and our eye contact held until your eyes fluttered closed as your chin touched my thigh. They stayed closed then—in concentration or bliss, I couldn't tell—while your lips grew redder in the lamp's glow as you moved up and down the dildo's length. I swore I could feel the rhythm of your sucking on my clit, and I longed for you to touch me.

As though you could read my mind, you sat up, straddled me, and grinned at the flush on my cheeks. "It's so hot," you said, fucking yourself on the mouth-warmed silicone. I could only whimper in response as you folded four fingers into me. Watching you made me so wet there was almost no friction as you slid inside, just the slight coolness of your fingers turning to heat as you stretched and filled me. There was no room for coordinated movement in all that sensation; I was capable only of quivering thighs and mindless thrusts against your hand, but you seemed not to mind doing all the work, watching my face as you fucked us both. With your fingers curled inside me and your thumb chasing my clit, I thought I'd never stop coming, but when I did, you sucked my taste off your fingers as you came shuddering against my thigh.

Now I'm watching you sleep in the late-afternoon sun, wanting to tangle my fingers in your hair, which is far too many shades of gold and bronze and copper to be natural, though it is. It curls onto your cheek, and it's just long enough that I'll bet anything sometime this week you'll say, "Evie, it's time for a haircut. Do you want me to book you a pedicure?"

You like to watch me in the mirror, teasing me with the point of your tongue between your lips, while Shawn cuts your hair and Rose paints my toes. I think Shawn likes to watch you watching. I wonder if that's what his boyfriend means when he calls you "Shawn's guilty pleasure."

I know I should probably let you sleep, but I can't resist you, idle fingers playing with your curls tightening to a tug until the curve of your neck is exposed. The little murmurs of protest you make are too sleepy to be genuine and only make me want you more, so first with my eyes and then with my tongue I trace that graceful line of muscle between your shoulder and your jaw. Protests become moans when I reach the not-so-secret spot under your ear; your hips shift against me, and our legs intertwine. When my hair falls on your breasts, you squirm. "That tickles," you say, and you gather it up and tie it in a knot as I continue to map your collarbone with my lips.

I have to abandon my hold on your hair as I move down your body, but my hands find as much pleasure in the curve of your shoulders and the plane of your ribs as they did in the silk of your hair. My nose seeks the postorgasm softness of the skin under your breasts. Nothing else makes you this soft; it's as though the blood that flushes your chest when you come is infused with almond oil.

I rub you with my cheeks like a cat. I can feel your laugh in the bones of my face.

"I'm starving," you say. "What will we eat?"

I tell you I plan to watch you eat with chopsticks tonight. You lick your lips in anticipation.

UNDRESSING TED POWERS

by Layla Briar

"What is your most erotic memory?" Kendra asked. It was the question of the week that Friday afternoon; we'd met in the pub after class to play the little game we'd devised to jump-start the weekend. That particular week, it was Kendra's turn to ask the question, and to my embarrassment—but the guys' delight—she asked for the goods on our most erotic memory. We had to answer truthfully, no matter what. It was the only rule of the game.

Andy had finished his story and sat back, self-satisfied, crossing his arms over his chest.

"No way! She didn't!" Ron leaned across the table, the buttons on his oxford shirt clattering across the glass.

"I swear to God. She walked right up to me at the buffet table—without even looking at me—and got in front of me like this." Andy demonstrated, using two fingers on the table for each pair of legs, his together, hers apart on either side of his. "And, well, bingo."

Ron looked as if he were about to explode. "But, uh, wasn't there a puddle? You'd think everyone—"

"Nah, it was outdoors. There was grass. And it was dark, kinda. Except you could hear it, like, *sissss* . . ."

Kendra snorted. "So your most erotic memory is of a chick pissing on your shoes."

"Not my shoes, my feet. I was barefoot. It was an *outdoor* wedding. A pool thing."

"A pool wedding. I see." Kendra rolled her eyes in disbelief. "Next." She lifted her beer and pointed the mouth of it toward me like a wand. "Jane?"

I shifted in my seat. Andy's story had been, well, *out there*. Who wanted to know about my little schoolyard discovery? I felt the blood rise in my neck. "*You* go next. I need time to think about it."

Kendra shook her head. "No thinking allowed. It has to be the truth, remember?"

"I know, but . . ."

She shrugged. "Okay, fine. I'll go. You guys remember the ski trip last year? Mont-Sainte-Anne?"

I'm not much of a skier, and hadn't gone. But Andy had. He'd told me that Kendra had fallen the first day—just a little spill—but that she'd spent the rest of the weekend lying around on the couch, demanding hot chocolate and showing off her bruised hip for anyone willing to look. He made a face. "The ski trip where you didn't do any skiing?"

Kendra smirked mischievously. "Doesn't mean I didn't get any exercise."

"Do tell."

"Do you remember the nanny at the house where we stayed? Dominique?"

Ron growled his appreciation. "Who could forget those legs?"

"Well, let's just say she took very good care of me while I was laid up."

Ron looked momentarily confused, then raised an eyebrow. "Ahh . . ." He nodded. "Explains why I couldn't get anywhere with her."

Andy nearly choked on his beer. "That, and your haircut's stupid, and you can't ski worth shit, and you talk too much, and um . . . she just didn't like you at all, actually."

"Well, according to Kendra, she was a *lesbian!*"

Kendra shook her head. "Nah. Just bi. Curious. And she didn't like you."

"She never *said* that!"

"Did *so*," simpered Andy. "She said, 'Ooh, Kendra, I'm sorry about your bruised bum. May I kiss it better? May I squeeze your boobies? Mmm . . . Oh, yeah, baby . . . Ron sucks! Oops, I mean, may I *suck* on your tootsies? Ron's haircut is sooo stupid. . . . Mmm . . .'"

"Jane's turn!" Ron barked.

"I don't want to. This conversation's juvenile."

"Immature," Kendra added. "But don't mind Andy, Jane. He wouldn't know an erotic moment if it walked over and peed on his foot."

I took a deep breath and waited for the laughter to stop. "Well . . . the first time I ever, uh . . ." I cleared my throat.

"Tried bestiality?" Andy offered.

"Came," murmured Laleh helpfully.

I nodded. "Right. Was alone, on a swing, in Wilmot Park, when I was thirteen." Ron paused, his drink in midair. The others looked at me expectantly.

"And . . . that's it?"

"That's it. Ron's turn."

Kendra shook her head. "Uh-uh. Laleh next. Leave Ron for last."

Laleh looked up from her corner of the booth and nervously tucked a ringlet of hair behind her ear. She wore tiny earrings, some kind of gold filigree, shaped like a flower set in a ring of leaves. I must have been smiling at her; she smiled back.

"My most erotic memory?"

We nodded.

"It's nothing special. . . ."

We waited.

She blushed. "It's about Edward."

Unlike Kendra's high school beau, or Andy's incontinent stranger, Edward Powers was someone we knew. Well, sort of. He was a business columnist for a national paper—one of those Waspy, tie-clad, utterly unremarkable severed heads that you see printed above articles you wouldn't read, unless the business section washed up onshore two years into your stint of stranded-on-a-desert-island. Edward was recently separated, and twenty-five years older than Laleh. As far as we were concerned, he was a different species.

Andy shifted in his seat. "You have something erotic to say about Edward Powers? I need another beer. And earplugs."

Laleh bit her lip. "I'll pass then."

"No!" Kendra pounded the table. "Don't listen to him. He's puerile. Homophobic."

"And an ass," Andy added helpfully. "You go, girl. If I'm gonna barf, I'll aim for Kendra."

Laleh looked rattled. I wished the waitress would come and save her, but no such luck. She cleared her throat.

"Well . . . like I told you, I had to interview Edward for that journalism assignment. I did the interview, and then he asked me out for *another* lunch. . . ."

We remembered. At the time, we'd advised her not to accept. What kind of forty-something-year-old guy dates a twenty-year-old college girl? Laleh is beautiful and smart, but kind of naive about some stuff. Her parents live in Iran, and so she's alone here; Kendra and I had taken her under our wing a little bit. But when it came to the subject of Edward Powers, Laleh could be stubborn. She didn't want us telling her not to date him, so she just avoided talking about him at all. We leaned in for a rare chance to hear about the mysterious Edward.

"So we went to that restaurant at Harbourfront. It was nice. . . . The ice was breaking up in the bay. The sun was coming in through the window, and it was just the teeniest bit warm . . . like the first moment when you can imagine that winter really is going to end. You know?"

I nodded.

"But anyway, I didn't know what to make of Edward. He was

so comfortable, and I was so . . . not, you know? I mean, he was talking to me the way you talk on a date. He was being funny. But it felt so unreal. I was making conversation, but it was like I was watching us from the outside— Andy, what's that?"

Andy had his elbow on the table, wrist drooping downward, all but his index fingers curled in a fist. His index pointed limply at the table. "It's a sexometer. It measures the eroticism of your story." He demonstrated, stiffening his finger and letting it rise toward the ceiling. He let it flop it back down again. "So far, not a flicker."

Laleh ignored him. "Like I said, I was watching us from the outside looking in, and I could see me—looking like me"—she looked down at her slight but curvy body, clothed in a faded cotton T-shirt and gray cords—"and this . . . man in a suit."

Kendra laughed at this, and I think we could all imagine him perfectly, cuffs raised fastidiously above his plate, his head seeming to sprout from the buttoned top of his collar like a plant from a pot. Men in suits have always seemed, to me, organic only at the extremities—robotic except for the vulnerable pink bits that extend past collar and cuffs.

Laleh gave my thoughts voice: "A suit is like . . . well, a disguise. You know . . . 'Jus' bizness, ma'am.'" She blushed, and the next bit tumbled out quickly: "You see a man in a suit and it's impossible to imagine that he has a penis."

She laughed along with us, her hand flying up to cover her mouth in embarrassment. "I couldn't reconcile it. He was flirting with me, but it was almost shocking. I swear, if he'd touched my hand I would have jumped out of my skin."

Andy leaned forward. "And did you?"

"Did I what?"

"Jump out of your skin."

"He didn't touch me. At least, not for a couple of weeks. We just had lunch. And breakfast, and coffee . . . We talked for hours."

She'd already told me, in private, that Edward had been troubled by their age difference; that he'd suggested, in those early weeks, that perhaps they ought to simply be friends. Laleh had been hurt, and deep down, they both knew that you couldn't make a friendship out of what they had. You just can't twist lust into a shape that it's not.

Though they hadn't even kissed, Laleh longed to reach underneath that suit, to put her hands on the man beneath.

"It wasn't desire yet," she told us. "He was still completely theoretical to me, as a lover. You men like to say that women are not visual." She looked at Andy, then Ron. "But that doesn't mean that we don't use our senses. We just need to touch what we see, and taste it. . . ." She blushed.

A little shiver rippled through me when she said *taste*. And I noticed that Ron sat immobile on the other side of the table, staring at her as though they'd never met.

"We'd been dating almost a month," Laleh said, "before he booked us a hotel room. . . . Edward had a penthouse apartment overlooking the Don Valley, but he'd sensed, Laleh explained, that she might be more comfortable on neutral turf. "He wanted to put me at ease. But I was still so nervous. I don't know why; it's not like it was my first time. I'm not a virgin or anything. But you have to realize, at that point, we'd never even *kissed* before. During dinner, I kept thinking, 'Two hours from now, we'll be naked together. . . .' Then, 'Ninety minutes from now . . .' I tried to imagine what it would be like, but I couldn't. There he was, smiling at me across the table, but I couldn't see past the tie. I was almost starting to think, you know, that maybe I'd made a mistake." She looked over at me, as though she were back in that moment. "I knew he was a good man," she continued, "and that he made me happy, and that I loved the way the corners of his eyes crinkled when I make him laugh. But did that make him a *lover*? We'd never even kissed. . . ."

But she'd decided, she told us, that it was too late to back out. She was a big girl, and she was going to go through with this. What was more, she desperately *wanted* to go through with it. Her heart pounded through the ride up in the elevator, the long walk down the elegant hotel corridor. She remembered tucking her purse neatly under the bathroom counter, and walking resolutely over to the end of the bed.

"The bed was so high," Laleh recalled, "that when I leaned against it to take off my shoes, my bum was lower than the edge. There was this beautiful, pure white coverlet. . . . Anyway . . ."

I smiled to encourage her. The truth was, by now, we were all on the edge of our seats. People like Kendra and Andy talked about sex all the time. Their sex stories, though graphic, were only mildly interesting, kind of predictable, like a porn channel. But listening to timid Laleh was utterly erotic.

"Ted came right in close. Very close, almost nose-to-nose,

even though we were in this giant room. He had his shoes and jacket off, but nothing else. I almost thought he was shy, you know? That he wanted to stand too close for me to be able to look down and see his body, the way he trapped me between him and the bed.

"Usually, my first time with someone, I'm the one who's shy. The guy takes off my top and all I can think about is, 'Are my boobs too small?' And I've had my appendix out, so I have this scar that I hate. . . .

"But with Ted, I didn't even register my clothes coming off. The way he was kissing me, it was hypnotic; I barely knew where we were." Laleh shifted slightly in her seat, pressing her thighs together. Just remembering his lips on hers was turning her on.

"Before I knew it, I was completely naked. He stopped kissing me for a moment and I opened my eyes, and he was smiling this questioning kind of smile. I realized he was waiting for me to undress him. I could feel the cloth of his suit trousers against my bare thighs, and the buttons on his shirt were rubbing against my nipples. . . ."

Ron was immobile beside me in the booth. He was aroused and trying to hide it, and he was hanging on her every word.

"And so I started at the top button. My hands were shaking. I can still see that button, it was real mother-of-pearl. I undid the top one, and suddenly he had a collarbone, and then a chest . . . and his skin was so much warmer than I expected. I thought it would be white, 'cause it was just barely spring, and when does a businessman ever go outside?"

She realized she was rambling and closed her eyes again for a second. "But his skin was golden, like butterscotch. He has the softest skin I've ever touched. I started kissing his neck and his chest; I've never tasted anything so good.

"I was undoing buttons as fast as I could. It was killing me, suddenly, having that shirt between me and the rest of that delicious skin. As soon as I got it halfway undone I pressed myself against him, and where my nipples brushed him, he got goose bumps. I could feel, umm . . ." She paused. ". . . him . . . then, through his pants, against my belly, and I couldn't wait for him. I couldn't wait. I've never felt that way before. And the whole time I was kissing him, it was strange; he never stopped smiling, like a kid at a carnival. And I was so wet.

"I pulled his shirttail out of his pants. I didn't even bother to take the shirt off his arms. I couldn't take my eyes off his body, and I was fighting with his belt buckle, because he wouldn't let me see. He was kissing me hard—still smiling—and he wouldn't let me look down at my hands.

"And so I touched his cock before I saw it. I tugged his boxers down over his bum. . . . I could see his bum in the mirror behind us, and my hands on his body. And then I slowly slid my hands across his hips. I couldn't wait, but I was so shy, all at the same time. My heart was pounding. And he made this little moan, very quiet and low, when I finally put my hands on him. I couldn't see; I could only feel.

"And he felt *huge*. And so hard, and so smooth. I remember exactly how he felt to my touch. I could sculpt his cock out of marble with a blindfold on. I'll never forget how he felt in my hands."

Nobody laughed.

"And I was shaking all over, and then I was off the floor. My bum hit the coverlet, his lips left mine, and he entered me, all in one motion, and . . ."

We nodded, transfixed. Ron held his breath.

"And we came, just like that. Both of us, instantly."

Laleh smiled with satisfaction at the memory of her passion for her unlikely lover. We stared at her, speechless, seduced.

She took a dainty sip from her beer. "He still had his suit trousers around his ankles."

MARS WITH MARS AND VENUS

by Alana Noël Voth

To Dennis Cooper

When Mason got bored, he practiced sketching. Mason was a tattoo artist. He'd always wanted to tat a pair of lovers, and often jerked off to the thought of being sandwiched between them, a guy and a girl.

DOONE FELT BORED TO DEATH sometimes. Rather than write lately, Doone watched gay porn. She didn't have to convince the performers that her interest was genuine. What if she got a tattoo of two interlocking male symbols on her left shoulder? Right *there*. She tried to envision it in the mirror.

LUKE COULDN'T TELL ANYONE HOW bored he was. Nobody listened to a pretty boy. Lately, Luke awoke in a cold sweat, nobody with him. He was becoming increasingly afraid of people. They said dumb shit like, "You actually speak?"

Before he left his apartment, Mason thought about an underage male prostitute he'd inked two months before: Christ with darkish hair and an erection. Getting into his VW bus, Mason cried about a kid having to prostitute. He should have *saved* that kid.

On her bed in her room in her parents' house, Doone masturbated picturing Colin Farrell fucking Jude Law up the ass. *God, let the men fuck each other.* Doone came as Colin Farrell filled Jude Law's ass with spunk.

On set for a photo shoot, Luke tried to read a Dennis Cooper novel while another dumb stylist admired his hair. Then she teased him: "You really reading that book?" Luke asked the stylist, "Want to suck me off?" *I hate you*, he wanted to say. *Bitch.*

Why hadn't Mason saved that kid? He couldn't see through his tears as he drove.

In bed, Doone curled up on herself in a fetal position.

Luke dug his fingers into the stylist's hair and hoped she choked on him.

Mason had chosen his apartment because it overlooked a cemetery. He wanted to get acquainted with death. Since he was twelve, he'd had heart trouble and was told he would die before he turned twenty-five. The doctors had all said that. The cemetery wasn't sprawling green but small and overrun by noisy-ass crows. Mason believed that after he died he'd come back as a noisy-ass crow, a human imprint, meaning he'd attempt to bond with a human lover.

From his window, Mason saw a headstone that read, *Dammit, Linda, I Loved You*. Actually, Mason couldn't read it. Weather had beaten the inscription away, and it was now lost to all but imagination. When Mason died, he wanted his lovers to put something like that on his headstone. *Dammit, Mason, We Loved You, Man*. Actually, they should get tattoos. Immortalized in ink.

DOONE'S MOM SAID, "YOU'RE A smart girl. You should be in college." Her dad said, "I think she let the pretty go to her head." Doone hadn't told her parents she'd been raped by her brother's best friend. While she watched gay porn, her brother beat on the door: "What are you watching?" She was sorry she hated her brother.

Doone wanted to be a writer but couldn't write about being raped because it was clichéd. She knew because she'd joined a writers' workshop thinking she'd meet a cool gay writer like Dennis Cooper, and instead it had been all women who wrote Ann Beattie–type stories in which nothing happened. Doone hadn't read Ann Beattie. Of course, *they'd* never heard of Dennis Cooper. When Doone had offered her rape story for critique, a woman in a black turtleneck had said, "This is *sooo* Dorothy Allison." The other women had given Doone tight-lipped smiles that had made her feel incredibly malevolent and totally dirty.

LUKE DIDN'T MIND THE MONEY he made as a model, but he thought it was basically stupid, looking good as a job. Even more stupid was how people reacted to him. One dude had scratched Luke's arm and then said, "Now I've got your blood under my fingernails." And a chick had said, "I was going to commit suicide, but then I saw your picture and knew I had a reason to live." That scared the shit out of Luke.

Sometimes, Luke imagined getting fucked up the ass by a huge line of people who took turns at him and said things like, "You aren't as hot as you think, bitch." Sometimes during photo shoots, Luke pulled the ugliest faces: tongue, teeth, rolling eyeballs. He'd pull out his cock and piss. But photographers liked that. "Do you think you could get hard?" they'd ask. Luke wanted to blow people away with his mind. Instead, he'd asked the last photographer, "Want to blow me?" while thinking, *You fucking dick.*

AT A BAR, LUKE WATCHED a threesome dance, girl in the middle. He liked the song. "Darling, come here; fuck me up the . . ." Lords of Acid. Luke didn't feel like looking anyone in the eye, because he felt out of place, which was stupid. Everyone here was a model, actor, artist, or lost soul. Basically, they were different versions of himself, echoes, perhaps wishful thinking.

DOONE HEADED FOR THE BATHROOMS and ran into a guy who said, "Take my card." She did a double take, but he was gone.

Like, damn! Did he totally look like Joseph Gordon-Levitt, or what? While Doone peed in a bathroom stall, she listened to two girls talk about Nordstrom, on and fucking on. Doone looked at the card in her hand. *Mason Carr. Tattoo Artist.*

THE SONG IN THE BAR changed to Ministry's "Stigmata." Mason dug this song. Like Jesus Christ on acid. Mason noticed a knock-you-over-make-you-stupid hot guy near the dance floor. Dyed black hair. Tall. Mason ordered a beer and then moved closer. The guy wasn't making eye contact with anyone. Instead, he watched a threesome on the dance floor make out, and yet this modelesque guy seemed sad. Mason got a lump in his throat, and thought maybe his cock was hard.

Somebody touched his shoulder. The girl he'd given his card to at the bathrooms. Mason nodded to her. "Hey, Pretty."

Pretty smiled.

His dick *was* hard.

"You good?" she asked.

"What?"

"Tattooing. You good at that?"

"Sure, I'm good."

"I want something done on my shoulder."

Mason looked closer. Irish red hair, green eyes, habit of gnawing her lip. "Tell me your name first."

"Doone."

"Cool name—Doone."

"My parents used to be cool."

"Got that." Mason lifted his beer, drank it. Doone watched

the tendons in his neck move in a single, fluid motion, pushing the beer through to his stomach.

"See that guy over there?" Mason nodded at a guy by the dance floor.

Doone nodded.

"I want to put a tat on him, too."

"I want to be there when you do," she said.

Mason smiled. "I dig that," he said.

Doone was suddenly happy.

AT LAST LUKE CAME OUT of his stupor and glanced around the bar. He noticed a guy and a girl across the dance floor. Guy: cute, black clothes, shaggy brown hair. Girl: redhead, forlorn face, big eyes, sexy. They had an amped-up, nervous, nice-to-meet-you energy about them, and yet nothing about them was corny. The girl talked in the guy's ear; the guy kissed her forehead. Luke strolled to the bar, then walked back and made eye contact with the guy. Luke stalled. He felt nervous. Why? When they didn't approach, Luke took a breath and walked over, but then didn't know what to say. If he said something stupid they'd think, *Figures, dumb model.*

The girl said, "Hi."

Luke nodded.

Mason said, "Beers?"

Luke nodded again.

Doone smiled at him. He was ethereal-looking, she thought, but sad in his eyes.

Luke tried to appear relaxed.

The girl said, "I'm Doone."

"Cool name," Luke said. That was easy. "Luke."

Mason passed around beers. "I'm Mason," he said.

Luke smiled.

"Cheers," Mason said, lifting his bottle.

The three of them drank and then glanced around the circle.

"Excuse me, I've got to belch." Mason covered his mouth. "Have either of you belched on a first date?"

Luke was still too nervous to say much.

"No, but I farted in a movie theater once," Doone said. Luke couldn't take his eyes off her. She blushed under the lights.

"That's golden," Mason said.

Luke relaxed enough to laugh. Chicks didn't usually admit to farting. Heck, nobody did.

"Everybody farts," Mason said.

"Yeah," said Luke. Did he just say that?

Doone laughed. "This is cool," she said.

Mason stood between them, Doone on his right and Luke on his left. He moved so his arms brushed them both. Doone gave him a nudge. Luke wondered what would come next.

Mason had parked his VW bus in the parking lot. Everyone climbed in front. Earlier in the week, Mason had made a mix tape for an unidentified special occasion, and now he knew this was it.

"What's this?" Luke asked about the song.

"Sunshine Superman," Mason answered.

Luke looked confused.

"By Donovan," Mason said.

"I've heard of him," Luke said. "From a Dennis Cooper novel."

"You have not," said Doone.

"Have too," Luke said.

"Who's Dennis Cooper?" Mason asked.

"Writer," said Luke.

"Insane," Doone said. "Total genius."

"Ever notice geniuses are generally nuts?" Mason asked, smiling.

Luke said, "Maybe because they think so deeply about stuff."

"Introspection," Doone said. "Like a connection with the universe."

"Doone writes," Mason said.

"Yeah, but not like Cooper," she said.

"So," said Mason, "write like you."

"Yeah, I know." Doone gnawed her lip.

The guys watched. And both felt something like wanting to protect her.

"I was raped," Doone said.

"Shit." Mason put his arm around her.

Luke took a breath. "Fuck." And then he didn't know what else to say.

"I'm all right. Seriously. But it's like, living at home with my brother, my parents, it makes it hard, makes it worse somehow."

"Hey, you can live with me if you want," Luke said.

Doone checked him out. "Serious?"

"Totally," Mason said.

"How do you know?" Luke looked at Mason and then couldn't help zeroing in on his mouth.

Mason smiled. "Because you're lonely," Mason said.

Luke dropped his eyes. Mason was right.

"Everyone's lonely," Doone said.

Luke sat back in his seat and then floated for second, soaking up vibes. Doone leaned her head on his shoulder, comforted by his warm, melting sweetness. Mason stared out the window and saw a split in the sky, something opening between the stars.

He said, "If you guys could have anything right now, what would it be?"

Doone giggled.

"What? Corny, right?" Mason laughed a little but still didn't take his eyes off the sky. He felt like if he put his hand out, he'd touch a heart inside a universe. A kind of heart that beat forever and was infinite, not like his at all.

All of a sudden Mason's chest hurt. Maybe he couldn't breathe. Lump in his throat.

"Depth," Luke said. "I wish my life had depth." Luke turned his head. "You?"

Doone thought a moment. "Probably . . . I guess peace, you know, like, inside."

Luke nodded, then looked at Mason. "You, dude?"

Mason took a breath. Okay, easy. The lump was gone. "I

want to live through this night." He took his eyes off the sky. Everyone was quiet.

AT THAT MOMENT, IN FACT, Mason wished it were possible to stay forever in the front seat of his VW bus with these two perfectly imperfect, therefore perfect people on each side of him. Obviously, true love didn't happen that fast, but tonight it did, which was so fine Mason felt like glowing from the inside out, invincible, beyond death.

On the stereo, Donovan's "Sunshine Superman" changed to the Dandy Warhols' "Not If You Were the Last Junkie on Earth."

"This is a radical tape," Doone said.

She put a hand on each guy's knee, then pressed her palms down and curled her fingers around their flesh and bone, felt warmth, and felt the solidarity.

She wanted in on a scene.

Threesome.

Her choice.

Big difference.

Inside, like a ribbon pulled through her middle, she felt a tickle. She wanted to see the guys fuck. How could she explain that an act labeled perverse by most of the world was in fact so lovely that it had become holy to her?

Luke felt himself shiver under Doone's hand. The shiver started at his knee, then went up his leg through the crack of his ass, around to his balls, before hitting his gut. Doone kissed his forehead. She kissed the edge of his nose where his left nostril flared.

"I'm sorry," Luke said, "that anyone hurt you."

"I'm sorry anyone hurt you," she said back.

Luke felt Mason's hand travel behind Doone to touch the back of his head. He felt Doone's lips on his jaw, Mason's fingers in his hair, touching his scalp.

"I don't want either of you to have to feel sad again," Mason said.

Nascent quiet.

Distinct Ink: It was a small, neat parlor. The guy who owned it, Ross, had taken Mason on as a protégé.

"I'm going to tat you tonight," Mason told Doone.

"Okay." She smiled. "My shoulder."

Mason went to work on a sketch to stencil onto Doone's skin; the other two admired the art on the wall. Luke noticed one in particular. "Who did the Jesus?"

"Me," Mason said.

Doone traced an outline of male thigh on the sketch. "He's beautiful."

"He looks . . . I don't know . . . very human," Luke said.

"Because he was human," Mason said. "Liberal, underestimated, tortured." Mason nodded at a small refrigerator. "Beers in there." He turned back to his sketch.

Luke opened the fridge, pulled three out. Mason focused on drawing. Doone watched Luke drink. Mason looked up and watched, too. Luke was definitely drunk now and felt sweet. Comfortable. Horny.

Doone sat on a stool. "I'm ready for my tattoo."

Mason walked over and showed her the sketch.

"Oh, man, it's cool." She kissed him straight on the mouth.

"Thanks, babe." He kissed her back.

"Does it hurt?" Luke asked. "You know, getting inked?"

"The needle doesn't hurt any worse than a bunch of bee stings," Mason answered. "Some people say it itches intensely."

Mason looked at Luke. "Check out what I'm going to do, her tat."

Luke leaned forward. "What is that?"

"Mars with Mars and Venus. The three signs interlocking."

Doone looked from one to the other.

Luke considered the idea. "Like two guys and a girl?"

"Yup." Mason smiled into Doone's eyes.

Doone looked at Luke. "What do you think?" She gnawed her lip.

"Yeah," said Luke. Sublime. He kissed Doone on the mouth.

"Now you guys," she said.

Luke put his hand around the back of Mason's head. They kissed.

MASON RUBBED SHAVING CREAM ONTO her shoulder and then used a disposable razor to shave the tiny hairs there. After Mason dried her off, he began to stencil his sketch to her skin. Doone thought this part tickled. Her nipples got hard. Mason pulled back the stencil, then put on latex gloves before picking up a tat gun. "Baby, this will hurt."

Doone didn't gnaw her lip. "Don't mess it up," she joked.

The whir of the tat gun wasn't sexy like a vibrator; it sounded more like a dentist's drill. The needle puncturing her skin felt like a million pinches. Mason guided the needle along his outline and felt goose bumps along his arms. Pinpricks of blood appeared on Doone's skin and stuck to the fingertips of Mason's gloves. Her shoulder was as delicate as a painting in its curvature. Ink filled her dermis, the second layer of skin. Luke felt his cock go hard. Doone felt water leak stickily through her lashes. Mason stopped the gun. Luke wiped her face with a tissue; there was a vague river of makeup.

Doone opened her eyes. Luke thought they looked brighter.

"I'm almost done," Mason said.

AFTER HE SHUT OFF THE tat gun, Mason stood back. Removed his latex gloves.

Doone craned her neck, trying to see Mars with Mars and Venus.

"Want to see?" Mason asked.

"Yeah, of course." Doone squirmed on the stool, trying to see her shoulder again.

Mason gave her a mirror. Doone looked and then set the mirror down. "I love it."

"I need to put ointment on it," Mason said. He dipped his finger in a jar, then smoothed it over her skin.

Doone said, "Thank you."

"I'm going to cover it with a bandage."

While Mason bandaged her, they caught each other's eyes. Doone touched his face. Mason nodded. Doone got off the stool and walked right into Luke, pushed her cheek to his chest. The tattoo throbbed inside her skin like a heartbeat. Doone listened to Luke's heart and felt him tremble. Mason stood behind her and felt sweat collect above his lip. Yin and yang, something. Mason kissed Doone's shoulder, followed the ridge with his lips, then tongue. Then he kissed Luke; they kissed over her shoulder.

Mason pulled away. "I want to put a tat on you," he whispered.

"Okay," Luke said. "What?"

Doone felt Luke's cock against her stomach. Mason's cock nudged the small of her back. "Last Supper, with a few variations," he said. "It'll take weeks." Doone moaned. Luke pushed his cock harder against her, her pubic bone. Mason wrapped his arm around Doone, then grabbed Luke's ass. "First I'd have to sketch it," Mason said. "Then do the tat one character at a time." He pulled Doone's tube top down. Luke looked at her breasts. Mason cupped them with both hands. "Then I'd do the shading." Luke bent and licked one of Doone's nipples. "Then I'd add color," Mason said.

"Yeah," said Luke. A tat like that would make him appear deeper, more complex. "I want you to do it," he said.

Doone imagined Luke on his stomach wearing no shirt, and Mason leaned over Luke's back with a tattoo gun, the needle ejaculating ink into Luke's pristine skin.

Doone stepped from between them. She pulled her tube

top down around her hips and then kicked it off. After meeting their eyes a moment, Doone removed her jeans, too.

The guys watched.

"One of you inside me," she said. "The other inside him."

Doone sat on the stool with her elbows behind her on a table for support.

Mason cupped her face with his hands. "All right?"

She nodded. Mason kissed her as if he would kiss her forever, and she opened her legs, pulling him closer. Mason moved between her thighs, then smoothed his hands around the small of her back to her ass. Doone saw Luke behind Mason. Mason felt Luke's lips on the back of his neck. He felt Luke move his hands around to his stomach and touch his cock. Mason felt his heart beat stronger. He felt the flush he saw in Doone's face. Doone kissed Mason's nipple and then kissed Luke on the mouth over Mason's shoulder. Luke kissed the side of Mason's face. Then Mason felt Luke's wet finger between his ass cheeks.

"Use lots of spit," Mason said.

"I will."

Mason sucked in his breath. Luke lubed him up.

"All right?" Doone asked.

"Fuck, yeah." Then, "Can I?" Mason held his cock in his hand.

"Yeah." Doone felt his breath fan her face, neck, and she closed her eyes and wrapped her hand around Mason's as he eased his cock in. Doone kissed Mason's chin.

"That's nice," he said, and then kissed her ear, held her face in his hands. Behind him, Luke prepared to enter. Mason felt the other guy's cock against his asshole. He went still.

Luke held Mason's ass cheeks apart with his hands and then worked his cock inside, a little at a time, feeling some resistance. He'd never done this before. He was doing it. Doone opened her legs wider. Luke pushed Mason forward, deeper into Doone's cunt.

"Fuck," Mason said. His cock swelled inside Doone with more force than he was used to. "Oh, Jesus, fuck." It hurt a little. Back there. He kissed Doone on the mouth, harder.

"It's okay, baby," Doone said, and peppered his jaw with kisses.

Luke focused against an intense shiver. "Is it okay? Am I hurting you?"

Mason shook his head. "It's all good. Fuck me."

Luke kissed the back of Mason's neck again. "This is intense," he said.

"Yeah," Mason said. "Let's thrust together."

It took several tries. Luke didn't think he could coordinate his rhythm with Mason's. Mason's asshole hurt. Then it didn't. His cock felt fat, his ass deep. They found a rhythm and went. Mason kissed Doone. She watched Luke kiss Mason's shoulder, his neck. She felt him fucking Mason. Their eyes met. Luke nodded, then leaned his head back and drove his cock farther inside the warm, moist confines of Mason's asshole.

*　　*　　*

MASON HAD FINALLY OPENED THE way he'd always wondered about. He was the split in the sky. He felt as filled as a person's skin felt getting a tattoo. He could take this with him, right? He was going to be all right. Mason moved his hand across Doone's tits.

Doone felt him drag his fingers across her skin, from her tits to her neck to her face. She opened her mouth for his finger, caught it, and then sucked him. Right now, reborn, both child and woman. Fear changed to happiness inside her, and it coated Mason's cock and became frothy, sucking sounds from her cunt, like oil and sugar.

She said, "Fuck me."

"Yeah," Mason said. "Fuck me, too."

"Yeah," Luke said. Everyone heard him groan. A loud sound, and powerful. What did he look like? There was a mirror across the room, and when Luke glanced into it, he thought he looked like he had become an extension of something else. Shakespeare had called sex a beast with two backs. Three was better. Parts of a same whole. Larger than himself alone. Wasn't that weird? He was ugly and beautiful at the same time, and it pleased him. What a relief.

Luke pushed his mouth to the center of Mason's back, there between the guy's shoulder blades, tasted salt, licked the guy's skin, and pushed his cock into the friction of Mason's asshole. It felt like fucking a tornado or a reverse cyclone. Maybe that wasn't possible.

Luke threw his head back.

Doone couldn't speak. She came, like light bursting from a wound.

Luke groaned again and then shot off. When he pulled out, Mason's asshole farted jizz, so Luke went to his knees and licked Mason's ass. He'd never tasted himself before. It was better now; it was him mixed with Mason.

"Oh, God," Mason said. He fell against Doone.

She kissed his face while Luke cleaned his asshole.

Mason didn't want to pull out; he came inside her. *Jesus, I don't want to leave.*

THEY CAME OUT OF THE parlor and stood under a lush silver moon, at rest a moment, suspended.

The moon looked kind of yellow, Luke thought. Like platinum gold. On his tongue, like a wafer they used to give him as a kid in church, melting, the taste of his own come and Mason's asshole. Luke breathed through his nose and then smiled.

Mason knew the moon was always female, like Marge Piercy had said in her book of poetry. Mason blinked. Was it flashing in the sky? He closed his eyes and then looked again. Bright. Blinding. His two friends pressed up behind him. He felt a little weak, actually.

"Hey, dude," Luke said in his ear.

"Hi," Mason said. He felt himself leaning against Luke.

Under the bandage, Doone's tattoo itched. Actually, her whole body itched. Doone was high on endorphins, and it wasn't just the tattoo or what they'd done inside the parlor. Okay, it was partially that. All right, it was a lot that; after all, when had she ever dreamed *that* could happen? This was her happy family.

Doone threw her head back and howled at the moon.

A second later, the guys joined her.

Luke tightened his arm around Mason.

Their howls settled on the night air.

"Can one of you drive?" Mason said.

"I'll drive," Doone said.

Mason found the keys in his pocket and then passed them to her. They began to walk. Doone sprinted ahead. Luke was ahead of Mason.

"Hey," Mason said.

Luke turned. Doone stopped. Luke collided with her. They started laughing.

"I want to see you," Mason said. "Stand, you know, over there." And then he motioned the two of them toward the bus.

Doone did a couple poses, trying for silly. Luke stood beside her and started posing, too. Exaggerated. Like Sid Vicious or something. He tried to see Mason's face under the streetlights.

"Stand there and hold each other," Mason said. "I want to see how it looks."

Doone grabbed hold of Luke. Big, goofy hug. Then they got closer. Luke pushed the bangs off Doone's forehead. They could feel each other's heartbeats.

"You guys are so fucking beautiful together," Mason said. He hadn't meant for it to sound so goddamned choked up, but it had.

Doone stirred. "Hey. We're a threesome."

Mason stepped toward the bus, solid on his feet now. "Let's go."

"Where're we going?" Luke asked. For a second he wanted to rush Mason and grab the guy. For a second, he was coming down off his high.

"My place," Mason said. "Food there. And a bed."

"Big bed?" Doone said. And then she couldn't help it, her new life; she giggled.

Too big for one person, in fact. Why did he have such a big bed? Cheap at a garage sale, Mason remembered. He was inside the bus now. Doone was in the driver's seat, holding the wheel. Luke got in beside him. Right, Mason thought, it was all fate.

He woke later with two people, one on each side of him. Lovely as vampires in their sleep. Mason got out of bed. From a window in his kitchen, he gazed at the cemetery. Noisy-ass crows. Mason grabbed paper and pencils, thinking he'd sketch in preparation for the Last Supper. But he wrote a note instead. Within minutes, something went wrong—a signal between his heart and head. Words wouldn't come anymore. The last thing to enter Mason's vision was a crow cawing outside a window, but then he got confused.

"What am I doing out there?"

When he fell sideways he knocked his coffee over, which had begun to cool and dry on the floor by the time Doone sat up in bed and saw Mason through the doorway, slumped in a chair. He wasn't moving.

"Luke?" she said. "Luke?" She panicked.

Luke stood from the bed, narrow and white in the sunlight; he dashed from the room to the kitchen.

Doone screamed, "Is he okay? Is he?"

"No. Oh, fuck. I mean, oh, dude. C'mon, dude." Luke sobbed on Mason's feet.

AFTER THE FUNERAL, ROSS DID the tats on their shoulders. Headstones: *RIP, Mason. We fucking loved you, man.* Doone was pregnant. They left town, took the high road, in the VW bus.

RUSTY NAIL

by Neve Black

Johanna stood naked on the cold bathroom tile as she scoured the inside of her purse for the bottles of ibuprofen, acetaminophen, and aspirin. She'd have to use the "holy trinity" this time to kill the muscle aches, sinus pressure, and five-alarm headache. With the bottles opened, she selected one pill from each and swallowed, chasing them with tap water that she cupped into her hand from the sink faucet.

She caught a glimpse of herself in the mirror; she looked a mess. Bed-head hair, flattened in some places and sticking up in others. The bright red lipstick she had applied last night was faded and smeared to one side of her face. Black eyeliner and mascara lay in dark pools above her cheekbones, like eclipsed half-moons.

I should at least brush my teeth, she thought. She carried travel-size toothpaste and a toothbrush in her purse. She glanced down at the red chafe marks around her wrists and then turned around to see her backside in the mirror, letting her fingers trace the raised welts on her upper thighs and buttocks.

Ouch. Still tender even after twelve hours of sleep. That's going to turn black and blue, she thought.

She dug into her purse, searching for her writing journal. She wanted to jot down a few notes about the previous night's experience while it was still fresh in her mind.

Initially, I was nervous and scared, even though the women I've interviewed reassured me there was nothing to be alarmed about. Interestingly, I found the mixture of both anxiety and fear highly arousing. The women I interviewed had mentioned this feeling, as well. I was grateful my guide into the "deviant unknown" was accomplished, which was not only helpful, but necessary. The dread of the erotic unknown and the anticipation of exquisite pain only increased the unbelievable pleasure I felt. I've never experienced such gripping ecstasy from sex.

Looking around the hotel bathroom, her thoughts drifted back to how she had ended up here in the first place. *I have only myself to blame—my blind ambition.*

"JOHANNA, YOU DECIDED TO TAKE my advice and seek a more ambitious topic for your thesis work? 'The Sexual Psychology of Subcultural Sex and its Effects on Single Women.' I like it, Johanna. I like it a lot! It shows good initiative on your part,"

Johanna's psychology professor had enthused. "Have you narrowed down a branch of psychology yet?"

"Behavioral. I'm beginning to conduct my active field research tonight," Johanna said. "I'll touch base with you on the progress in a week." She collected her things and headed for the door.

Johanna wanted the teaching position at the university, and she knew that her thesis topic and paper were the keys to obtaining it. It was a risky topic to research and write about, but it was a risk she knew she had to take.

The idea for her thesis had been planted several years before. While at a coffee shop, she overheard two women discussing their BDSM sexual experiences. Since then, her little bud of interest in sexual fetishism had grown.

For her preliminary research, Johanna had placed an ad in the local newspaper requesting women's personal testimonials on subcultural, or BDSM, sex. Johanna was pleasantly surprised at how many women responded enthusiastically to her ad. Many wanted to remain anonymous, but were eager to meet with Johanna and talk about their trysts.

Johanna noted that the majority of these women felt that having BDSM sex with a stranger not only heightened the sexual experience, but both partners had a clear understanding of the expectations: nonvanilla, nonjudgmental, no strings, no emotional attachment, just the total sexual fulfillment of both partners. Johanna felt that these women and their experiences rubbed up against the grain of more traditional stereotypes regarding women and sex. Instead of constantly seeking a mate and a sexual companion, these women felt empowered and enriched after expressing their deepest sexual desires with a total stranger.

The second step in Johanna's research had her placing another ad in the local paper:

SWF seeks male dom for research @ university in social sexual psychology.

Contact SSP69@univ.edu for appointment.

It was raining on the night of her first meeting with an anonymous dom. The "Take Me to Bed Red" polish on her toes peeked through her black stilettos as she dodged puddles in the street like mines on a battlefield. The neon signs from the bars and restaurants reflected against the pavement and lit a path to the hotel bar.

Johanna reached the doorway, pulled the door toward her, and walked into the dimly lit foyer. Standing just inside, she shook the drizzle from her long, naturally curly hair. Just to the left of the entrance, large, high-backed booths swathed in deep red leather enclosed and separated the bar from the hotel lobby and the single elevator door.

She found an available seat at the very end of the bar. Untying her raincoat, she slung it over the bar stool next to her. She wore a sleeveless, short black dress that clung to her well-toned, slender body. She felt the silkiness of her freshly shaved legs as she crossed them and seated herself on the tall bar stool. The

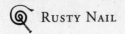

neckline of her dress plunged into a vee, intentionally revealing the cleavage of her large, firm breasts. Nervously, she drummed her fingers against the bar's oak countertop as she waited.

```
To: SSP69@univ.edu
Message: Tie and tease.
From: flogger@hipmale.com
```

The bartender nodded, acknowledging her as he finished serving a drink to a gentleman seated at the other end of the bar. The bartender's long sleeves were rolled up to his elbows, exposing well-developed forearms. He was a handsome guy. His nose was slightly crooked in a way that would make one think it had been broken on more than one occasion. His cheeks, nose, and forehead were slightly reddened from too much sun exposure, maybe from playing contact sports outside. He reminded her of the jocks she saw on campus.

The bar was somewhat disheveled: Bar napkins and empty glasses littered the empty tables. Johanna ordered a dirty vodka martini with three olives from the bartender, then pulled her journal from her purse and began scribbling notes about the night thus far.

Her thoughts were jarred when the door opened and the cool, wet air blew in, carrying with it a man wearing a long black trench coat, a panama hat, and loafers. He was dressed like Dick Tracy or Mickey Spillane, and her thoughts raced humorously: *Private detectives with their little memo pads, sharp pencils, and handcuffs, oh, my!*

He walked toward the bar, removed his coat, and sat on the stool beside her. Her drink arrived, and he glanced at her, tipping his hat before removing it and placing it on top of his coat. The bartender approached him and he abruptly placed his order: "Rusty Nail."

She choked a little on her drink. A shiver ran up her spine, back down again, and settled, pulsing between her legs.

```
To: flogger@hipmale.com
Message: Meet me at Salisbury Sq bar 6/06,
9 p.m. sharp! Order a Rusty Nail.
From: SSP69@univ.edu
```

Johanna turned for a better look at the man beside her. He was her date for the night.

He casually sat down, draping his left arm over the back of the bar stool that held his wet coat and hat. He didn't speak, but his body language said, *I have grit and I'm ready to play.*

She uncrossed her legs and turned her body to face him. The soles of her shoes sat perched on the bottom rung of her seat. Parting her legs slightly, she let her dress ride up to expose her bare thighs.

His drink arrived, and he stirred it with the swizzle stick, his sidelong glances betraying his tense awareness of her. She held her martini, looked directly at him, and purred, "Rusty nail?"

Raising his left eyebrow, he took a sip of his cocktail and smiled at her. His eyes slid over her body. Johanna's olive-

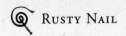

colored skin flushed plum-pink under his scrutiny. Her eyebrows arched perfectly over her soft brown eyes, and he noticed the small mole that sat to the right of her long, slender nose. She had a wide, voluptuous mouth, and her lips were pursed and a succulent red. She was tall, standing about five-ten, and she had a willowy build with long, lithe arms and legs.

"Rusty Nail" had chunky, short fingers. He was a large-framed man, and it looked like he was twenty to thirty pounds overweight. His thick, dishwater-blond hair was parted to one side, framing his bright blue eyes and light complexion. The waves of his hair brushed his collar at the back of his shirt. If she had to describe him to someone, she would have said he looked a little like Robert Redford—a shabbier version, perhaps. He wore a gray suit and a white button-down shirt. Purple and red flecks of color bounced from his tie. He possessed an air of confidence. She made mental notes, as all of this information would make it into her journal at some point.

He finally spoke: "Your ad in the paper intrigued me. I've never been part of a social study before."

"Well, here's to first times, then," she said, smiling generously. She raised her glass to touch his.

"I have a room upstairs," he said.

"Great. Let's finish our cocktails and go." She tried to speak calmly in order to hide her tension.

Johanna's real-life knowledge of the BDSM lifestyle amounted to an occasional slap on her ass cheek from a past boyfriend who awkwardly attempted to experiment with her sexually, but who really didn't know what the hell he was doing.

This was entirely different, and she knew it. Johanna thought she might chicken out at the last minute, but after interviewing so many women on the subject, she knew something in her had been stirred. Her curiosity and arousal were winning the battle over her anxiety and fear.

Rusty Nail pushed himself back into the bar stool, leaning slightly over the bar now. One hand held his cocktail, and he took another long sip before speaking. He spoke thoughtfully and slowly. "That's it, huh? You don't want to know my name, my mother's maiden name, where I live, or what I do?"

Johanna had taken explicit direction from the women she had interviewed: Each woman had explained clearly to Johanna that the less information a woman receives from her partner, the easier it was to disengage emotionally and fully engage sexually, releasing her mind and body to the experience of both the pleasure and the pain during the sex. She had decided to take their advice.

"Would it make a difference to you if I did?" she asked.

"Well, I guess not," he said as he reached for his wallet. He finished what was left of his drink and motioned to the bartender that he was picking up both tabs.

She put her journal away, stood up, and reached for her coat.

"You're very beautiful," he said, watching her move.

He led the way to the elevator, holding the door open for her. It was a quick ascent to the second floor. He raised his left eyebrow for the second time as the elevator arrived and opened. Holding his hat in his hand, he laid his coat over his arm and motioned for her to step off first. She obeyed his instructions and stepped out of the elevator. Soon, he was at her side, and he eagerly pulled the hotel room key from his pants pocket, guiding her to their door. He slid the magnetic key into the door slot; green buttons flashed, and he pushed the hotel room door open.

Johanna followed her date into the room, the door closing behind them. They stepped through a narrow tile walkway that had a bathroom on one side and a closet on the other. He paused only for a moment, flipping the bathroom switch on and keeping the door slightly ajar. Johanna took a deep breath as they moved into the main bedroom.

Two overstuffed chairs and a table sat beside the window, and a large armoire stood against the wall opposite the bed. The king-size bed stared back at her. There were several items placed on the tightly pulled bedspread: rope, handcuffs, paddle, a bottle of lube, and a large vibrator.

"I see you came prepared," she observed.

He looked at her and said nothing. The silence grew between them, and it made the tension in her belly blossom.

Finally, he said, "First lesson: Don't speak unless you're spoken to."

He moved toward her and smacked her ass with his hand. She flinched. The warm sting moved in between her legs. She blinked hard, looking up at him, saying nothing.

He walked to the minibar and pulled out two airplane-size whiskey bottles. He poured their contents into a glass, adding ice from the bucket that he must have filled earlier. Then he pulled the curtains together over the window, shutting out the light pollution from the street below, and settled himself into one of the overstuffed chairs, sipping the whiskey.

Her eyes needed a moment to adjust to the darkness, and she squinted to see the outline of his colossal frame. He seemed much bigger to her now, and more commanding.

"Get undressed." His tone was absolute.

She pulled her purse from her shoulder and let it drop to the floor by the bed. Balancing on one foot, she started to remove her shoes.

"Not the shoes," she heard him say.

She bent forward and clutched the hem of her dress with her fingers, pulling it over the top of her head, letting it drop to the floor by her purse. Johanna stood in front of him wearing black lace panties, a sheer black bra, and a tiny diamond belly-button ring that shimmered against her flat stomach.

Johanna heard his breath quicken, and she could see his hand moving back and forth across the groin of his pants, rubbing his cock. She heard him moan, or maybe she heard a growl, and her nipples hardened, exposed through the sheerness of her bra. She stood still, staring at him, her hands falling placidly to her sides.

"Did I tell you to stop?"

Startled, she unlatched her bra. Her large breasts, now uncontained, spilled out in front of her. This time she was sure she heard him growl.

Her eyes were adjusting to the light as she stood there watching him watch her. The bathroom light glowed behind her. She heard the ice cubes tinkle against the glass as he lifted it to his lips and said, "Pinch your nipples using just your thumb and forefinger until I tell you to stop."

She reached for her breasts, feeling the hardness of her nipples. She pinched them over and over, and every pinch sent an electric surge between her legs. Her breathing became labored, and she felt her heart beating. She heard his body weight shift from the chair. He was approaching her.

He stood in front of her, and she could feel him; his body temperature smoldered. He smelled of a long day of work, sweat, sexual anticipation, and whiskey. He was fully dressed as he pressed his body to hers—her hands, still pinching her breasts, were sandwiched between them.

His stiffened cock knocked loudly at the front door of her panties. His breath sizzled on her neck while his hands found her ass, squeezing and pulling her up onto her tiptoes. She felt his hands and fingers as they charted the outline of her panties, seeking her womanhood. Shifting her panties to one side, his fingers eagerly dipped in between her legs and grazed over the folds of her wet pussy.

"You're very wet," he whispered as he bit into her shoulder. She could feel one of his hands moving from her ass toward the inside of her thigh. Gripping firmly, his hand moved farther down and toward the outside of her thigh and hamstring, and farther still until it reached behind her knee and pulled it upward, so that her leg wrapped around his leg. She felt his fingers as they probed, rubbed, and glided against the wetness of her pussy. His forefinger touched the bud of her clit and he rubbed it back and forth. It felt incredible and she moaned.

"I'm going to tie you up," he whispered hotly into her ear, and her body shivered with anxiety and lust. He stepped away from her, reached into his shirt pocket, and removed two nipple clamps, deftly placing them on her breasts. The rush of pain pierced her body. He lifted her up and tossed her onto the bed. She landed, bouncing onto her side, and then settled on her ass and the small of her back. He walked toward her, still fully clothed, and picked up the rope that sat on the end of the bed. He ran the rope back and forth through his hands, teasing her with what he had planned. She looked up at him.

"Slide closer to me, turn around, and put your hands behind your back," he instructed.

Her nipples were no longer shrieking, but throbbing with a low, pulsating beat. Doing as she was told, she scooted toward the end of the bed where he stood. She turned around, faced the wall and the front of the bed, and placed her hands behind her back. He took both her hands together, but instead of rope, she felt metal clasp at her wrists, and heard the cuffs click as he tightened them. The metal was painful against her skin. Her heart was pounding now, and her thoughts raced: *What am I doing? I don't know this guy. I'm naked, clamped, and handcuffed!*

He walked away from her for a moment, and she could see him reach for the glass of whiskey he'd left on the table close by.

"Face me."

She turned around, and her legs slipped over the side of

the bed, her shoes touching the floor. He moved toward her again. He knelt down in front of her and pulled her toward the very end of the bed so his face was between her legs. He slid the panties down her legs and moved in closer. She could feel his breath, hot and sticky on her inner thighs.

He licked her pussy back to front, the way someone would lick an ice-cream cone, occasionally pointing and dipping his tongue inside her pussy, sometimes teasing her clit.

He has a way with his tongue, she thought. It felt unbelievable.

Johanna's residual fear and misgivings fell away. She became lost in the intense narcotic of pleasure. Yet, a tiny, dispassionate part of Johanna's brain reminded her to pay attention to this feeling for future transcription into her journal. She could relate to the women she had interviewed. Johanna now understood how anxiety and agony mixed with writhing, teeth-gritting pleasure were by far the best aphrodisiacs she had ever experienced.

She melted into the rhythm of his tongue against her, and she knew he knew that if he continued, it would be a quick road to orgasm. Just as she moaned and felt her climax rising, he stopped, pulling his tongue away.

He grasped one of her ankles and ran his hand along her calf, reaching her knee. He bent her knee so that the heel of her shoe sat just under her upper thigh, and he fastened the rope at her thigh and ankle. He did the same to the other leg. *Frog tie,* she thought. During her research, she had read about this bondage method on one of the BDSM Web sites.

He casually stepped back, looking at her. He stood there for what felt like an eternity. She lay before him, tied up and immobile, clamped breasts pulsating feverishly, pussy, clit, and asshole completely exposed. The cutting pain that the handcuffs had initially inspired in her wrists was now reduced to an indolent low throb. Her vulnerability was shocking, and she was surprised to feel highly aroused by it all. She wished could pause to write in her journal.

Finally, he moved close to her again. He placed one of his hands on her knee and pushed her to one side. He picked up the paddle and brought it down hard on her ass, just above the rope on her thigh. She squeezed her eyes shut and muffled a scream. He hit her again.

"You're a bad girl," he said in a growling, low tone. He held on to the rope between her feet with his free hand, lifting and rocking her from one side to the other, hitting her again and again and again. The paddle burned and stung as it struck her soft skin. Her handcuffed wrists dug into the small of her back. She shuddered, and the burning in her wrists sprang back to life. She yelped in pain with each smack, fighting back tears.

Then he stopped.

She felt his hands gently rub her swollen, red ass, felt his lips tenderly kiss the pain away. He carefully rolled her onto her back, and his fingers moved in between her legs. She was dizzy with euphoria, trying to find the balance between the two extremes of pleasure and pain. She closed her eyes. His wet lips and tongue touched her again as he probed and flicked her clit, and two of his fingers pushed into her, fucking her pussy. She arched her back and tried to thrust her hips against the bindings.

His mouth left her and she heard the low hum of the vibrator. He traced the toy down her neck, in between her breasts, and across her stomach, until it rested vertically against her clit and pussy, the handle thumping at the hole of her ass. He removed the vibrator, and then gently pressed it against her again, teasing her and watching her wriggle and squirm.

He stood up from his kneeling position and fastened the vibrator to the binding around one of her thighs so that the head of the vibrator pulsed at her clit. He stepped back and watched her while she panted and moaned. She feverishly tried to buck to the motion of the vibrator, but the restraints made it difficult, teasing her and delaying her orgasm. Unzipping his trousers, he pulled his pants and boxers off at the same time and stepped out of them. He stood at the foot of the bed, still wearing his shirt, tie, socks, and shoes, and his hand slid up and down his hard cock; he masturbated while he watched her writhing body.

She moaned in mounting pleasure as the vibrator continued to pulse against her engorged clit. At last, her body surged against the ropes in release. She screamed, "Oh, God! Oh, God! I'm coming!"

He knelt in front of her and his rigid cock pulsed. He removed the vibrator and grappled for the bottle of lube, pouring it onto her pussy. He rubbed his hand into her and she pulled back, still sensitive from her orgasm. His hand rubbed the juices from her wet pussy, mixed with the lube, onto his throbbing dick, and he quickly slid on a condom. She felt the head of his cock as it touched the opening of her ass. She was tense, but her recent orgasm had opened up her muscles. He slid the tip of his cock inside.

Slowly, he pulled the head out from her asshole and then pushed it in deeper. She gasped and gulped. Surprised at how good it felt to her, she closed her eyes. He grunted like a wild beast as he pulled out again, only to thrust himself ferociously back into her ass. She inhaled and her body opened, letting him in. She heard him grunting and breathing hard, and she could feel his balls thump up against her. He pulled himself completely out and then drove himself into her, filling her up. He was in a rhythm now, and she felt his long, stroking thrusts change to shorter, faster, more fervent movements. His cock pulsated. He made one final, deep thrust into her and then he stopped, as if in midair, floating. He let out a loud groan, orgasmed, and then collapsed on top of her.

Minutes passed before he lifted himself up from her. He stood at the end of the bed and removed the condom from his penis. She heard the rustle of clothes and lifted her head to see him pulling his shorts and pants on. Stepping toward her, he gently removed the nipple clamps. Her nipples felt scorched again as the blood rushed back into them. He untied her bound legs and carefully stretched them out in front of her. Finally, he uncuffed her hands from behind her back, massaged her wrists, and softly kissed them.

She lay there, arms at her sides, legs shaking slightly, saying nothing, only breathing. She watched as he put the vibrator,

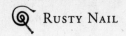

cuffs, rope, and lube into a bag and reached for the coat he'd left on the chair by the window. He turned to her. "You can stay here as long as you want. The room's paid for until noon tomorrow," he said.

She closed her eyes and rolled onto her side. She heard more rustling, heard the front door open and then close.

Silence. He was gone.

Sore and exhausted, Johanna finally moved very slowly. She turned the lamp on next to the head of the bed and spotted her purse on the floor. She took out her journal, untied her shoes, and pulled the covers over her body. Somehow, after dangerously giving a stranger complete control over her body, she felt safe. She poured the events of the night into her journal until her eyes could no longer stay open, and then she fell into a deep, dreamless sleep.

SWIMMING LESSONS

by Jane Anderson

THE WADING POOL

The main problem with being butch is the bruises.

Let me explain. I'm sitting on the edge of my bed (a lovely, king-size extravagance), looking at my right foot. On the top, dead center, is a dark purple bruise about a centimeter square. The bruise deepens to a cut on one side and has perfect corners.

Damned femmes. They get me every time. I go to a dance club looking to have some fun, and the next thing I know I've picked up some flirt sporting her short spring skirt and high heels. The problem increases as the weather warms, as it has during these past few April weekends, and my shoes become less protective. I've never noticed the actual moment of impact, but four out of five Saturday nights result in my having geometric bruises on my feet that can leave me limping down the unforgiving sidewalks of Chicago for days. I'm afraid that last night may end up having a similar effect on my heart.

Last night's conquest, Brianna, is beyond adorable. Girl-next-door blond, compact, rounded body, big eyes—all my major weaknesses. From a distance, the disjointed glimpses I had of her between the frantic posers on the dance floor, she was fantasy-inducing. Up close, she smelled of citrus and sea air, clean and glowing with health, sweat, and frantic fun.

Oh, but vulnerable, soul bruises lurking just behind her baby blues. So I did what I always do with wounded creatures: I swooped down and scooped her up, nourished her with strawberry daiquiris, and petted her. Stroking a soft thigh or "accidentally" brushing my arm against a peach-perfect breast isn't exactly like picking burrs off a stray dog—in one case, getting bitten is bad, and in the other, it's fabulous—but the underlying need to groom and help is the same.

I've been like this since I was a child. By the time I was ten my father knew not to park the car in his garage, as he'd had too many close encounters with stray animals. I was a tomboy (I know, I know, a stereotype) and used to drag home all the wounded creatures I found on my adventures. Funny, I had no problem throwing rocks at friends or school buddies—small Midwestern towns don't tend to bring out the geniality in kids—but I never aimed at animals.

So, in typical form, last night I adopted and nourished. At first, success was effortless—coaxing Brianna to the bar was much easier than wrapping a wounded tomcat in my T-shirt and carrying it home. Brianna was, she informed me, out to have fun, and anyone offering a drink or a dance was fine by her. At the bar she ordered a strawberry daiquiri, biting into the strawberry with relish and lapping the frozen drink out of the glass like a kitten, which earned her an eye roll from the bartender but hooked me.

We danced, and on the dance floor, her blue cotton scoop-necked blouse slid around as she swirled and swung her fabulous hips and toned torso. First, an ecru bra strap bisected a round shoulder. Then the front of the blouse gaped, showing the same ecru lace bra and the top of a firm, cuppable breast. I wanted her naked and horizontal. I wanted that delicate kitten tongue in my mouth. So when she leaned into me and pressed her soft lips against my ear, I had no problem giving her what she wanted.

Which is probably why, as sometimes happens, my stray eventually turned against me. I guess I overnourished. Strawberry daiquiris are, at least in this case, more a sedative than an aphrodisiac. And while there's definitely something to be said for spending the night together on the first date, last night's episode was not exactly something out of *On Our Backs*. It was more like something out of a grocery store magazine, the advice from one of those helpful articles about saving a relationship in which the individuals live in separate bedrooms.

So here I sit, trapped in my apartment by someone else's hangover, contemplating my abused foot. I need to tread carefully for the next few hours—I think my stray will wake up soon, and that's when the fight-or-flight instinct should kick in full force. Perhaps some coffee will help. Hell, cheerleader good looks or not, this relationship will go nowhere if she can't handle the sound of a coffee grinder in the morning.

THE SHALLOW END

THE PROBLEM WITH WRITING AD copy is the brilliance-on-demand factor. Not too brilliant—Oscar Wilde would have been fired in a day—just brilliant enough to sell a billion dollars' worth of the product. In this case, the product, delivered just this morning to my Michigan Avenue office, is a lovely new brand of bottled springwater. Beautifully packaged, judging by the prototype sitting on my desk, and a veritable steal. It's certainly a bargain, considering that the spring is far north of Chicago and Lake Michigan, so a person can actually drink the stuff. The water company needs the perfect campaign to induce a frenzy of purchasing, as if midsummer in the Midwest isn't incentive enough.

You'd think that some quip or tagline about the joys of water would be easy for me this afternoon. July in Chicago is never exactly pleasant, but for the past few days the lake hasn't even offered up a breeze, and the humidity is bearing down on the city like an ex-girlfriend determined to have closure: impossible to avoid, even if you keep ducking phone calls, or into air-conditioned buildings, as the case may be.

Also, I'm hostile about water right now. Brianna and her request for water marked the end of my dancing, the last of my attempts at spring flings. It's been three months and counting since I last hit my favorite clubs. Never mind how long it's been since I last had an orgasm that wasn't self-induced.

The morning after the fateful daiquiri-interruptus night, Brianna woke and beelined for the bathroom. The tease of gold hair that flashed at me when she swung her legs out of the guest room bed, and the briefest glimpse of her round bottom as it peeked out from under her (borrowed from me) T-shirt, made my mouth dry. I swallowed compulsively and headed for the kitchen and my faithful coffeepot. Few things stop me from tackling beautiful blondes, but a steaming cup of coffee has been known to do the trick. Graduate school memories of an ill-timed, burn-inducing assault usually penetrate my lust-fogged brain before I do something stupid.

So I stood in my kitchen, pretending to admire my new oak cabinetry and cheery yellow walls, all the while clutching my coffee and letting the heat of the mug chase the memory of Brianna's warm breast from my hand, and the brown, toasted taste of the brew wash away her strawberry-candy kisses.

Even now, months later and in my overtly professional office, I find myself shifting in my chair and crossing my legs, trying to relieve the swollen, damp pressure of remembered pleasure. The misty weather outside is nothing compared to what happens between my legs every time I think of Brianna.

She'd found my bathrobe, which practically swallowed her in its creamy silk folds. Lucky bathrobe. But either the color didn't suit her or she was worse off than I thought; she had the pale green tinge of the truly hungover.

"Good morning." I tried to speak gently, in case the concept of morning wasn't one she could deal with yet. She offered a tremulous smile, then visibly took a deep breath.

"I'm sorry about—"

"It's okay," I cut her off. As much as I wanted to get my robe off of her, or maybe get her off on my robe, gratitude fucks from damaged femmes weren't up my alley. So, the trick was to see if the good parts of last night could be highlighted—the dancing, the drinking, the grinding (oh, the fabulous, torturous grinding!)—and the bad parts, like the crying and the passing out, downplayed.

"Look, it happens to everyone. Don't worry about it." It's important to reassure all sick animals. They need soothing tones and nourishment. "Can I get you something? Coffee or tea, or maybe some juice?" I opened my cabinet and pulled out another ceramic mug.

Brianna eased herself into one of my almost-antique kitchen chairs. "Just some water would be great." She didn't sound tearful, and that was a start. One of last night's drunken revelations involved the ending of a relationship.

"Okay, water it is." I swapped the mug for a glass and filled it from the kitchen tap. Then I set my offering on the table in front of her. I tried not to notice the way the robe gaped, exposing her thigh. "Need any ice?"

"Um, actually, do you have any filtered?" Her baby blues beseeched me.

"Oh, no, sorry. I had one of those pitchers, but I never replaced the white part, you know, the filter, so I got rid of it."

I watched as she took a tentative sip of the tap water and

shuddered. I had felt that shudder last night, and would have mistaken it for passion if my tongue hadn't been in her mouth and I hadn't felt her reflexively swallow at the same time.

I didn't know color could visibly drain from a person's face, but I swear I saw it happen. Then she stood and fled to the bathroom. After a minute, I followed. Standing outside the door I listened for clues about which hangover activity was going on. Nothing but ominous silence. I knocked.

"Brianna?"

The sound of a toilet flushing.

"Brianna, um, there's some ibuprofen and some antacids in the medicine cabinet."

"Thanks. I'm okay."

She did not sound at all okay, but she was at least able to speak.

"May I borrow your shower?"

Speech and the desire for a shower, both good signs.

"Sure, need any help?" I wasn't sure how stable she'd be on the tile.

"No, actually, I think I'm feeling better now. I just want to clean up."

"Okay. Go ahead and use any of the dark blue towels; they're clean." Beautiful, blond Brianna wrapped in soft, midnight terry cloth. I put my hand on the doorknob, then paused. She didn't need any help. But I did; I needed to step away from the door. And then brilliant inspiration struck. "How about I go get you some bottled water. The mini-mart is right around the corner."

"Yeah, that would be great. Thanks."

"No problem." I was impressed. I was behaving myself and I was being helpful. I was the embodiment of the courtly ideal of love; she wouldn't be able to resist me.

I heard the shower water start to run, and I let myself fantasize all the way to the store and back. Brianna tipping her head back and letting water hit her breasts, the hot drops teasing, pearling her pink nipples into cotton candy–flavored jelly beans, perfect for sucking and gently chewing. Brianna's wet hair wrapping around my thigh when she knelt before me. The slick feel and soapy tang of her skin when I reached the point where I couldn't keep my hands and mouth off her. Even one quick flash of a truly unhygienic use of my shampoo bottle.

I was floating on a pheromonal cloud produced by my own hormones when I got back to the condo.

"Brianna?" The shower was off, so she had to be in the bedroom.

She wasn't.

She also wasn't in the kitchen, in the living room, in my office/guest room, or sitting on the deck gazing at the lake. There was, however, a banal yellow sticky note stuck to the mirror of the medicine cabinet in the bathroom.

Thanks.
Bad relationships are a bitch, especially when they're almost over. I hope you don't mind if I wear your shirt home. You're very nice, and I'm sorry we didn't meet under better circumstances. Brianna.

I brought the note to my downtown office and put it in my desk drawer. I like to think of it as an excellent example of not enough product information. For instance, note the lack of a last name. No way to trace her.

The bathroom, however, was immaculate, and the bed in the guest room neatly made up. Whatever else you could say about her, at least she cleaned up after herself.

SWIMMING LAPS

ONE OF THE PROBLEMS WITH having good friends is that they give you advice. And in my case, I'm prone to listen. Which is why, on a sweltering Saturday night best spent with a beer in my hand and several more in the ice-filled cooler at my feet, I'm at a book reading in a great little store on Fifty-seventh Street.

This is all Joan's fault. Joan is my married, DINK, Martha Stewart–wannabe friend. On that fateful Sunday afternoon, several hours after Brianna bit the hand that held her up, Joan arrived at my condo so that we could venture into the wilds of Wisconsin searching for antiques for her new country kitchen with built-in breakfast bar.

Joan was patient; Joan was sympathetic; Joan was ruthless. My problem was that I was acting like I was twenty years old. I was a successful, adult woman, and I needed to meet other women like me. No, not gay and horny—intelligent and dynamic. Maybe I didn't realize it, but I'd been searching for a relationship for over a year, and relationships, the good kind, not the kind that begin in a bar and end in a bedroom, take some time and effort.

Somewhere between Rockford, Illinois, and Madison, Wisconsin, I found myself nodding my head in agreement. Mute and rhythmic, like one of those plastic birds that dips its beak into a glass of water. Up and down, bobbing and dipping, until finally it just tips forward and rests with its beak in the water and its neck on the edge of the glass. Waiting and staring at nothing. That was me, nodding and staring out the car window and not seeing the acres of cornfields broken up by summer-dry, grassy hills.

In the bookstore, the attentive women and the few men around me blur as though I'm looking at them through vapor. There is a soft "oh" emitted when the author reads a particular line, and then the solid "hmmmm" sound of agreement that I've begun to think of as the base chord of the lesbian book chorus.

Over a year and no relationship, only a few safe lunch dates. Many more months than that since I last got laid properly; an ad campaign for bottled water that is sinking fast; too many nights fantasizing about blue-eyed blondes; and eight days and counting of temperatures in the high nineties. I have to get out of the bookstore. I need the familiarity and the energy of a club—it's time to sweat this malaise out of my system.

OFF THE DEEP END

The only problem with my favorite club is that it tends to be everyone else's favorite club, too. So even though the hour is early by club standards, I still have to battle through a sweaty crush to get to the bar. The bottle of beer in my hand is better than finally getting my chance to stand in front of the air-conditioning vent. I take the time to run the cold, wet bottle up the side of my throat to my temple and across my forehead before tipping it into my mouth. Nothing like it. Out of all the salty, tangy, yeasty flavors on the planet, including come, nothing satisfies like a cold beer on a hot night.

"Darcy!" My name reverberates through the booming music. I'm tugged onto the dance floor by Kevin, a young, slender gay man with Elvis-inspired hips. Makes no difference; dancing is dancing, and with the beat driving up through the floor and grabbing me by the groin, any partner will do.

The music cycles into its hip-hop segment. The DJ Divas like to do that, mix it up and give everyone a chance on the floor. Kevin leaves me to make kissy-face with one of his many amours. My beer is half-gone, and given the crowd at the bar, I think it might be best just to finish the bottle while in line for the next.

Stillness has a way of standing out in a vibrating crowd. You notice the void of movement and the change of traffic flow around the area. Pausing at the edge of the dance floor, I instinctively turn my head and my eyes snag on the calm in the storm and then stick, magnets to metal. Brianna has entered the room. I actually hear the announcement in my head as though I have an internal speaker system.

She looks much better than the last time I saw her. Even better than she looked in my fantasies, in spite of the fact that, in reality, she's officially fully dressed. Although tiny, tight denim shorts and a familiar white T-shirt don't really count as actual full-coverage clothing.

I sink into the crowd at the bar, but I don't struggle to move ahead. I watch Brianna scan the room. She shakes her head as though waking up, or physically shaking off a thought, and navigates her way to the stairs.

Upstairs, there's a small cocktail lounge area. One can hang out on the balcony and ogle people on the dance floor, begin or end relationships at one of the small tables set back from the railing, or just nurse a drink in the relative quiet. I tell myself that finishing my beer in a quieter spot is my goal, and don't bother to acknowledge the lie when I drop the empty bottle into the mesh trash can at the foot of the stairs.

Brianna is leaning over the railing, her already short denim shorts riding even higher up her legs. I create and discard five or six witty opening lines and just walk over and stand next to her.

"Buy you a drink?" It's quiet enough that I don't have to raise my voice too much.

She turns, unsurprised, like we've been standing next to each other for hours. She smiles. "Hi."

"Hi." Caution stands briefly on the balcony railing,

then gleefully suicides into the gyrating crowd below. "Nice T-shirt."

"Thanks, I borrowed it from a friend." The smile reaches her eyes.

"A friend who didn't get your last name or your phone number." Cut to the chase, that's me. Why waste time when your heart is at stake?

"I didn't think you'd want it. I mean, you left the apartment so quickly, and I was so . . ." She catches her lower lip between her teeth.

"Hungover. Forget about it. Let's dance."

She hesitates, then takes a step, then stops. "You weren't mad or freaked out or anything? I'm really sorry; I don't usually—"

"Look, I mean it: Don't worry about that night. How did things work out . . . with the girlfriend and all?"

"Oh, her. Over. Very over. Over, done with, completely moving on."

"Great! So, you're unattached and emotionally available. The dream date."

I pushed her toward the stairs, savoring the contact between my hand and her butt. "Let's dance, or drink, or something."

She turns and looks up at me, cocking an eyebrow, forties-movie-star style. "Something?"

"Well, I am going to reclaim that shirt sometime soon." I hope I don't completely lose control and do it on the dance floor.

The hip-hop has transitioned into something techno-like, and it's definitely danceable. The noise doesn't allow for much conversation, but the six square inches of dance floor allotted to the two of us force us closer than if we were whispering in each other's ears. A few minutes on the floor and the white T-shirt is damp and clinging to Brianna, showing off the cropped sports bra underneath. So that's what happened to her breasts.

"You work out?" I shout.

"Yep, martial arts. Tae kwon do and some kickboxing."

I'm jostled from behind and our legs tangle. I can feel the heat of Brianna's crotch through my linen pants, and I see no reason to remove her from my thigh when the song switches to a popular Latin tune. Nobody bumps and grinds like Shakira, and who am I to argue with the trend?

Brianna ebbs and flows against me like the tide taunting the shore. She drags me toward her, millimeter by millimeter, and I literally turn liquid against her. My back drips with sweat, my hand slides across her waist, and her wet legs stick like Velcro to my slacks. Heat rises off of us and joins the miasma of human humidity that separates the swampy dance floor from the rest of the club.

Only a few feet away, on the balcony or through the open door to the street outside, is relief. But I don't want that relief. I want the relief of stripping off my drenched clothes and having the sweat licked off my body, a cool, soft tongue lapping at my hot lips, coaxing the wetness from me and then sucking me dry as my muscles clench and my body shakes.

"Let's get a drink," Brianna says against my ear, so that I can hear her. Her chest rises and falls rapidly; she's panting like a distance runner.

"Okay," I say, and wrap my arm around her, guiding her to the bar—again. The bartender asks us what we want, rolling his eyes at me as I reluctantly unwind from Brianna.

"Water. Two bottles of water," Brianna says while I fumble, trying to detach the soggy money from the soaked lining of my back pocket.

"Huh?" I shove the bill across the bar and follow Brianna to the corner of the room, near the currently vacant coatroom.

Brianna leans against the redbrick wall, twisting the plastic cap from her water, and tilts her head back to drink. I watch, mesmerized by the movement of the muscles in her neck and throat as she downs half the bottle. She pauses for breath and licks her lips.

"*Eau de vie*, the true champagne of life, second only to air."

She isn't just the lust of my life; she's a genuine muse. I file her phrases away for later plagiarism.

I take the other bottle. "Let me try." I tangle my hand in her hair and tug gently, forcing her head back. She opens her mouth, a little surprised, and I pour the water carefully between her lips. Before she can swallow, I cover her mouth with mine and drink. The water is still cold and clear; her mouth is hot and open and relaxed until my tongue dips into its depths, and then her lips tighten and the kiss begins.

"More." Her eyes are closed and water dribbles down her chin. I lick it off, tasting the salty sweat and the water all at once. I lick down her jawline, lapping at her like she's a Popsicle, and settle next to her ear.

"More water or more kissing?"

She grabs my hand, the one with the bottle in it, and drinks again. She pulls me to her. "Both," she growls against my mouth.

I sandwich Brianna between my soft, sweaty body and the hard, dry brick wall. We kiss and pet, and whenever I change my grip on her, the rough bricks scrape my hands and arms. I even bang my head on the wall while trying to get to her neck, the vulnerable spot just above her collarbone. Intermixed with our intense, sweat-slick groping are sips and glugs of the bottled water. The clean coolness of the water heightens the rich, musky taste of her skin and the slickness of her mouth.

I reclaim my shirt, and use it to pillow her head against the concrete of the coatroom floor. I'm drizzling the last drops from the bottle into her perfect, round belly button when a throat clears above us.

"Excuse me, ladies, but this room is not for rent." A fuchsia Lycra-clad transvestite, her fake eyelashes highlighting her wide-eyed gaze of disapproval, looks down at us from the doorway.

Brianna jumps, opens her eyes, and blushes with her whole body. I scramble to my feet and hold out my hand to her, always the gentleman. Brianna tugs her shirt on, not bothering to tuck it in, and accepts my hand. We push past the smirking diva and weave our way through the crowd on the dance floor.

The Chicago night air offers little reprieve for our dance-damp, hormone-heated bodies, even compared to the swamp of the dance floor. The "sorry, fan broke this afternoon" cab ride from the north side to my Hyde Park condominium takes an interminable twenty-five minutes, during which time I alternate between holding Brianna's hand and stroking her thigh. There isn't a nonsweaty, unturned-on part of my body by the time we hit the elevator.

The stuffy heat of the dark apartment hits me with a rush when I open the door. I turn on the table lamp next to the door and enter the room.

"Sorry." I start across the living room, but Brianna tugs me back, so I gesture at the air conditioner in the window. "I don't have central air, and I turn the units off when I leave—trying to keep my electricity bill from looking like the national debt."

Brianna smiles and gives me a look that brings my nipples to attention. "Leave it. Let's just open the door to the balcony and see if we can get a breeze."

She heads for the sliding glass door and I follow, the mighty jungle hunter pushing her way through the tropical night, braving all just to keep her prey in sight. My coffee table leaps out and attacks my shin, making me stumble and then hop ungracefully to the door. The quarry has already vanished into the inky blackness of the balcony.

I settle myself on the wood-and-iron bench, next to Brianna. There's a brief pause that is almost awkward until Brianna saves the mood by picking up my feet and nestling them in her lap. Carefully, she rolls up my pants leg and rubs the injured shin. Knowing there is no way I will regret this, my most recent bruise, I lean over and kiss her.

The heat of the night, the remembered energy of the club, and the distant boom of thunder make my hands fly. I break the kiss to pull off her shirt, and she struggles with the small buttons on my silk tank top while trying to kick off her shoes. I pull her across my lap, nestling her butt against my thighs, and cradle her head in the crook of my elbow. Now, between kisses, I can look down at her face and watch her eyes close as I brush my thumb lightly over her sports bra–bound nipples. Each beads in its turn and Brianna squirms, her body mimicking mine as her thighs rub against each other, seeking the fleeting relief caused by the friction.

Much too soon into my explorations, Brianna sits up and straddles me, pulling her bra off over her head. For one gorgeous moment, her back is arched and her smooth, white breasts with their straining strawberry nipples are perfectly highlighted by a splash of light from the living room. Her bra hits the balcony deck, and I finally get my lips and tongue on her ripe nipples. Tugging, tonguing, and sucking, I'm too preoccupied to pay much attention to the hands that fumble at my own bra until my mouth is abruptly deprived of its flesh candy.

"Hey, I'm not done with you yet."

Brianna ignores my halfhearted protest and hops off my lap, pulling me to my feet with her. I stumble and she catches me, and then I'm lost in the sensation of her hard nipples and dewy breasts pushing against my own, creating a sweaty slick of desire that drips down my stomach. We kiss like we have no need for air, and the humidity outside has hit such a level that breathing is almost impossible. I push her away so I can hold her breast, cupping and molding it in rhythm with her swaying body. She pinches my nipples in a staccato counterbeat to my pelvic thrusts against her thigh.

My pants fall with surprising ease to the deck, but Brianna's shorts snag on her sweat-drenched thighs. We wind up side by side on the rough wooden floor of the balcony. I resume the delirious activity of kissing Brianna's nipples, sucking and nipping hard enough to make her cry out, but her pleasure pleas are lost in the increasing cracks of thunder that boom over us.

She beats me to the next step, sliding under my thong and tickling my clit with a delicate finger. Mindless and on the edge, I wedge my hand into the small space between the tangle of her underwear and denim shorts, and the juncture of her thighs. I rub her crotch with my hand just long enough to feel her swollen wetness, her clit pressing into my palm like a slippery pearl in a newly opened oyster. I find my bearings and slide my fingers home.

Her own fingers work electric magic, sliding in and out of me, pausing to return to the delicate rubbing. She pushes herself onto me, gasping and moaning. A huge crack of thunder explodes overhead, followed immediately by a bolt of lightning that lights up the balcony just as I feel Brianna clench around me. I see the ecstatic expression on her face and watch her shake as the first cold drops of rain hit my steaming skin, and I lose myself in my own release.

DIVING IN

THE MAIN PROBLEM WITH A long-term relationship is that eventually your boundaries blur to the point of being one body; you cannot imagine separating the way you cannot imagine living without water or air.

Let me explain. It starts in the beginning, when you pour your passion into each other the way a river pours into a lake. You trade sweat and saliva and tears and come until all your bodily fluids are mixed. The human body is 98 percent water. How long does it take until the water in you is the same as the water inside your lover?

Habits lap at you the way waves lap at a shoreline, wearing you down, reshaping your borders. The experience of dinners out and movies seen, job triumphs, and shared friends rain down on you both, filling the reservoir of your soul. When do you finally fill to the brim and either break through the dam, destroying the relationship, or overflow and just admit that you're now one body of water? One liquid, salty, constant, and ever-changing ocean?

Brianna is asleep on her side of the bed. She has a habit of barely rousing in the middle of the night and reaching, still asleep, for the glass of water on her nightstand. I started bringing her the full glass each night after she crawled into bed, about the same time I cleared out a few dresser drawers for her clothes. I don't know how she manages to find the glass, drink from it, and put it back without fully waking up or spilling it, but she does. The water, of course, is filtered, and the glass is always back in its place on the nightstand in the morning. I usually pick it up on my way to make the coffee, and there's always water left over. Half-empty or half-full, I'm not sure I've decided. Either way, it's enough.

ABOUT THE AUTHORS

Jane Anderson has published several nonfiction articles, and she won a national contest with Romance Writers of America, in addition to publishing with Oysters & Chocolate last year. Jane has lived and traveled all over the world, and currently resides in Tucson, Arizona.

Neve Black has been writing since she can remember and opted for a degree in English literature. She mostly enjoys writing about subjects that scratch the underbelly of society; thus her love of erotica. Neve currently resides in Cleveland, Ohio, with three adopted pussy cats.

Often described by reviewers as "shocking," **Iona Blair**'s erotic novels have been published by Pink Flamingo, CF Publications, Amatory Ink, Phaze Books, Amira Press, Carnal Desires, Total-E-Bound, and Siren-BookStrand. Her short stories have appeared in a variety of publications including Oysters

& Chocolate, Ruthie's Club, *Good Vibrations* magazine, Erotic Dreams, *Whispers*, STARBooks Press, and the Velvet Mafia. She lives in an old converted lighthouse on the Pacific Coast, where her thoughts run as wild as the weather. www.ionablair. blogspot.com.

Layla Briar's alter ego writes textbooks for lawyers and police officers. Finding time for a little erotic fiction keeps her sexy and sane!

By day, **Callie Byrne** is a respectable journalist; by night, she enjoys writing articles and reviews for Oysters & Chocolate; and it's when her husband is away that she delves into the fantastic act of writing erotica to keep herself company.

Sarah Carter has stories in *BENT* magazine and in the upcoming *Tough Girls 2* and Alyson Books' *Best Lesbian Love Stories: Summer Flings* anthologies. She lives in California and is studying creative writing.

Chelsea Comeau was born in New Westminster, British Columbia, and currently lives with her boyfriend, mum, dad, and lovebird. She has completed a year of English and creative writing courses at Douglas College, and will be continuing her education there beginning in September 2008.

Brian K. Crawford lives in Marin County, California, with his wife and college-age son. He has written two novels and many short stories—erotica, science fiction, mystery, and historical—as well as essays, poetry, and memoirs of his rather adventurous life. You can read some of his writings at www. BrianCrawford.info.

Jeremy Edwards is a pseudonymous sort of fellow whose efforts at spinning libido into literature have been widely published online. His print appearances include the anthologies *A Is for Amour*; *Coming Together: At Last, vol. 2*; *Coming Together: For the Cure*; *Coming Together: Under Fire*; *Erotic Tales 2*; *F Is for Fetish*; *Five Minute Fantasies 1*; *Five Minute Fantasies 2*; *Frenzy: 60 Stories of Sudden Sex*; *Got a Minute? Sixty-Second Erotica*; *J Is for Jealousy*; *K Is for Kinky*; *The Mammoth Book of Best New Erotica 7*; *The Mammoth Book of Best New Erotica 8*; *Open for Business: Tales of Office Sex*; *Rubber Sex: A Collection of Erotic Stories*; *Satisfy Me (Aphrodisia)*; *Screaming Orgasms and Sex on the Beach*; *Seriously Sexy 1*; *Seriously Sexy 3*; *Sex & Satisfaction: Twenty Erotic Stories*; *Sex and Seduction*; *Tasting Her*; *Tease Me*; and *Ultimate Burlesque*. Jeremy's greatest goal in life is to be sexy and witty at the same moment—ideally in lighting that flatters his profile. Drop in on him unannounced (and thereby catch him in his underwear) at www.jerotic.blogspot.com.

Aimee Herman is a poet from Brooklyn or New Jersey (or her mother's vagina—depending upon whom you ask). She has been published in several publications, including Cliterature, Origami Condom, the Pregnant Moon Poetry Review, and, of course, Oysters & Chocolate. She has freelanced for *Out Front*

Colorado and has performed on radio shows and at various clubs and cafés in New York, New Jersey, Connecticut, Massachusetts, and Colorado. Aimee has two chapbooks of poetry currently out: *Tastes Like Cheesecake* (Butcher Shop Press) and *If These Thighs Could Talk* (RoseWater Publications), as well as a spoken-word CD available through www.cdbaby.com/AimeeHerman. Her current publication of poetry, with spoken-word CD, *self-diagnosed lactose intolerance,* was released this year from Baobob Tree Press. Aimee can be reached at writerslashpoet@gmail.com.

Kay Jaybee is the author of the erotic anthology *The Collector* (Austin & Macauley, 2008), which features the adventures of a writer forever in the pursuit of tales of sexual adventure. As well as being a regular contributor to Oysters & Chocolate, Kay has had a number of stories published by Cleis Press (*Lips Like Sugar: Women's Erotic Fantasies; Lust: Erotic Fantasies for Women; Best Women's Erotica 2007, 2008, 2009; Best Romantic Lesbian Erotica 2008*), Black Lace (*Sex and Music*), Xcite Books (*Ultimate Sin*), and Mammoth Books (*The Mammoth Book of Lesbian Erotica).*

Gwen Masters writes. And writes. And writes. Hundreds of her short stories have been published in anthologies, magazines, and online venues. Her novels have met with rave reviews and a vast readership. To find out more about her naughty words, visit her Web site at www.gwenmasters.net. When she's not writing, Gwen loves kicking through the fallen leaves of autumn, music cranked up as loud as she can stand it, and homemade lemonade with just enough gin to make things interesting—and not necessarily in that order.

Heather Monaco lives, writes, and seeks new varieties of pleasure in Denver, Colorado.

Alicia Night Orchid's mainstream fiction has appeared in several literary journals under another name. Her erotic stories have appeared online at Clean Sheets, Ruthie's Club, Sliptongue, Oysters & Chocolate, and the Erotica Readers & Writers Association. Her story "Savage Nights" took first prize in Desdmona's 2007 Sixties Erotic Story Contest. Another story, "A Lover in the House of Spies," was runner-up in the For the Girls 2008 Fiction Contest. Ms. Orchid's first novel, an erotic legal thriller, is expected out late 2008. She's currently at work on a second novel. Visit her Web site at www.anightorchid.com.

Terri Pray has been writing professionally for a little over five years. As of August 2008 she has sixty-two novels and novellas in both e-book and print with eight different publishers. Her work ranges from sweet romance to BDSM inferno-level fiction. Originally from the UK, she now resides in Iowa with her husband and their two children.

P. Alanna Roethle has published nonfiction work for *Road & Travel* magazine and worked for a weekly newspaper in New Mexico called the *Round Up*. She has had poetry published in various collections and anthologies, she is currently working on a screenplay, and she has recently completed a novel, *The VIP Room*.

Alice Sturdivant lives and works in South Carolina, where she drinks too much sweet tea, attempts to garden, writes erotica when no one is looking, and occasionally wrestles with her muse. Her work has appeared on various Web sites; most recently, her short story "Modern Cinderella" appeared in the best-selling anthology *Succulent: Chocolate Flava II*.

Alana Noël Voth is a single mom who lives in Oregon with her ten-year-old son, one dog, two cats, and several freshwater fish. Her fiction has appeared in *The Mammoth Book of Best New Erotica 7*; *Best Gay Erotica 2004, 2007,* and *2008*; *Best Gay Bondage Erotica*; *Best American Erotica 2005*; *Best Women's Erotica 2004*; and online at Clean Sheets, Eclectica magazine, the Big Stupid Review, and Literary Mama.

Belle Watling is a Southern gal from Georgia who loves the finer things in life, including chivalrous gentlemen, romance, fine clothes, and barbecues. She also loves being naughty, because it just isn't fun being nice all the damn time.

Jordana Winters is a thirty-something Canadian writer of women's erotica. Jordana's print credits include *Ultimate Sex, Best Women's Erotica 2008, 2007,* and *2006, Sex & Seduction, Uniform Sex,* and *Erotic Tales*. Her online credits include Tassels & Tales, A Woman's Goodnight, Lucrezia Magazine, Forbidden Publications, the Erotic Woman, Ruthie's Club, Oysters & Chocolate, eXtasy Books, and Thermoerotic.

Jordana likes working out, chillin' out, tattoos, doing as much and as little as possible, drinking coffee and tea, bubble baths, and anything that makes her think. When not hiding behind her computer telling filthy tales, Jordana is an often-disenchanted administrative whore. She isn't much into following society's rules and rarely does as she's told. She admits to being jaded and cynical about almost everything and wonders if life will ever make sense. Contact her at jordanawinters@yahoo.com, and visit her online at http://jordanawinters.tripod.com/.

ABOUT THE EDITORS

Jordan LaRousse and **Samantha Sade** (the pen names of Naomi Tepper and Yvonne Falvey Mihalik) created and launched Oysters & Chocolate (www.oystersandchocolate.com), the online magazine for women's erotica, in July of 2005. Both women are graduates of the University of Colorado at Boulder and lifelong friends, and have cumulative experience in editing as well as nonfiction and fiction writing. Oysters & Chocolate is now home to over seven hundred erotic stories, poems, and articles and fifty art galleries created by over four hundred contributors.